D0016049

THE LEAGUE OF
BEASTLY
DREADFULS
The Witch's Glass

⟶❖ WARNING: ❖⟵
Read These Beastly Adventures—
At Your Own Risk!

HOLLY GRANT

pictures by

JOSIE PORTILLO

THE LEAGUE OF BEASTLY DREADFULS

The Witch's Glass

· BOOK 3 ·

Random House New York

Text copyright © 2017 by Holly Grant
Jacket art and interior illustrations copyright © 2017 by Josie Portillo

All rights reserved. Published in the United States by Random House Children's Books, a division of Penguin Random House LLC, New York.

Random House and the colophon are registered trademarks of Penguin Random House LLC.

Visit us on the Web! randomhousekids.com

Educators and librarians, for a variety of teaching tools, visit us at RHTeachersLibrarians.com

Library of Congress Cataloging-in-Publication Data is available upon request.

ISBN 978-1-101-93366-4 (trade) — ISBN 978-1-101-93368-8 (ebook)

Printed in the United States of America
10 9 8 7 6 5 4 3 2 1
First Edition

Random House Children's Books supports
the First Amendment and celebrates the right to read.

for

NICHOLAS

❧ CONTENTS ☙

❋ 1 ❋
The Marvelous Flop

A NASTASIA WAS DREAMING about her father.

She was back in the McCrumpet house, back on the morning before tragedy had turned her life upside down. Rain spattered the windows, but the kitchen was warm and homey and smelled of waffles. Anastasia had not yet been kidnapped. She was sitting at the table eating marmalade. Mr. McCrumpet had not yet vanished. He was slopping cinnamony batter onto the griddle.

It should have been a cozy dream. And yet somewhere in the depths of her slumbering brainbox, Anastasia was uneasily aware of the grim events that, in reality, had followed this ordinary breakfast. Dream-Anastasia stared at her flour-dusted father, knowing she wouldn't see him again for many months. Perhaps she would never see him again.

In fact . . . his face was growing hazy right before her eyes. The harder she looked at Fred McCrumpet, the foggier he became. "Dad!" She blinked—and blinked—

Anastasia blinked awake, her heart thumping a panicked little tattoo. Sleep still fuzzed her peepers; she blinked again. Something felt different. Something felt *wrong*. Her bones ached. Her head throbbed. Green and pink shapes wobbled in her vision. Her eyelids stuttered as she strained to focus, the blurs finally crystallizing into a design of roses and briars pricked out in nimble stitches. It was, she realized, the embroidered canopy on her new bed in her new home, thousands of miles away from the McCrumpet abode. But why did the roses look so *big*, floating above like squashed pink clouds?

Anastasia swallowed and called to her lady-in-waiting: "SQUEEEEEAK!"

If she had been possessed of hands, Anastasia would have covered her mouth in shock. However, she now discovered, *she didn't have hands*. She had great bulky flaps—*wings!*—and these she rustled in alarm.

Anastasia McCrumpet had turned into a bat.

For the first eleven years of her life, Anastasia played the part of an ordinary child to perfection. She played it so well that even *she* believed she was utterly average. She had mousy-brown hair and mousy-brown eyes and exactly 127 freckles. Were you to bump into her at the ice cream parlor or the post office or the library, you probably wouldn't give her a second glance. Anastasia didn't have what the bigwigs in Hollywood call *star quality*.

But all the time she was brushing her teeth, tripping over her shoelaces, and attending to the thousands of other tiny chores that make up a normal human life, a potpourri of secrets simmered in her blood—secrets so secret that even *she* didn't know them. However, by age ten and three-quarters, these hidden truths had started bubbling up into her daily existence.

I wonder, dear Reader, what sort of secrets might be brewing inside *you*.

Perhaps the biggest, strangest, most shocking secret of all was that Anastasia McCrumpet, despite all outward appearances, was not entirely *human*. But you already knew that. After all, how many humans wake up as fuzzy, pointy-eared, moth-craving bats?

"Squeak! Squeak! Screeee!"

Anastasia tumbled from the bedstead and onto the floor, landing in a tangle of wings. "Peep!" Her mind twirled in a wild carousel of shock and confusion and fear: *It's happened, just as they said it would. . . . Why does everything hurt so much? . . . I'm a bat I'm a bat I'm a bat!*

"Princess Anastasia! We've come for your morning toilette!"

CLUNK! CLUMP! STOMPITY-STUMP! Anastasia swiveled her head to glimpse a herd of monstrous silk slippers, buffalo-big, stomping across the marble floor.

"And I've brought something to—why, where *is* the little twerp?"

Anastasia's sensitive bat eardrums amplified the irritation in her aunt Ludowiga's voice. Even in the midst of her shock and fear, Anastasia cringed. She had two aunts, one good and one bad, and Ludowiga *wasn't* the good one.

"Are you *hiding,* you silly twit?" Ludowiga demanded. "Show yourself, girl! You've already weaseled out of one bath this week—"

"Squeak!" Anastasia cried.

"Well, well. What do we have here?" Ludowiga stooped. Her face (enormous—she was bigger than the Statue of Liberty!) lurched into view. "Look who *finally* metamorphosed."

Anastasia let out an unhappy peep.

"Well?" Ludowiga glowered at her. "Why are you lying on the floor like a senseless banana peel? Get up. *Fly!*"

With great effort, Anastasia wriggled her wings. Ludowiga gawped, aghast. "Princess! *Can't you fly?*"

But at that moment, in a flash and a twinkling, Anastasia morphed back into a girl.

"Anastasia!" Baldwin Merrymoon exclaimed, his voice warm with admiration. "Just *look* at your mustache!"

Baldwin possessed a beautiful ginger-colored mustache of his own, and he took great joy in its everyday grooming and display. Unlike her uncle, Anastasia had never sported whiskers of any kind. She was, as you will remember, a normal-looking eleven-year-old girl most of the time, and most normal-looking eleven-year-old girls do not have enormous handlebar mustaches sprouting from their upper lips. But this morning, she did.

"Oh my!" Penny Merrymoon cried, staring as Anastasia slunk into the dining hall. Penny was Anastasia's *good* aunt. She was lovely and patient and full of hugs.

Over the previous three months, Anastasia's family tree had plopped forth all kinds of heretofore-unknown relatives. Some of them were sweet peaches, like Aunt Penny, and some of them were bad apples, like Ludowiga. Uncle Baldwin was another of these strange fruits. Fortunately, he was a peach.

"My darling, did you *shift*?" Penny asked.

"Of course she shifted, Penny!" Baldwin said. "Where else would she have gotten that splendid mustache?"

"When you first start morphing, a bit of animal fluff sometimes sticks to you," Penny explained to Anastasia. "Back when I was your age, I'd keep a few whiskers after shifting into a mischief of mice. Don't worry, dear. That mustache will fall out by the end of the day."

"Pity," Baldwin said. "It's a beauty! If I didn't have such wonderful mustaches myself, I'd be *chartreuse* with envy."

Anastasia groaned, sitting down at the table. "I don't want to go to school with a mustache!"

"There, there," Penny consoled her. "I'm sure your classmates will understand. They're all starting to morph as well, you know."

Anastasia moped. "I've never seen a fifth grader with a mustache. And it's *itchy*."

"One must suffer for beauty," Baldwin rhapsodized, patting his own cookie-duster.

"I *am* suffering," Anastasia said. "I feel like I have the flu."

"You're going to ache for a few days. It's no small feat, shrinking an eleven-year-old girl into a little six-ounce bat body and back again!" Baldwin beamed. "Ah! Your first morph! It's a landmark event in a Morfo's life!"

"Winthrop." Penny signaled to one of the white-wigged servants stationed in the dining hall. "Would you please bring some of Dr. Lungwort's Miracle Fizz? That will make you feel better, Anastasia." She reached over to squeeze Anastasia's hand. "How I wish your father could be here. He'd be so proud."

After discovering she was a Morfo, Anastasia had dreamed of the glorious day she would shift into another creature. Some Morfolk, like Baldwin, changed into wolves. Some metamorphosed into mice, like Penny. Two of Anastasia's very best friends, Ollie and Quentin Drybread, turned into shadows. However, most Morfolk, like Anastasia, changed into bats. A Morfling's first shift was generally the subject of hugs and hoorays. It was better than a birthday.

Anastasia, however, did not feel like jubilating. She felt as if someone had squished her through an old-fashioned clothes wringer.

Winthrop whisked back into the dining hall, bearing a domed platter. He removed the dome to reveal a goblet of water and two purple tablets on a saucer. Penny dropped the tablets into the goblet. The water started to fizz.

"Oh, the fun you'll have!" Baldwin said. "We'll take you abovecaves for moonlit flits—"

"Ahem." Ludowiga stormed into the dining hall. "Don't make any grand plans yet, Baldy. The princess *can't fly*. I discovered her this morning sprawled on the floor. She lay there and wiggled. And I've seen better wiggling in a *worm*!"

"We-ell." Penny hesitated. "The first few shifts are always awkward."

"This morning's performance was *beyond* awkward, Penny," Ludowiga snapped. "It was a *disaster*. It was, quite literally, a *flop*. It was a *parody* of proper metamorphosis."

"Oh, shove it, Loodie," Baldwin retorted. "Your *wig* is a parody of a stupefied poodle."

Ludowiga ignored him. "My Saskia flew *laps* around the palace the first time she metamorphosed. She zigzagged through the corridors like a stunt plane. She did loop-the-loops and barrel rolls and climbing spins and lazy eights. And then she adjourned to her chambers and morphed back into a well-bred girl and put on a charming gabardine gown for the Duchess of Cummerbund's tea party. It was all entirely *dignified*."

Cheeks flaming, Anastasia slouched lower in her seat.

She was now decently clad in her school uniform. However, at the moment of her shift from bat to girl form, she had been buck raving au naturel. She had crouched on the floor in her birthday suit, naked as a jaybird, before Ludowiga and the astonished maids.

Clothing was a cumbersome point of metamorphosis: one's duds didn't morph along with one's body. This irksome little detail yielded endless opportunities for embarrassment. Morfolk learned to control their morphs over time, but young Morflings' blood was unruly and mercurial and triggered shifts with neither rhyme nor reason.

Anastasia suddenly yearned to be one hundred years old. To a Morfo, that was still pretty young. Most Morfolk lived for centuries.

"Yes," Ludowiga said, "Saskia's first morph was a tour de force."

Anastasia winced and slugged down Dr. Lungwort's purple medicine, stifling a belch against the back of her hand. *Saskia.* Was she doomed to constant comparison with her cousin? She hadn't even met Saskia until three months earlier, and yet people constantly measured them against each other like specimens in a science experiment. Saskia had beautiful moon-blond hair (Anastasia's was mouse-brown)! Saskia glided like a swan on a cloud of silk (Anastasia clumped around in galoshes)! Saskia this; Saskia that. It was unbearable.

"I wonder," Ludowiga said, narrowing her eyes, "whether Anastasia will *ever* learn to fly. She is, you will remember, only half Morfo."

"Anastasia will be a proper aeronaut in no time," Baldwin huffed.

"I certainly hope so. It will shame the Crown if she sprawls on the floor like a dazed rat every time she shifts." Ludowiga sniffed. She was a big sniffer, Ludowiga. One whuffle of her pinched nose could express anything from disdain to delight. "You know, my Saskia is to dance the role of Vespertina in the Twinkle Toe Ballet's upcoming production of *Dance of the Sugarplum Bat*."

"Bully for her," Baldwin said.

"Bully, nothing! Saskia's triumphs bring glory to the royal family. What has *this* one done to honor us lately?" Ludowiga aimed her nostrils at Anastasia. "You'd better shape up, Princess!" With one final, scornful snort, she sailed from the dining room.

Baldwin clapped Anastasia on the shoulder. "Don't let Loodie spoil this momentous occasion. That woman could find fault with *anything*, even a happy event like your first morph. Think of *that*, Anastasia: *you turned into a bat!* That's something *big*."

"Something *marvelous*," Penny agreed.

"A marvelous *flop*," Anastasia said, Ludowiga's scorn still reverberating in her aching ears.

"Pshaw. Don't you start quoting Ludowiga to me! No, my girl, you're becoming a proper Morfo!" Baldwin enthused. "We need to get you abovecaves and into the moonlight. Moonglow is mother's milk to Morfolk. I know—let's go moonlight sledding tomorrow night! The Swiss hills are chock-full of top-notch sledding spots!"

Anastasia perked up. *"Moonlight sledding?"*

"Anastasia can't go gallivanting through the Swiss hills right now, Baldy!" Penny protested. "CRUD is still hunting her."

Anastasia shivered, her memories scrolling back to her recent brush with the Committee for Rubbing-out Unnatural Dreadfuls. It had all started with a ride in a pink station wagon. You *must*, prudent Reader, keep your eyes peeled for these sinister vehicles! If you happen to see one, peek to see whether a child of perhaps ten or eleven or twelve years of age is sitting in the backseat. Look closely!

The sad statistical truth is that you are probably-most-definitely spotting the victim of a diabolical kidnapping scheme.

Now, if you can: get a glimpse into the front seat. That nice lady driving the car? She's the kidnapper. Even worse, she's a *murderess*. She's one of the most accomplished and dangerous murderesses you could ever meet.

You are shocked. You are, perhaps, even scandalized. But pink station wagons and sweet-faced murderesses are just one of the thousands of unpleasant facts of life, much like ingrown toenails and tonsillitis and expired milk.

Not every kidnapper drives a pink station wagon. This particular automobile is the preferred mode of transport for the crème de la crème of kidnappers working with CRUD. Have you heard of it? I suspect not, because CRUD is hush-hush. It *needs* to be, because CRUD is a villainous society devoted to abducting Morfolk like Anastasia. In CRUD's perspective, the more Morflings snatched and snuffed, the better. Each kidnapping brings joy to the members' hearts and delight to their souls. The minions of CRUD celebrate squelched children with cake and confetti and cards of congratulations. And CRUD rewards its most successful Watchers with a jolly pink station wagon, the perfect vehicle with which to lure children to their doom.

So, good Reader, I implore you: no matter what anyone tells you—

even if—

especially if—

she's a little old lady with rosy cheeks and a purse full of sugarplums—

NEVER GET INTO A PINK STATION WAGON.

Anastasia had, and all sorts of ghastliness ensued. And even though she had escaped CRUD and moved halfway across the world, she still had to be careful. CRUD was looking for her, and they had agents in every nook and cranny you could spot on globe or map.

Fortunately, Anastasia now lived in a village that showed up on neither globe nor map—at least, not any of the globes or maps CRUD Watchers might have at their disposal. This village was, you see, entirely *underground*.

"Anastasia should stay in Nowhere Special for now," Penny said, a fretful little line creasing her brow. "Especially while she's growing into her morphs. Imagine if she turned into a bat in the middle of Dinkledorf!"

"Anastasia can't stay underground *forever*, you know. That's no kind of life for a child." Mischief twitched Baldwin's mustache. "Besides, the sledding season isn't going to last much longer. Spring looms nigh, Penny! And *I* want to go sledding, too."

Penny bit her lip. "I'm not sure. . . ."

"It's settled," Baldwin proclaimed. "You can bring your friends, Anastasia. When it comes to moonlight sledding, the more, the merrier!"

Penny frowned, her gaze twitching to the stack of cold pancakes on Anastasia's plate. "You haven't touched your breakfast, child. My goodness, you don't look well at *all*. Should you stay home from the academy today?"

Most children would leap at the opportunity for a day off from school, but Anastasia did not make this leap. Despite the collywobbles curdling her tummy and the headache hammering her brain and the mustache bristling upon her upper lip, she was bursting at the seams to get to school. This was not, as you might think, because Anastasia was an especially diligent scholar. She wasn't.

Nope; Anastasia yearned to hightail it to Pettifog Academy for a different reason entirely. She was anxious to see her friends, aka the League of Beastly Dreadfuls. In the grand tradition of all great secret societies, the Dreadfuls had a Matter Most Urgent to discuss. They needed to work out the nitty-gritty of a Secret Mission of Life-and-Death Importance.

"I'm fine," she fibbed. "Dr. Lungwort's Miracle Fizz really helped."

"Oh, good," Penny said.

"Splendid stuff, that fizz," Baldwin declared. "Just a sip peps me full of get-up-and-go."

Anastasia nodded, even though Miracle Fizz had nothing to do with the moxie now propelling her school-ward. Her get-up-and-go issued from something far more potent than any potion or pill: a mixture equal parts love and fear, the powerful combination of which has propelled many brave souls directly into the waiting arms of Doom.

"Ready to go?" Penny asked.

Squaring her shoulders, Anastasia patted her mustache with her napkin. "Ready."

❧ 2 ❧
Practical Survival

HOW DO YOU travel to school, dear Reader? Do you walk? Do you ride there in a car? If you, perchance, descend from an illustrious family of acrobats, do you torpedo to school from the barrel of a cannon? For the first six years of her educational career, Anastasia had jounced to Mooselick Elementary in a yellow school bus. However, those days were long behind her. She now sailed to school in a glossy black gondola. A gondola, as you may already know, is an elegant boat.

As her aquatic chariot pushed off from the dock, Anastasia snugged into the cushion of its velour seat and stared at her new home. Just as she had not always traveled to school in a fabulous boat, neither had she always lodged in a magnificent palace rising from the gleam of an underground lagoon.

That was another of the secrets that had simmered so deep inside Anastasia that she had had no idea of its existence. She was a *princess*. She had learned this gobsmacking fact just a few months earlier, shortly after discovering the heretofore-unknown branches of her family tree. Anastasia's surname wasn't really *McCrumpet* at all; it was *Merrymoon*, and the Merrymoons were *royalty*. Anastasia's grandmother Wiggy was Queen of the Cavelands, and that made Baldwin a prince, and Ludowiga and Penny and Saskia and Anastasia were princesses. Anastasia even had a lady-in-waiting, although that lady was a little brown bat. Her name was Pippistrella, and she was roosting under Anastasia's braid at that very moment.

Anastasia's father was a royal, too. However, he didn't bunk at Cavepearl Palace. Nor did he bunk in the humble family abode back in Anastasia's hometown of Mooselick. Unfortunately, those two depressing facts constituted the sole information anyone had regarding Fred's whereabouts. He had vanished without a trace, you see, on the same fateful day two CRUD snatchers lured Anastasia into their sordid pink station wagon and whisked her off to their ramshackle, authentically Victorian kidnapper lair.

Had CRUD Watchers seized Fred as well? Or was he in hiding? Was he wandering the globe, scouring the earth for Anastasia? Nobody knew. Nobody even knew whether he was *alive*. And the one person in the world endowed with a curious, infallible ability to locate Fred was missing, too. That person, as it happened, was Anastasia's grandpa Nicodemus.

Remember that Secret Mission of Life-and-Death Importance I mentioned a few pages ago? As you may have already guessed, Anastasia's vanished father and gramps centered at the shadowy heart of that very mission.

Anastasia unbuttoned her satchel and tugged forth her Cavelands history textbook. Nestled within the heavy tome's pages was a picture of Nicodemus Merrymoon, and at this picture she now peered. A curious design of concentric circles and stars gilded the elder Merrymoon's hand. Anastasia swallowed. Could Nicodemus's extra-special tattoo really illuminate the path to Fred?

Boohooohoooooohooooooo . . .

"The lagoon's been downright woebegone this morning," observed the black-clad figure at the gondola's stern.

"Oh, Belfry, you know the lagoon doesn't have feelings." Penny smiled at the gondolier. "Odd drafts sometimes pipe through the Cavelands. There are so many tunnels and holes and passages down here that the acoustics produce some strange noises."

"Like a great big French horn." Baldwin nodded. "Tootling away with us inside!"

Ooooo . . . ooooo. . . . Melancholy ululations rose from the silvery lake, sending shivers down Anastasia's spine until the gondola glided from Stardust Cavern into the murky maze of canals beyond. The twenty-minute cruise to Pettifog Academy took them through pitch-dark ducts and tunnels a-twinkle with chandelier-lit windows, beneath clouds of squeaking bats, and past Morfolk-crowded plazas.

"*Awooo!* Hey, Roger!" Baldwin hollered at a white wolf trotting across a limestone bridge. "Don't forget our whist game next Thursday!"

The wolf rounded his fuzzy lips into a howl and then padded into a coffee shop.

"Old Crescent Lagoon," Belfry announced. "Pettifog Academy."

"Have a lovely day, dear," Penny said.

"Thanks, Aunt Penny." Anastasia pulled a wig over her head. Pettifog Academy required its students to wear a school uniform, and that uniform included a curlicued white wig of the sort gentlemen sported in George Washington's glory days. The wig was itchy and hot, and Anastasia considered it her nemesis. *Nemesis* is a fancy word for *enemy*.

Two of Anastasia's other nemeses came into view as the gondola neared the dock. Cousin Saskia simpered at the center of a cluster of girls, and Marm Pettifog glowered at her pocket watch, marking the seconds until she could ring her handbell and summon the schoolchildren to another day of misery. Anastasia's gaze ricocheted among the crowd outside the academy until it settled on three other Pettifoggers. Oliver and Quentin Drybread and Gus Wata—the Beastly Dreadfuls—stood apart from the other students, their wigs bent close in a huddle.

Anastasia hopped up to the dock. "Bye."

"Belfry will come to fetch you after school," Penny said. "Baldwin and I have extra meetings in the Senate Cave today."

"If Dellacava and his supporters keep quibbling over the Merrymoon Militia Bill, we'll have *plenty* of these long nights," Baldwin groused. "Oh well. Farewell, my girl. Give old Pettifog what for."

Marm Pettifog was Baldwin's nemesis as well. He shot a dirty look at the starchy schoolmistress, and then he winked at Anastasia. "Put a thumbtack on her chair in my honor."

"Anastasia! Peeps!" Ollie tugged Quentin and Gus toward the pier. "We were just talking about our mission. I say—" he broke off. "Anastasia, did you know you have a *mustache*?"

Anastasia clapped her palm over her mouth, blushing.

"Does this mean you *morphed* today?" Quentin asked. "Congratulations!"

"Did you shift into a bat? You've always struck me as a sometimes-bat," Ollie said.

"I'd rather not discuss it," Anastasia muttered from beneath her fingers. "It didn't go well."

"At least you morphed," Gus encouraged her. "I never will."

"Really?" Ollie yawped. "Why not?"

Gus shucked his wig, revealing the green snakes coiled amidst his dark tufty hair.

Only a few gorgons lived in Nowhere Special, and Gus Wata was one of them. His mother was another. As you already know from peeking under Gus's wig, gorgons have snakes growing from their scalps. And that, dear Reader, isn't even the strangest thing about them! Just *one glimpse* of a lady gorgon's face would transform you into a lump of stone. Mrs. Wata wore a sack over her head almost all the time because she didn't want to petrify her friends and family. She was very thoughtful in that regard.

Gus didn't have to mask his face, however, because male gorgons didn't pack the same wallop as their female counterparts. They couldn't petrify anyone, even if they wanted to. And now Gus informed them, "Gorgons can't morph."

"But you're still half Morfo," Anastasia protested. "Just like me!"

"My *snakes* aren't," he said. "They're one hundred percent gorgon."

A striped fellow near his ear yawned.

"Your *clothes* don't morph with you when you shift," Gus went on. "Well, my snakes are *attached* to me. They can't morph, so neither can I." He replaced his wig, tugging it firmly in place.

DING DING DING DING DING DING DING!

Ollie grimaced as the last toll jangled from Marm Pettifog's handbell. "I wonder what tortures old Pettifog has planned for us today?"

Heavy wooden spiral staircases dominated the academy's cavernous front lobby, and these staircases twirled up to various classrooms, including the candlelit chamber where Marm Pettifog tormented Anastasia's fifth-grade class. Still clasping her upper lip, Anastasia took her seat beside her cousin-nemesis. Saskia leaned over and drawled, "Mumsy told me all about your little episode this morning. It sounds like the only thing you got out of morphing was that *lovely* new mustache."

Taffline Plimsole, one of Saskia's loyal minions, giggled.

"Why are you covering it up?" Saskia crooned. "Worried your gorgon boyfriend won't want to kiss you?"

"Gus is *not* my boyfriend," Anastasia mumbled.

"Anastasia!" Marm Pettifog said. "Stop whispering! Class has begun, and I have two important announcements.

First: next month our class shall go on a field trip to Dinkledorf."

"Are we going to the Dinkledorf Chocolate Museum?" Ollie cried.

"Or the fondue farm?" asked Jasper Cummerbund.

"Or the snowshoeing camp?" asked Parveen.

"None of the above," Marm Pettifog said. "We shall visit the Yodeling Museum."

The Pettifoggers harrumphed and slumped in their seats.

"Yodeling is an important part of Dinkledorfer culture," Marm Pettifog admonished. "And Dinkledorf is our gateway to the world abovecaves. As you get older, you'll be going to Dinkledorf with greater frequency. As you know, many Morfolk live in Dinkledorf now, passing as humans. If *you* sorry lot are to pass as Dinkledorfers, you'll need to know about yodeling. Dinkledorfers *love* yodeling." The headmistress shuddered.

"*Chocolate* is also an important part of Dinkledorfer history, Marm Pettifog," Ollie said hopefully.

"Stuff your face on your own time, Drybread." Marm Pettifog whisked around the room, scattering permission slips. "Make sure your parents sign these. Anyone without a permission slip shall remain at Pettifog Academy and muck bat guano from the science cave."

Gus's head drooped.

"Pay attention, Wata," Marm Pettifog said. "I'm about to

make my second announcement, and it's of utmost importance! Ahem. Today we begin our Practical Survival unit."

Practical Survival? What did that mean? Several children leaned eagerly across their desks, as though Marm Pettifog had just proclaimed a Pettifog pie-eating contest.

"I'm pleased to tell you that we've hired a new fencing instructor," Marm Pettifog said. "Your lessons commence next week. And this morning, you'll start Applied Navigation."

"Hooray!" shouted Jasper Cummerbund. "Hooray! Hooray! HOORAY!"

Many teachers would be delighted to think their assignments inspired joy in their young pupils. Marm Pettifog was not delighted. It was all the same to her whether her students liked or lumped their schoolwork, so long as they remained quiet and obedient. "Shut it, Cummerbund," she snapped. "As I was saying: for the remainder of the academic term, your rowing sessions shall be devoted to learning the central zones of the Nowhere Special canal systems, and some of the secret passages up to Dinkledorf."

"HUZZAH!" Jasper howled.

Marm Pettifog rolled her eyes. "You can't always count on a gondolier or parent to shuttle your sorry rumps around town, and you need to know where to go in the event of . . . a *witch attack.*"

A few children squealed, and Anastasia's stomach executed a wobbly somersault.

Witches! The word alone hammered a spike of sheer terror into the heart of each and every Morfo in the world, whether tiny tot or battle-hardened knight. Witches haunted Morfo dreams. Witches prowled the darkest annals of Morfo history books.

Once upon a time, Morfolk and witches had lived together peacefully in Nowhere Special. Nowhere Special was the perfect spot for peculiar sorts to go about their business without attracting the suspicion of humans. Sadly, this hunky-dory state of affairs was not to last.

It started with the cheese. Hard cheese turned to jelly, cream cheese thickened into tasteless cement, and stinky cheese didn't stink anymore. It smelled of peppermint. The Great Cheese Blight only lasted a few weeks, but then a rash of fever pox pimpled Nowhere Special. Everyone was itchy and sweat-sodden for months.

Suddenly, nothing seemed to go right. Wigs frizzed. Underpants pinched. Gondolas sank and clocks ran slow or fast or not at all. A mysterious fire melted the Nowhere Special chocolate reserve, and a freak cold snap plugged half the town's toilets with ice. Seeds of doubt began to sprout in Morfolk minds. Was it a run of bad luck? Or was it magic gone amok?

And then came the deaths. A smattering of Morfolk perished of pox, which puzzled doctors and alarmed their polka-dotted patients. Then a Morfo fell to his doom from a witch's balcony, and a weird sinkhole swallowed up two Morflings. After a Morfo baker choked on a donut he refused to share with a wizard, the Cavelands started buzzing with rumors of poisonous, deadly-as-dynamite magic. Suspicion festered. Fights erupted.

Finally, one fateful day in 1756, a powerful warlock named Calixto Swift cast a spell so vile and villainous that Morfolk declared Perpetual War on witches. Queen Wiggy (aka Anastasia's grandmother) banished witches from the Cavelands for good—or so the Morfolk hoped.

"Marm Pettifog—" Parveen faltered. "Do you really think the witches will come back?"

"They might, and they might not. There hasn't been a witch in the Cavelands for over two hundred years, but that doesn't mean a nasty witch won't show up in *that* doorway"— Marm Pettifog indicated the classroom door—"tomorrow during Echolalia lessons."

Gasps wheezed across the cavern.

"Should witches invade, you must be versed in fight and flight," Marm Pettifog said. "The fencing lessons will prepare you to *fight*. Knowing the canals will prepare you for *flight*. Now, I don't give two hoots about any of you individual sprats." The headmistress glared at them. "However, I'll be darned if any of you little twits croaks in a witch invasion under *my* watch. Pettifog Academy has a reputation to maintain, and blast me if the painful death of a student should besmirch it. Anyone who dies during school hours receives detention. Is that clear?"

"Yes, Marm Pettifog," the students chorused.

"Good." Marm Pettifog rustled papers on her lectern. "Now, you'll stay in your rowing teams, and your ninth-grade coxswain will guide you through the waterways. Your assignment is to *memorize* the routes through Nowhere Special, and you'd *better*! You won't get to use maps during your final navigation exam."

"No maps?" Taffline protested. "But Marm Pettifog, the canal system is a *maze*!"

"And lots of it goes through dark tunnels!" Parveen added.

"You wouldn't have time to consult a map during a witch attack, would you?" Marm Pettifog demanded. "You have to make a *mental map*. So pay attention during these rows— and *no lollygagging*! I don't want to hear that any of you has gone rogue and spent your rowing time munching taffy at O'Cavitee's Sweet Shop." Here her chilly eye fell upon Ollie, the most notorious sweet tooth at school. "If I find out that anyone has deliberately strayed from their assigned canal course, you'll flunk Applied Navigation."

Anastasia gulped. Although she had been an average-to-goodish student back in Mooselick, she was woefully behind at Pettifog Academy. Her scores in Subterranean Geography and Morfolk Literature were rather poor, I am sorry to say.

Her score in Echolalia, the squeaky bat language, was even worse. Our freckled hero now teetered on the brink of failing fifth grade.

Mind you, even though Anastasia lagged behind her classmates in most Morfolk subjects, she had a scoop unbeknownst to even the brainiest Morfo scholar: *the location of Calixto Swift's secret study.* Oh, but Calixto Swift had been an old slyboots!

The war-sparking wizard had devised a hidden den in which to craft his strangest, most sinister spells.

And within this mysterious hidey-hole, amidst who knew what sort of witchy badness, nestled all the Dreadfuls' hopes for tracking down the missing Merrymoons.

"One hour is just enough time to row to your destinations and back. If you return even *one millisecond* late, you'll spend your afternoon scrubbing stalagmites in the loos." Marm Pettifog smiled nastily.

"That's *disgusting*," Ophelia Dellacava objected. "My daddy wouldn't stand for that. He's a senator, you know!"

"I don't care if your daddy is the Archbishop of Canterbury," Marm Pettifog growled. "I don't tolerate disobedient children, and I *certainly* won't tolerate disobedient parents! Now get down to the docks!"

3

Witch Things

"**W**HY ARE WE learning how to build fences?" Anastasia asked as the Pettifoggers clambered down the staircase to the lobby. "Are we going to build a fence to keep out the witches?"

"Fences?" Gus's eyebrows drew together in puzzlement. "Oh! No, Anastasia: we're going to learn how to *fence*. With *swords*."

"Swords!" Anastasia exclaimed.

"Yep," Ollie said. "Duels, you know."

Anastasia blanched. "I can barely *skip rope* without tripping! I can't fight with a *sword*!"

"Well, you'll have to learn," Ollie said ominously as they tumbled out the academy entrance. "In case you run into a bloodthirsty witch. Oh—there's Q!"

A small fleet of pink Pettifog rowboats bobbed in the lagoon, and a ninth-grade coxswain waited in each one. After grabbing their oars, Anastasia and Gus and Ollie hopped aboard the vessel helmed by Quentin.

"Tallyho!" Quentin greeted them. "I'll be escorting you to Mudpuddle Cavern today."

"Mudpuddle Cavern?" Anastasia echoed.

"Yep. It's one of the exit routes to Dinkledorf," Quentin explained. "There's a secret stairwell up to the cuckoo clock shop. Ready, all! Row!"

The Dreadfuls flurried their paddles.

"Harder on starboard!" Quentin called, directing them across Old Crescent Lagoon and into one of the canals. Now he leaned forward and lowered his voice. "I didn't want to say anything too close to the academy, but Mudpuddle Cavern is in the same direction as the Cavepearl Theater."

"Really?" Anastasia's eyes glinted. "Should we hop out and visit you-know-where?"

"But what if Marm Pettifog finds out we—er— lollygagged?" Gus asked. "She'll flunk us for the entire Applied Navigation project!"

Ollie snorted. "Here's our grand chance to get cracking on our secret mission, and you're worried about *schoolwork*? Marm Pettifog won't find out."

"Even if she doesn't, we still need to memorize the canal system," Gus quibbled. "We're going to be tested on it."

"I can take you out some afternoon in Uncle Zed's gondola," Quentin offered. "We'll get plenty of practice before your final exam."

"And I know all kinds of shortcuts," Ollie boasted.

Gus considered. "We-ell . . . okay."

Quentin reeled off instructions as they zigzagged deeper into the tunnels. "Take the second left off Limestone Alley—no, that canal doesn't have a name; you just remember it's the second left—and then turn right down No Name Way. But there's no sign for it; you just have to remember that it's the first right off the nameless canal."

Anastasia was completely muddled by the time the Dreadfuls scudded into Rising Star Lagoon. She rubbed her temples. How would she ever forge a tidy mental map of the tangled canal system?

The Cavepearl Theater loomed upon the lagoon's far shore. The theater was closed up tight during the day, so no gondolas clustered along its quay, and no playgoers queued at its box office. Quentin quickly leashed the pink Pettifog boat to the dock. "We'll go through the side entrance," he said as the Dreadfuls scrambled up the deserted pier. "This way."

They charged down a narrow alley, halting at a small black door nooked on the theater's stone flank. Gold letters gleamed in the light from a nearby lamp:

AUTHORIZED PERSONS ONLY
(ALL OTHERS: SCRAM!)

Quentin withdrew a key from his pocket. As first chair saw in the Nowhere Special Orchestra, he was authorized indeed to pass through this grim and forbidding door. The rest of the Dreadfuls, on the other hand, *weren't*.

"The orchestra doesn't start practicing until afternoon," Quentin said, "so hopefully we won't run into anyone. But there might be costumiers or prop people working, so be quiet."

The Dreadfuls nodded, and Quentin fitted his key into the lock.

Were you to enter the Cavepearl Theater through the great arch of its front entrance, you would behold a rococo lobby dripping with chandeliers, and beyond this lobby the great gilded yawn of the playhouse itself, toothed with gilded stalactites. Upon its hallowed stage hundreds of opera singers had bellowed and thousands of silk-slippered ballerinas had pranced. However, not to any of these attractions were the Dreadfuls drawn. No, dear Reader: as is often the case in life, the most important element of the Cavepearl Theater lay behind the scenes.

Quentin cracked the door open, and the Dreadfuls slunk into a tunnel lit with greeny-glowing luminescent moss. The tunnel curved into the cavernous backstage area, deserted and eerie in the doldrums between performances. They pussyfooted through a forest of papier-mâché pines and past racks of ghostly white tutus, all the way to the darkest and farthermost corner. In this corner lay the jewel of Cavepearl Theater, as far as the Beastly Dreadfuls were concerned. Hidden behind the boughs of an artificial tree lay a small chink in the wall, and through this chink the children crept, one by one.

"Ugh!" Ollie said as he squeezed out on the other side. "Sickle Alley still gives me shivers."

"It's *ominous*," Gus agreed, eyeing the cracked streetlamps. "But Marm Pettifog is much scarier. Let's hurry."

"There's a rumor that some of the merchants along here sell black-market witch goods," Quentin said.

"Really?" Ollie's eyes rounded. "But wouldn't that be illegal?"

Quentin grinned. "Sure. That's why it's the black market, silly."

"Having old witch stuff is treason," Ollie said. He pressed against a grimy shop window and peered into the darkened cavern beyond. "It looks like this shop sells Shadowsilk. I don't see any witch things."

"They wouldn't exactly have a big display of potions out,

would they?" Gus said. "Come on, Ollie. We don't want Marm Pettifog to hear that we were hanging around Sickle Alley during school hours."

But Sickle Alley was abandoned. No pedestrians hustled down its muddy cobbles, perhaps because most of the shop windows lay shuttered or unlit. Anastasia wondered whether the sorts of customers who ventured into the creepy shopping district reserved their errands for the wee hours. Did the Sickle Alley dealers really peddle witch paraphernalia? Queen Wiggy had banned magic from the Cavelands at the beginning of the Perpetual War.

Of course, there were still pockets of magic tucked away in Nowhere Special, forgotten or hidden, lurking like poison ivy creeping around a picnic site. If you didn't watch your step, you just might rub up against something nasty. Most Morfolk avoided magic like the plague.

However, the Dreadfuls weren't like most Morfolk.

They edged through a crevice in Sickle Alley's craggy wall and sidestepped down the narrow passage beyond for a few breathless minutes until blurting into a musty little cavern. The cavern had once belonged to a witch named Mrs. Honeysop, and it was chock-full of old magic. This magic grabbed the Dreadfuls by the scruffs of their necks and set them adrift among clouds of luminescent twinkling beetles. Mrs. Honeysop's parlor, you see, wasn't bound by the normal laws of gravity. Witchcraft, like nimble fingers untying a tricky knot, had untethered the peculiar chamber from the earth's gravitational pull. Anyone visiting the cavern floated around much in the manner of astronauts in a space shuttle. However, few Morfolk dared set foot into the enchanted nook. As you will remember, Morfolk steered clear of magic; in fact, entry to Mrs. Honeysop's former abode was strictly forbidden, just like owning witch artifacts.

"Whee!" Ollie twisted into a slow-motion somersault.

"We don't have time to horse around, Ollie," Gus said sternly, brushing a floating cuckoo clock out of his way.

Anastasia frogged toward the silver grille spanning Mrs. Honeysop's fireplace. She removed a screwdriver from her satchel (she kept it handy for just this purpose) and made quick work of removing the bolts fastening the screen across the hearth. As she twisted the final screw loose, the screen detached from the wall and drifted aloft.

"Well done," Quentin praised, lighting the tapers of a candelabrum and handing it to her.

"Thank you." Anastasia ducked under the mantel and, lighter than a wisp of smoke, floated up the chimney. She floated all the way to its tippy-top, to the secret trapdoor discovered by the Dreadfuls only four days before. She twisted its knob. She took a deep breath. She steeled her resolve.

And up Anastasia popped into the secret lair of history's most notorious witch.

❧ 4 ❧

The Glass Conundrum

ANASTASIA HOVERED, HER petticoats puffing up around her waist (she was glad, today, for her silly pantaloons), and gazed around the snug beyond the trapdoor: the floating carved desk and matching chair, the library of drifting books, the witchy trinkets and knickknacks and doodads suspended midair. Shadow puppets glided about like big, slow black angelfish.

It was, Anastasia fancied, like swimming in a cabin of a wrecked ship. She crossed her ankles and bucked her legs, pretending for a few seconds to be a mermaid. Something slithered against her knee, pricking her skin into goose bumps—just one of the puppets, she realized, heaving a sigh. The warlock's hollow had her properly spooked! Anastasia swatted the paper figure away and paddled across the study to its far wall.

Bracketed in place by stalactites and stalagmites, gleaming in the flicker of the candelabrum, was a cabinet wrought entirely of glass. It was a peculiar, baroque thing. Clouds of spun glass crowned its top, and great ribbons of glass, stretched like glass taffy, curled round its curving flanks. The cabinet was unlike anything Anastasia had ever seen, and she had beheld some wondrous strange stuff in the Cavelands.

However, fantastical as the glass chest was, the Dreadfuls were far more interested in its contents. Anastasia peered beyond branches of coral and floating seashells and little bottles, deep into the cabinet's shadowiest nook.

"The Silver Hammer," Gus murmured behind her.

Morfolk had speculated for centuries about the Hammer's whereabouts. Knights and explorers and detectives (and detective-knight-explorers) had combed the globe seeking it. People had *died* looking for it.

Why, you might ask, would anyone risk their life hunting for a *hammer*, of all things? Ah, but my good Reader: the Silver Hammer was no ordinary nail-walloper! It was the weapon Calixto Swift wielded to execute his Dastardly Deed. It was the key, you must understand, to Anastasia's grandfather's freedom.

Nicodemus Merrymoon's whereabouts were a great mystery, but all Morfolk knew he was trapped in a magical silver trunk. Calixto Swift had put him there. Eight spellbound nails studded the lid of this trunk, and only the Silver Hammer could prize these nails loose. And the Dreadfuls had found the Hammer.

They just didn't know how to get it.

Calixto Swift's curious cabinet lacked a door.

"Maybe the door just blends in. . . . It must be concealed. . . ." Gus ran his palms over the glass.

"Don't you think it's odd that Calixto Swift left the Silver Hammer in a *glass* case?" Ollie asked. "Anyone who came up here could see it!"

"But *no one* comes up here," Anastasia said. "At least, no one has for hundreds of years. This is a *secret* study, after all." She stifled a shudder, imagining the odious Calixto Swift lurking within the murky lair, plotting to zonk Grandpa Nicodemus.

"Still, you'd think a mighty warlock would come up with a better hiding place. When I hide something, I put it well out of sight," Ollie said. "Like my secret stash of Toffee Mucker bars. I wouldn't just leave them sitting out in a glass jar, plain as the nose on your face! What if a sweet-toothed burglar broke into our apartment?"

"So what's your great hiding place, Ollie?" Gus asked, diving beneath the cabinet to examine its base.

Ollie darted a look at Quentin. "Not telling."

Quentin rolled his eyes. "You keep them in your pillowcase," he said. "And I don't know *how* you can sleep on that lumpy thing. Any luck, Gus?"

"Nope. I don't see a door, or a keyhole, or *anything*." Gus emerged, a fine layer of dust coating his wig.

"But how did Calixto take things out of the cabinet?" Anastasia asked. "And how did he put them inside in the first place?"

The Dreadfuls stared at the glass conundrum.

"It's just like Uncle Zed's ship in a bottle," Ollie declared. "Very mysterious, how that schooner got inside."

"This is a bit more complicated, Pudding," Quentin said. "If there isn't a door, Calixto must have used magic."

"Like a magic key?" Anastasia asked.

"Maybe," Gus said. "Or maybe he just chanted a spell and made a door appear."

Ollie chewed his lower lip. "*We* don't have magic."

Anastasia frowned. "Well," she said, "glass *breaks*, after all."

As a Beastly Dreadful and budding detective, Anastasia was inclined toward trespassing, eavesdropping, and general sneakery. She was not, however, prone to vandalism— usually. Desperate times call for desperate measures, you understand, and Anastasia was desperate indeed to find her father. And Nicodemus Merrymoon, trapped inside Calixto's Silver Chest, was the only person equipped with a foolproof way to do so.

The tattoo upon Nicodemus's right hand was no ordinary ornament. It was no run-of-the-mill skull and crossbones, nor heart emblazoned MUMSY, nor any of the other usual doodles you might spot upon your friends and neighbors. Nicodemus's tattoo was a compass, and it was *magical:* it always pointed the way to Fred. If Anastasia could find her grandpa and release him from the Silver Chest, then she could find her father.

"You think we should just *smash* the cabinet?" Gus asked.

"We *need* the Hammer. My dad . . ." Anastasia's thoughts flitted back to Fred's face evaporating from her dream. She swallowed. "The longer my dad is missing, the worse it is. If CRUD has him, he's trapped somewhere bad. And if he's *hiding,* then I have to find him before CRUD does."

"Breaking a warlock's cabinet seems *dangerous,*" Ollie protested. "What if it's hexed? Maybe any Morfo who shatters that glass will be cursed, just like the archaeologists who opened Tutankhamen's tomb!"

"There wasn't really a curse," Gus said. "That was a myth."

But the group fell into uneasy silence.

"You can wait in Sickle Alley," Anastasia said. "But I'm taking the Hammer *today.*"

"We'll stay," Quentin said. "Credo of the Beastly Dreadfuls: all for one, and one for all—right, Ollie?"

Ollie huffed. "Fine."

Anastasia snatched up a massive bust of Shakespeare. Outside Mrs. Honeysop's house and burdened by gravity, the statuette would have been heavy indeed; however, in Calixto's weightless lair, the Bard's marble noggin was featherlight. It was nonetheless very solid. Clutching the bust with both hands, Anastasia raised her arms above her head.

"It seems a shame to smash that beautiful case," Quentin murmured. "It really is a work of art."

"Like something out of a fairy tale," Ollie agreed wistfully.

Anastasia hesitated.

"You have to break a few eggs to make an omelet," Gus prompted.

"Gus!" Ollie said. "I didn't know you were interested in cooking."

"I'm not," Gus said. "It's just an expression. Go on, Anastasia. Smash it."

Anastasia closed her eyes. She swung the bust.

CLUNK! Shakespeare's face skidded across the cabinet. Anastasia blinked and stared at the Bard's nose, or rather, she stared at where his nose had once been. The force of the impact had knocked it clean off. Contrarily, Calixto's glass case remained completely intact. It wasn't even scratched.

"Try again," Quentin urged.

CLUNK!

"Why isn't it breaking?" Ollie asked.

CLUNK!

"Let me try." Gus took the statuette from Anastasia.

CLUNK!

"Oh, for Pete's sake," Quentin muttered. He pulled his foot back, aimed it at the cabinet's crystalline front, and kicked. "Ow!" His foot skated across the glass, and he flipped into a backward somersault.

"It must be the *magic*," Ollie said. "That's *magic* glass."

Anastasia touched the cabinet with the tip of her index finger, thinking. How might Francie Dewdrop, the hero of her favorite book series, approach the puzzle of a cabinet without doors? Over the course of her distinguished career as a detective-veterinarian-artist, Francie had contended with plenty of mysterious chests and coffers. In *The Case of the Tight-Lipped Tooth Bandit*, Francie discovered a code nestled within the scribblings of a murdered dentist (*"Miss Knox has gold fillings in left molar 17, right molar 32, and right molar 1"*), and she used this code to infiltrate a vault full of pirates' doubloons. In *The Ink Slinger's Cipher*, Francie had realized a mammoth old typewriter was actually a combination safe, and the combination was an odd sentence found typed on crumpled pages throughout the author's study (*unlock my writer's block with my black and many keys*). And while solving *The Candle Maker's Secret*, Francie discovered a tiny key hidden inside a wax votive, and with that key she had unlocked an intriguing jewelry box.

Yes, Francie Dewdrop had sniffed out plenty of codes and keys squirreled away in ingenious hiding spots. Anastasia now swiveled her gaze around the warlock's study. While Francie had never contended with magic, perhaps her ace snooping methods could help with unlocking the glass cabinet. "If there *is* a key to the chest, maybe Calixto hid it somewhere in here," she suggested. "Or we might find an 'open sesame' spell in one of his books."

The Dreadfuls set to plundering the study. Gus grabbed a promisingly thick tome full of handwritten notes and began perusing, and the others rummaged through nooks and pigeonholes. Anastasia opened the desk drawers, and out drifted loose papers and half-full bottles of ink and a sheaf of black-feathered quills. Really, a zero-gravity chamber was rather an *unpractical* place for an office! How had Calixto sat at his desk without floating up from the chair? Just the simple task of scribbling a few words would be difficult! As soon as the warlock uncorked the bottle, wouldn't the ink spill upward and into the air? Maybe, Anastasia reasoned, the cunning warlock used a bit of witchy magic to keep his work things from floating away midtask.

"This journal reminds me of Leonardo da Vinci's notebooks," Gus said. "There's all kinds of diagrams and drawings in here. . . . Here's a blueprint for some kind of flying machine. . . . I think Calixto was a *genius.*"

"An *evil* genius," Ollie corrected. "*Ooooh,* do I have the collywobbles!"

"How much time do we have to get back to school?" Gus asked.

Anastasia took out her pocket watch. "Fifteen minutes."

"We'd better leave," Quentin said. "I don't fancy spending an afternoon mopping out the Pettifog loos."

"But we're no closer to getting the Silver Hammer!" Anastasia protested.

"Anastasia," Gus said softly, "even if we could open the cabinet and grab the Hammer right this second, we wouldn't be able to *do* anything with it. We have no idea where Calixto hid the Silver Chest."

"Right. We still have to figure that out!" Ollie complained. "Cripes! This Daring Search-and-Rescue Mission has ever so many steps!"

"Maybe Calixto left some clues about the Chest's hiding place in these journals." Gus touched Anastasia's arm. "Next time, we can read them more carefully."

"But when *will* there be a next time?" Anastasia asked. "We can't come here during every navigation session."

"And we can't pretend to follow Quentin to orchestra practice every day," Gus said. "That fib worked last time, but our families will get suspicious if we use that excuse too much."

Quentin nodded. "I really can't skip any more orchestra practices, anyway. Maestro Flootwit can be pretty strict.

Last month he poured pudding down the tuba of a musician who hadn't learned the coda to 'Waltz of the Wayward Walrus.'" He cringed. "I'm anticipating a scalding this afternoon about yesterday's absence."

"You mean a *scolding*?" Gus asked.

"Believe me," Quentin said darkly, "with the maestro, it's a *scalding*."

"We'll just have to find chances when they come up," Ollie said.

"But we'll need to use the theater shortcut," Gus said. "I checked a map of the Nowhere Special pedestrian routes earlier this week, and Sickle Alley doesn't actually connect with any Cavelands passageways. It starts in a Dinkledorfian wine cellar and dead-ends not too far past our secret crawlway."

"That complicates matters," Quentin brooded. "With *Dance of the Sugarplum Bat* coming up, Cavepearl Theater's about to get really busy. It might be hard to find opportunities to sneak backstage when stagecraft really gets cracking on the sets."

Anastasia stared at the glass case in despair, imagining the weeks and months unfurling before them. How long might it take them to solve the twin puzzles of Calixto's mysterious glass cabinet and the missing Silver Chest—that is, if they ever solved them at all? And in the meantime, her father was who knew where, and ditto for Grandpa Nicodemus!

Gus seemed to be considering the same problems. "For now, let's take a couple of these books. We can study them at home." He stuffed Calixto's codex into the inner pocket of his school jacket. Anastasia followed suit, selecting two books from the floating library and shoving them into her satchel.

"No!" Ollie squeaked. "Witch stuff is strictly forbidden *by rule of the queen*! Do you know how much trouble you'll get into if anyone catches you with those creepy witch books?"

"If that happens, we'll just say we didn't even know they were witch books," Gus reasoned.

"Well," Quentin cautioned, "find a good hiding place for them. Better than your pillowcase." He winked at Ollie, then dived toward the trapdoor.

As Anastasia turned to follow them, she cast one last, longing look at the Silver Hammer, safe behind the unbreakable glass wall.

"We'll come back soon," Gus promised. "We'll find a way."

Ollie nodded. "We always do, you know."

5

Snottites

"**FOUR MINUTES!**" **MARM** Pettifog screeched from the academy pier. "Four minutes late!"

"Late?" Anastasia grabbled for her pocket watch, letting out a groan upon glimpsing its face. "Crumbs! I forgot to wind my watch this morning. It's stopped—"

"Spare me your excuses, Merrymoon. Would a *witch* take mercy on you and your lousy timepiece?" Marm Pettifog demanded. "That's detention for all of you! Assemble at the loos at three o'clock, *sharp.*"

Horror curdled Anastasia's soul. The students of Pettifog Academy avoided the loos as best they could, you understand. Most children tried to "hold it" through the school day. This was because the loos were in the academy basement, and the academy basement was *sinister.* It was dark and dank and potted with mud puddles, and sulfuric smog belched from the toilets and sogged the tunnels with a rotten-egg stench.

"Jasper Cummerbund says Marm Pettifog has a torture chamber hidden down here," Ollie divulged as the Dreadfuls descended to their punishment that afternoon.

"Why?" Anastasia whispered back. "The *entire academy* is a torture chamber."

Marm Pettifog awaited them at the lavatory doorways. "There are buckets and scrub brushes in the girls' loo. You may not leave until those stalagmites are spotless, understood?" She pointed at the rock formations spiking around the washbasins.

"Ugh! They're covered in *slime!*" Anastasia yawped. "What *is* that stuff?"

"Snottites," Marm Pettifog said briskly. "Bacteria colonies. You'd know that if you paid better attention in biology, Princess."

"Marm Pettifog, I can't go into the *girls'* loo!" Ollie protested.

"You can and you shall," the schoolmistress retorted. "Don't make me say it again, or I'll triple your punishment." And with that, she turned on her heel and departed.

"Better get to work." Quentin heaved one of the soapy buckets toward the sinks. "Pettifog isn't bluffing. She'll lock us down here overnight if those snottites aren't gone by the time she leaves to go home."

Ollie edged cautiously into the lavatory. "Home? Where do you suppose Marm Pettifog lives?"

"She probably lurks under a bridge somewhere," Gus grumbled.

"Like the troll in *Three Billy Goats Gruff*?"

"Exactly."

Ollie harrumphed. "Did you know Miss Candytuft's class gets to do a scavenger hunt for every Applied Navigation assignment? Miss Candytuft says learning should be *fun*."

"Miss Candytuft gives her students jelly beans for *good effort*," Gus said.

"And Miss Candytuft is taking her class *ice-skating* for their Dinkledorf field trip," Ollie groused above the *SWISH-SCROOSH-SCROOSH* of the scrub brushes. "Why do we get stuck with the *Yodeling Museum*? It's not fair!"

"At least you get to go to Dinkledorf," Gus mumbled. "My parents will *never* sign that permission slip. They'll never let me go abovecaves, *period*."

"Why is your dad so twitchy about leaving Nowhere Special?" Quentin asked. "I understand why your mom can't go abovecaves—she's a *gorgon*—but your dad could pass for a human."

Gus sighed. "It's because of what happened to my grandma."

"Your grandma?" Anastasia echoed.

The corners of Gus's mouth drooped. "She was burned at the stake."

"Like a *witch*?" Ollie squeaked.

Gus nodded. "Back in the seventeenth century, my grandparents lived in Italy. Grandpa Baba taught astronomy with Galileo at the University of Padua."

"Galileo?" Anastasia exclaimed. "The famous astronomer?"

"Yeah." Gus paused, sitting back on his heels. "So, Grandpa Baba and Galileo made a telescope and went to demonstrate it in St. Mark's bell tower in Venice. While my grandpa was peeking through the telescope, he turned it toward Padua and saw smoke rising above the rooftops. . . ."

"Your grandmother?" Quentin asked.

Gus bit his lip. "Some snoopy townspeople spotted Grandma morphing into a bat, and they thought she was a witch. There wasn't a trial or anything."

"Crumbs," Anastasia whispered. "That's horrible, Gus."

"Witches ruin everything!" Ollie said angrily.

"The people who did this were *humans*," Anastasia pointed out. "Not witches."

"But if witches didn't go splashing their bad magic around, maybe humans wouldn't be so suspicious and afraid," Ollie argued. "Maybe they wouldn't panic the second they saw something strange."

"Maybe not," Gus said. "Grandpa Baba and Galileo had

already gotten into trouble for their ideas about stars, and that didn't have anything to do with witchcraft—just science." He leaned forward and swiped his scrubber against a dangly bit of ooze. "Anyway, my family came to Nowhere Special after all that."

"I guess I can understand why your dad is so protective," Quentin murmured.

Gus scowled. "I understand it, too. But I don't want to live my entire life without seeing *anything* except Nowhere Special. I don't want to hide forever because of something that happened four centuries ago."

"But it's *still* happening," Ollie said. "Humans are still hunting Morfolk! CRUD kidnapped Anastasia and Q and me just five months ago."

"*You* still want to go abovecaves, don't you?" Gus pointed out with a huff.

"Yes," Ollie admitted. "Not to the Yodeling Museum, but I'm dying to go sledding."

"Oh!" Anastasia cried. "Baldwin and Aunt Penny promised to take me sledding tomorrow night. And you're all invited!"

"Smashing! Brilliant! Hoorah!" Quentin and Ollie chorused, but Gus's frown deepened.

"Couldn't your dad make one little exception?" Anastasia asked. "Penny and Baldy are *knights*, you know. They fought in a lot of battles in the Perpetual War. . . . We'd be safe with them."

Gus shook his head. "Dad thinks humans are *barbarians*. He'll never let me go, no matter what I tell him."

"Well . . ." Ollie wrinkled his nose, peeling a snottite from the wall. "Then why tell him anything?"

Gus crinkled his eyebrows. "Are you saying I should just go into Dinkledorf without telling my dad?"

Ollie grinned. "That's exactly what I'm saying."

"*Shh!* Marm Pettifog's coming. Look busy," Anastasia hissed.

But the footsteps clumping down the hallway proved to belong not to the academy schoolmistress but instead to its art teacher. Miss Ramachandra poked her face around the doorjamb and peered at the Dreadfuls. "Is this the right place for detention?"

"Yep," Ollie said. "Marm Pettifog is making us muck out these snottites."

"Well, I'm going to join you." Miss Ramachandra held up a scrub brush and winced. "I'm afraid I have detention, too."

"But you're a teacher!" Anastasia said.

"I spilled paint all over Marm Pettifog's favorite book on military strategy," Miss Ramachandra confessed, plunking down beside them. "And you know how fond she is of history.

My goodness—what *is* this stuff? You wouldn't find anything like this in London, except perhaps inside your nose."

"Aren't you from Nowhere Special, Miss Ramachandra?" Anastasia asked.

"No, dear. I just moved here a few months ago," Miss Ramachandra said. "I was very happy to get a job teaching here. In fact"—she wriggled in delight—"I'm starting the first official Pettifog Academy Art Club! Would you like to join? The first session is after school next Monday, and we'll explore the *wonderful world of creative expression!*"

There, amidst the snottites and the sulfuric toilets, Anastasia's spirits perked. Art club? She aspired to be a detective-veterinarian-artist when she grew up, just like Francie Dewdrop. On the other hand . . . the Dreadfuls' Secret Mission of Life-and-Death Importance didn't really leave Anastasia with much spare time. She needed to focus all her energy on plotting her next visit to Calixto's study.

"We'll have ever so much fun," Miss Ramachandra persisted. "Have you heard of Claudio Mezzaluna, the great painter? He's designing the sets for *Dance of the Sugarplum Bat,* and he's agreed to let the Pettifog art club help! It should be *inspiring!*"

The boys eyed Miss Ramachandra doubtfully, but Anastasia's thinker jerked into action. "*Dance of the Sugarplum Bat?*" she asked. "So will art club be meeting at the Cavepearl Theater?"

"Indeed we will," Miss Ramachandra thrilled. "Twice per week! Oh, I've always wanted a backstage glimpse of a world-class theater—"

"We'll join," Anastasia interrupted.

"We *will*?" Ollie squeaked. "But I'm not an artist!"

"Ollie," Anastasia urged, "haven't *you* always wanted an—um—backstage glimpse of a world-class theater?"

"Just think of all the—er—artsy *secrets* we'll learn!" Gus chimed in, nudging Ollie's side with his elbow. "The theater is the perfect place to *study* art."

"Oh!" Ollie said. "Right! I see what you mean. Okay, Miss Ramachandra. Count me in."

"Wonderful!" Miss Ramachandra beamed. The children beamed, too. I'm sure you, clever Reader, can guess the snoopy schemes already brewing in their Dreadful minds.

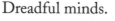

"Why, Anastasia!" Miss Ramachandra blinked. "My goodness, dear, that's *quite* a mustache! Did you morph today?"

The grin faded from Anastasia's face, and she twisted away, attacking the snottites with renewed vigor. "Not really."

"What shape did you take?" Miss Ramachandra asked. "Let me guess—you're a wolf!"

"No," Anastasia mumbled. "A bat."

"A bat! How lovely!" Miss Ramachandra said. "And how did you like flying?"

"I didn't," Anastasia muttered.

"You didn't like flying?" Ollie cried. "Did you *crash*?"

"No." Anastasia pulled her shoulders up around her ears, wishing to disappear completely. "I didn't fly at all. I just lay on the floor and wiggled."

"Everyone's first morph is awkward," Quentin consoled her. "You'll get it right next time."

"I don't think I will."

"Anastasia, dear, you mustn't say that!" Miss Ramachandra clucked. "Haven't you read your *Peter Pan*? *The moment you doubt whether you can fly, you cease forever to be able to do it.*"

"But I *can't* fly! That's the problem!" Anastasia said.

"Oh, but you *can*!" Miss Ramachandra said. "You just don't *know* it yet. But if you go on believing you can't—well then, it could become true. That's what happened to me."

"What do you mean?" Gus asked.

Miss Ramachandra hesitated. "You see . . . I *thought* myself out of flying. In fact, I thought myself out of morphing entirely."

"Really?" Ollie said.

"The first time I shifted, I flew into a car windshield and broke my arm," Miss Ramachandra explained. "It took two months to heal, and during that time I brooded and worried and convinced myself not only that I would never fly again but I would never even *shift*. And you know what? I haven't!" She shrugged sadly. "The doctors told me it's a psychological block."

Anastasia lifted her face so she could better see Miss Ramachandra. The art teacher smiled and patted her hand. "Next time you morph, dear, *just think happy thoughts*."

"That's from *Peter Pan*, too!" Ollie said.

"Of course it is," Miss Ramachandra said. "*All* the best advice comes from storybooks, don't you think?"

6

An Untimely Death

FROM KINDERGARTEN THROUGH fifth grade, Anastasia had known Penny merely as the school librarian at Mooselick Elementary. Only recently had she made the great switch from calling her Miss Apple to Aunt Penny. And Baldwin had entered Anastasia's life just a few months earlier. Nonetheless, Anastasia felt as though they had been family for years and years. Now that she knew Penny and Baldwin as her aunt and uncle, she couldn't imagine life without them.

Anastasia's grandmother Wiggy, however, was an entirely different ball of wax.

Perhaps, Anastasia mused, it was that she rarely *saw* Wiggy. Her Majesty was usually busy attending to queenly activities like presiding over Congress and reviewing bills and traveling to blab with diplomats and politicians. Before she'd descended to the Cavelands, Anastasia's notions of a royal's existence came straight from fairy tales: dancing at balls and wearing diamonds and sitting around munching tarts. Ludowiga and Saskia certainly lived up to those expectations, but Wiggy did not. Wiggy was pensive and preoccupied. Anastasia had never heard the queen laugh, and had seen her smile perhaps three times in as many months.

Sitting now at the long glass table of the dining hall, Anastasia edged a glance at her grandmother. Might the queen's solemnity stem from her husband's and son's absence from family fondue night?

"I had a meeting with the Wish Hags today," Wiggy announced.

The Wish Hags were three eccentric old ladies skilled in the art of brewing wishes. That sounds like a rather witchy talent, but the hags were not in fact witches.

"Did you make a wish?" Anastasia asked Wiggy.

"Indeed I did. I asked them whether I might wish to know your father's whereabouts."

Anastasia's heart lurched. Why hadn't *she* thought of it? It was so obvious! It was so simple! The Wish Hags could *brew up a wish* to find Fred!

"Alas," Wiggy went on, "that is not a viable solution."

"But *why?*"

Wiggy sighed. "The hags informed me that 'seeking' wishes are generally ineffective. They take months to brew for something so simple as a missing sock or set of lost keys; for a *person* it takes *ten years* for the wish-goop to—er—steep properly. And even then, the wish only reveals where the subject was *at the time the hags started mixing the goop.* Imagine if someone tried to find *you* now based on your location ten years ago."

Anastasia slumped back in her seat.

"Your Mommyness," Baldwin said, "we should still make the wish. If Fred is being held captive somewhere—"

"Then he might still be there by the time the wish comes true." Wiggy nodded. "I already thought of that. And I *did* make the wish." She turned her mirror-colored eyes back to Anastasia. "I hope my telling you this doesn't rub salt in the wound, child. But I did want you to know that your father is very much on my mind, and I'm trying everything possible to find him."

Anastasia swallowed, staring at her plate.

"What about Poppa?" Penny asked. "The Silver Chest has likely remained in the same spot since 1756. And it will probably be there ten years from now."

"But the Chest is *enchanted* to stay hidden, Penny," Baldwin said. "And you know the hags' wishes aren't powerful enough to undo witch magic."

"The *Chest* is enchanted, but *Poppa* isn't," Penny said. "We wouldn't wish to find the Silver Chest; just Poppa."

"Ah!" Baldwin marveled. "A clever loophole! Ingenious! Penny, you should have been a lawyer!"

"It *is* a good idea," Wiggy said. "I had it myself. Unfortunately, the hags' wishes can reveal neither the Chest *nor* its contents." She sighed again heavily. "Hag wishes aren't *omnipotent*. There are limits to what the hags can do."

Perhaps, Reader, you have heard the old proverb "If wishes were horses, then beggars would ride." It's another way of saying that wishing is silly and ineffectual. Anastasia did not agree that wishing was silly. She was not going to stop wishing and hoping to find her father. But she was also wise enough to know that wishes and hope often needed a little elbow grease to properly jell. And even if the hags couldn't supply the elbow grease required to reveal the missing Merrymoons' whereabouts, Anastasia thought, the *Dreadfuls* could.

Wiggy reached out to smooth Anastasia's braid. "The hags did mention that they would love a visit from you, my dear."

"Maybe they can wish up a unicorn for us," Baldwin mused. "I've always wanted a pet unicorn! I would name it Narwhal."

"Oh, Baldy," Penny said. "You know unicorns aren't real."

"If you don't change your attitude, Penny, I won't let you pet Narwhal," Baldwin countered. He clapped Anastasia on the shoulder. "Now, eat up this scrummy fondue. A growing Morfling needs plenty of cheese to keep up her strength!"

Penny dunked a morsel of bread into the pot of molten cheese. "This week's Pettifog newsletter mentioned a school concert next month, Anastasia."

Anastasia chomped her fondue. "Yep. We got a big lecture about it today. Marm Pettifog says we have to be on our best behavior because Superintendent Sternum is invited. I think she wants to impress him."

"Then you should put a whoopee cushion on his seat," Baldwin urged. "I'll lend you mine—it's extra-squishy."

Penny ignored him. "Now that Quentin is first chair saw in the Nowhere Special symphony, does he still play in the Pettifog orchestra?"

"Yes, he—"

"Your Mommyness!" Ludowiga gasped, bolting into the dining hall. "Your Mommyness, did you hear? Oh, disaster! Calamity!"

"Why, Ludowiga!" Wiggy said. "What's wrong?"

"Senator Gibbeous is dead!"

"Dead?" Wiggy echoed.

"Nonsense," Baldwin said. "We just saw him today in the

Senate Cave. He complimented my cravat. A man of excellent taste!"

"That's all very well and good, but he's dead now," Ludowiga said. "He croaked in the middle of a fondue course at the Gilded Cheddar one hour ago."

"Oh dear," Penny said. "Poor man. I did think he was looking rather frail lately."

"He *was* over six hundred years old," Baldwin mused.

"At least he died eating cheese," Penny said softly.

"A fine way to go," Baldwin eulogized. "A fine way."

"But still sad," Penny said.

"It's worse than *sad*," Ludowiga said. "It's *catastrophic*! Gibbeous couldn't have picked a worse time to kick the bucket!"

Baldwin shot her a dirty look. "Why? Are you worried his funeral will interrupt some important party?"

"Baldwin, don't you pay the slightest attention in Congress?" Ludowiga demanded. "Senator Gibbeous always backed the Crown. *Always.* And in case you haven't noticed, we need every bit of support we can get for the Merrymoon Militia Bill. The vote is in six weeks."

"This does tip the scales," Wiggy murmured. "The Dellacavas are campaigning fiercely against my proposed tax increase."

"They've even persuaded Larry and Linus Cummerbund

to vote against it," Ludowiga said. "Victoria Cummerbund hinted as much at my tea party yesterday."

"Cummerbund?" Anastasia piped up. "There's a Jasper Cummerbund in my class!"

Ludowiga nodded. "Linus Cummerbund is his father. Anastasia, sit near Jasper in the Pettifog caveteria this week, and keep your freckled ears pricked. See if he mentions anything about the bill."

"Ludowiga!" Penny cried. *"Really!* Anastasia is not a *snoop."*

"Oh, get off your high horse, Penny," Ludowiga snapped. "Every member of this family needs to do their part to protect the Crown's interests, including silly Halflings like Anastasia."

Anastasia ignored this barb. "What *is* the Merrymoon Militia Bill?"

"It's a proposal to increase our military budget," Wiggy said. "We would use the money to fortify the Cavelands army."

A shiver tickled Anastasia's spine as she remembered Marm Pettifog's Practical Survival lecture. "Because of witches?"

Wiggy nodded. "You understand, the witches consider these caves *theirs.* There's still a silver mine somewhere down here to fuel their magic, and plenty of space in which to practice it far from the prying eyes of humans." She steepled her fingers. "Should the witches ever return, I fear it shall prove the bloodiest chapter of the Perpetual War. I fear it shall prove the *final* chapter."

"Why?" Anastasia whispered.

"Because, my dear child, it would be a fight to the death. It wouldn't end until one side was utterly crushed. The witches won't come back unless they're prepared for that." The queen's strange eyes flashed. "And, as you know only too well from your experiences at St. Agony's Asylum, witches aren't the only threat to Morfolk safety. CRUD remains a constant menace. The Merrymoon Militia Bill would bolster our abovecaves espionage network, too."

Penny smiled sadly. "Unfortunately, we have quite a few enemies."

"Including the Dellacavas," Ludowiga snapped. "They're doing everything they can to sabotage this bill."

"But *why*?" Anastasia asked. "Don't they want Morfolk to be safe?"

"The Dellacavas put their pocketbooks before everything else," Baldwin gruffed. "They don't want to pay higher taxes, even though they're one of the richest families in Nowhere Special."

"But their main agenda is *political*," Ludowiga hissed. "The Dellacavas grasp any opportunity to undermine the Crown. They're certainly not going to support a bill that would strengthen the queen's army!" She slapped the table-top, jouncing the fondue pot. "Those silvermongers have been stirring up trouble for *centuries*!"

"So they have," Wiggy said wearily. "But let's put aside matters of state for the evening, shall we? Tonight, I am going to mourn the passing of a dear colleague." She stood and crooked a finger, summoning her bats-in-waiting to follow her from the hall.

"But, Your Mommyness!" Ludowiga wailed, scurrying in the queen's wake. "We need to strategize. . . ." Her protestations faded down the hallway.

"Thank goodness I've been blessed with a stalwart stomach." Baldwin reached for a lump of bread. "Otherwise, I would have lost my appetite after that little scene."

Anastasia frowned. "Why did Ludowiga call the Dellacavas *silvermongers?*"

Penny twiddled a button on her jacket. "Back before the Perpetual War, the Dellacavas exported silver for the witches."

"But silver is poisonous to Morfolk!" Anastasia cried.

"Indeed it is," Baldwin said. "But there was a thumping good trade in silver abovecaves back then, as now. The witches owned the silver mines in Nowhere Special, as you know. They used silver in their magic, but they also sold silver in abovecave markets. And the Dellacavas helped them."

"The Dellacavas blocked quite a few of the bans the

Morfolk Senate tried to impose on the witches' magic," Penny said.

"Hmph!" Baldwin harrumphed. "Witch sympathizers! They were just looking out for their own business interests."

Penny reached across the table to squeeze Anastasia's hand. "You mustn't worry too much about Caveland politics, my dear. You have your own concerns. For one: homework."

Normally, Anastasia would protest and bellyache and carry on in the face of homework, but this evening she kept her mouth shut. The sooner she muddled through her history paper and Echolalia worksheets and math problems, the sooner she could begin reading Calixto Swift's secret journals.

7

Silver-Bound Secrets

THAT NIGHT, BY the golden glow of her candelabrum, Anastasia munched a plateful of snickerdoodle cookies and pored through the fancier of the two books she had pilfered from Calixto's study. It was a lovely volume, leather-bound with silverwork filigreeing the cover.

Anastasia stared now at this delicate metalwork, thinking of witches and Dellacavas and silver mines. Nobody knew where the witches' old mines were now, which suited Morfolk just fine. You wouldn't catch a Morfo in a silver mine. Sometime around age eleven, Morflings developed a severe allergy to silver. Just *touching* silver made a Morfo break out in painful blisters and stinging rashes, and prolonged exposure to silver sapped a Morfo's strength. For this reason, Primrose and Prudence Snodgrass had clasped

a silver cage over Quentin's head back at the asylum. And Prim and Prude had packed their kidnapper lair with silver doodads and loaded their Watcher shotguns with silver bullets. Silver injuries were very bad for Morfolk.

In fact, a nefarious warlock had burned off Wiggy's eyelids with a silver spell many ages earlier, in the first battle of the Perpetual War. The queen had had them replaced with glass so she could always watch for the return of witches, even in her sleep.

Tucked now into the safety of her comforter, Anastasia scrutinized Calixto's silver-bound journal. She then reached out her right hand and pressed her palm firmly against the poisonous metalwork.

Perhaps you are bracing yourself for a scream of agony. Perhaps you're even expecting smoke to seep out from between Anastasia's fingers. However, neither of these things happened. *Nothing* happened. She didn't even feel itchy.

Anastasia stared at her palm, bemused. Why didn't she react to silver in the manner of every other Morfo in the world? The Merrymoons had explained to Anastasia that her Morfolky development might differ, since her mother had been a human. Anastasia, the Merrymoon princess, was a Halfling.

Anastasia was nonetheless puzzled. She had metamorphosed that very morning, after all.

"Most mysterious," she informed Pippistrella.

"Squeak!" Pippistrella replied from her nook in the canopy.

Anastasia shrugged and carefully opened the silver-bound book. After scanning the first page, she realized it was some kind of diary.

Now, gentle Reader, reading someone else's diary is usually a no-no. Diaries are sacred places in which to unburden one's heart and pour one's soul. Even the most hard-boiled detective or villainous rogue knows that opening someone else's journal without permission is a gamble with fate.

You might expect Anastasia to now hesitate. However, she didn't even bat an eyelash before diving into the jumbly cursive. She had no scruples about reading Calixto's diary, not if it provided a clue that would lead her to Nicodemus.

September 13, 1753

At breakfast this morning Nico bemoaned his craving for a proper beignet. Aha! thought I, 'tis the perfect opportunity for a little magic trick! I excused myself on the pretext of visiting the loo, but I actually whisked upon a whirlwind trip to visit Cousin François in New Orleans. Of course, I arrived in the middle of the night!

François lives in a grand mansion on the bayou, and he wears the same frilly fashions he wore back in France. He looks every inch the foolish popinjay, which is how he best camouflages his witchery from the humans. Nonetheless, I teased him about his silk stockings. Mind you, François's magic is powerful strange, and he's been training in voodoo. He's even hypnotized the alligators living in his swamp—he plays them a tune on a bewitched flute, and up from the mossy depths the beasts march like a small reptilian army. I wouldn't tease him too much.

Imagine Nico's astonishment when I brought a dozen beignets back to the breakfast table, still piping hot from François's griddle!

Anastasia goggled at the page. How could Calixto travel from Louisiana to Nowhere Special before his donuts cooled? It was impossible! Even a supersonic jet couldn't blast from New Orleans to Switzerland in the five minutes or so it would take for a pastry to lose its heat. And Calixto had written this in the eighteenth century, well over one century before the Wright brothers rigged up the first airplane. Was Calixto just exaggerating? Or had he used some kind of hocus-pocus to travel across the globe? Had he flown on an enchanted broomstick?

Anastasia plucked a snickerdoodle from her plate and crunched into it, leaning again over Calixto's journal.

October 24, 1753

Last Monday I received an invitation from my good friend Youssef, urging me to come to Morocco to admire his newest project: a rug enchanted to fly. All week I labored to craft a magic door to Marrakesh, and last night I set upon my merry jaunt.

'Twas a pleasure to see old Youssef, but a greater pleasure still to behold his magic carpet! Oh, what a ride it was! We loop-the-looped starry stories above the town, cloaked in the gloom of a night of new moon. I was positively giddy by the time we landed.

I implored Youssef to bind a magic carpet for me, and the good fellow agreed. We set off for the markets, and I chose a rug from one of the stalls. Zounds, I shall be on pins and needles waiting for Youssef to spellbind it!

Magic door! So *that* was how Calixto zipped across the globe so quickly. Her gaze drifting back to the Louisiana entry, Anastasia wondered just how many enchanted doors the old warlock had forged.

The following entries described similar trips. Calixto had gone to Egypt and Iceland. He claimed to have toasted marshmallows with Benjamin Franklin in Philadelphia. He had picnicked beneath cherry blossoms in Japan and sniffed roses in the gardens at Hampton Court Palace in England. The silver-bound volume was not, Anastasia realized, the sort of diary into which one scribbles their deepest, darkest secrets. It was a travel journal.

Still, she mused, it might provide a clue about the Silver Chest's whereabouts. She jotted in her sketchbook:

LOUISIANA—BAYOU
MOROCCO—MARKETPLACE
EGYPT—GREAT SPHINX OF GIZA
JAPAN—SHINTO SHRINE, CHERRY TREE
ICELAND—REYKJAVIK
ENGLAND—HAMPTON COURT PALACE
PHILADELPHIA—S'MORES?

Anastasia stared at her notes. She certainly *hoped* Calixto hadn't hidden the Silver Chest deep in a gloopy Louisiana swamp, guarded by beignet-chomping alligators. How on earth would the Dreadfuls ever manage to dredge out Nicodemus?

She shook her head and turned the page to the final entry.

June 9, 1754

Still squiffy after last night's gallivants with Nico . . . by the stars and the moon, that man can outdrink any pirate! Together we finished off two bottles of rum. Speaking of pirates, in the midst of our potted revelries we ventured to Penzance. (I blindfolded Nico for the trip—imagine his surprise when he found himself in the English port town!)

Many of the details of our great whoop-de-do eluded me this morning, until I glimpsed upon my forearm a mermaiden penned in emerald-colored ink. She actually winked at me, the saucy lass! Then bits and pieces of our adventure in Penzance came back to me, like fragments of a dream: Nico and I went to a tattoo parlor in the wee hours!

Now I remember: the tattoo artist inscribed a compass on Nico's hand—a compass to guide him to ever-wandering Fredmund, who ran away again last week after another quarrel with his twin, Ludowiga. I bound the ink with a finder spell, so the compass should work like a charm!

Nico and I have a little jest in mind for Fred. Tonight we'll challenge him to a game of hide-and-seek. . . . He may go anywhere in Nowhere Special, with a half-hour head start. . . . We'll astound the poor child with our "tracking skills"! Nico promised to wear gloves today to conceal the tattoo, so as not to ruin the joke.

He's still wondering about our trip to Penzance—he came by my workshop for brunch, full of curiosity. "By gum, Calixto," said he, "I'm simply dying to know how you got us a thousand miles away in the blink of an eye!" I told him I couldn't possibly reveal the magic mechanisms—that I derive far too much pleasure in surprising and confounding him. But really, there are some secrets I can't tell even Nico. I trust him with my life; I love him dearer than a brother; but I cannot make all my witchery plain. Like so many good and dutiful husbands, he tells his wife everything. And lovely though Wigfreda may be, she's still a Von der Mond, and the Von der Monds have made no bones about their distaste for magic. No, my magic doors are a secret between the Glass Lady and yours truly.

Anastasia looked up from the journal, her thoughts all out of kilter. Up until then, she had imagined Calixto Swift as a cardboard villain, a crafty witch who had cloaked evil intentions behind smiles and gags and puppet shows. However, through Calixto's jolly travel memoirs, she was beginning to glimpse a different character altogether. It was difficult indeed to reconcile the merry jokester of the journal jottings with the backstabber behind the Dastardly Deed.

What in caves had twisted the warlock's heart so horribly? What had provoked the donut-sharing, prank-playing wizard to consign his best friend to a fate worse than death? Anastasia was baffled, because one truth shone through page after page of the silver-bound chronicles: Calixto Swift had *loved* Nicodemus.

❧ 8 ❧

In Search of a Magic Door

THE LIBRARY IN Cavepearl Palace was, Anastasia reckoned, one of the coziest spots in the entire world. Packed with thousands of Penny's tomes, chockablock with Baldwin's collection of cuckoo clocks, crammed with old globes and brass telescopes and squishy chairs, the palace book nook was the perfect place to dive into a novel or a nap, or both.

It was also the perfect place to whisper about Secret Missions of Life-and-Death Importance, and whisper the Dreadfuls did the following afternoon.

"Did you find anything good in Calixto's notebooks?" Anastasia asked.

Gus frowned. "I'm not sure. There was some kind of plan for a flute that plays music on its own."

"Oh!" Anastasia said. "I wonder if Calixto wanted to hypnotize alligators?"

"Alligators?" Ollie asked. "What does a magic flute have to do with *alligators*?"

Anastasia told them about Calixto's journey to New Orleans and his cousin François's triumphs in reptile enchantment. Then she summarized Calixto's globe-trotting. "He even went to Iceland and Japan!"

"How could he have traveled so far so fast?" Gus asked.

"Magic carpet?" Ollie suggested.

"Calixto *did* fly on a magic carpet," Anastasia said. "One of his warlock friends in Morocco had one. But that isn't how he got around." She leaned over the table and lowered her voice. "He made magical doors that open up to different countries."

"Incredible!" Gus's eyes widened. "Do you think Calixto might have built a door that leads to the Silver Chest's hiding place?"

Anastasia's heart thumped. "That's what I was wondering."

Gus gave a little jump. "Maybe the magic doors are *somewhere in the castle*."

"Why would they be *here*?" Ollie asked. "Calixto's office is clear across Nowhere Special!"

"Yes, but this was his *home*," Gus pointed out. "Calixto

lived here before the Perpetual War, remember? He *designed* Cavepearl Palace."

"If there were any magic doors in this castle, don't you think someone would have found them by now?" Ollie asked. "The Merrymoons have been living here for over two hundred years. Surely someone would notice that one of the palace doors opened into a Louisiana swamp!"

"Cavepearl Palace is enormous," Anastasia said. "I bet there are all sorts of nooks and crannies that nobody's discovered yet. There could be secret doors and tunnels, too."

"She's right," Gus said. "Calixto was a *genius,* you know. He was great at hiding things. Who else would think of hiding a secret study at the top of a chimney? And even if we don't find a magical door," he went on, "we might find something else that belonged to him."

"It can't hurt to look," Quentin philosophized. "But where should we begin?"

Were you, dear Reader, an evil warlock genius, where might you hide your magical portals to foreign and faraway lands?

"In Francie Dewdrop mystery one hundred and one, *The Case of the Cryptic Cockatoo,*" Anastasia mused, "a bank robber melted down a million dollars' worth of stolen platinum bars and turned it into a big birdcage for his parrot. Lots of people ransacked his house looking for the missing platinum, but nobody paid any attention to the birdcage." She paused. "Until the cockatoo told Francie the secret."

"What does a birdcage have to do with magical doors?" Ollie demanded.

"Nothing," Anastasia said. "The point is: *sometimes the best hiding place is right in plain sight.* People overlook the obvious. Maybe the door is disguised as a window!"

"Anastasia!" Gus cried. "That's brilliant! I can just imagine Calixto leaping through a window and landing halfway across the world. You're really thinking like a witch now!"

"You're not going to jump out one of the windows, are you?" Ollie cried. "You'd land in the lagoon, and the lagoon is full of electric eels!"

Gus chewed his lip. "We could just throw something out and see if it disappears into thin air."

"Paper airplanes!" Quentin said.

The Dreadfuls spent ten minutes folding a sheaf of Anastasia's notebook paper into a squadron of airplanes, and then they set off in search of windows through which to fling them. As in many castles of yore, the windows outfitting Cavepearl Palace were not actually paned with glass. They were simply holes in the wall.

"No wonder this place is so chilly," Anastasia said.

"*Everywhere* in the Cavelands is chilly," Ollie said. "All right! Three . . . two . . . one . . . blast off!" He sent

an airplane sailing through the window, and the Dreadfuls gathered around the ledge in breathless anticipation.

"It just fell into the lagoon!" Anastasia groaned.

"But did you see how far it flew?" Ollie preened. "That was a pretty good airplane."

After they had torpedoed their entire stock of planes, Gus drummed his fingertips on his chin. "Hmmm. What next?"

"I suppose we'll just have to wander about and see if we spot anything interesting," Anastasia said. "Maybe Calixto hid his doors somewhere else."

Wander they did. They tiptoed betwixt armless statues in shadowy salons. They peered behind heavy tapestries embroidered with scenes of wolves galloping through midnight forests. They snooped beneath carpets in the hopes of glimpsing trapdoors. They even clambered into empty fireplaces and stared up the chimneys.

"Nothing," Quentin lamented, staggering from his thirteenth hearth and coughing up a handful of soot.

They roamed the winding corridors, discovering rooms Anastasia had never seen. Some were fanciful bedchambers similar to hers, and others were deserted hollows. An arch at the end of a quartz-encrusted hallway led into a long cavern chock-full of artworks.

"Mightn't Calixto have hidden a magical door *behind* a painting?" Quentin asked.

"Perhaps," Gus said. "I wonder whether the queen brought these paintings in, or if they were here when the palace belonged to Calixto."

The Dreadfuls prowled through the gloomy gallery, peeking behind the gilded picture frames.

"Anything interesting?" Gus called.

"Nope," the Dreadfuls chorused.

"Maybe the *paintings* are magical," Ollie said. "Maybe Calixto could hop into them, just like Mary Poppins!" He laid his palm flat against a still life of s'mores and roses. He pressed gently. To everyone's disappointment, his hand did not reach into a far-flung realm. It only left a few candy-sticky fingerprints on the canvas.

"Ollie!" Quentin scolded.

"*These* paintings definitely didn't belong to Calixto." Gus paused in front of a section of portraits. "They're all of the Merrymoon family."

There was an enormous oil of Baldwin in wolf form, and dozens of little portraits of noble-looking mice—Penny, Anastasia knew, from the intelligence gleaming in their bright mouse peepers. She stared at a painting of a solemn young woman dripping with armor and clutching a sword at her hip. A small golden tag bolted to the frame read WIGFREDA MERRYMOON AT THE BATTLE OF PENUMBRA CAVERN. It was Wiggy, girding her loins to chase witches from the Cavelands.

WIGFREDA MERRYMOON
AT THE BATTLE OF PENUMBRA CAVERN

Wiggy didn't match up with the cozy, huggy, cookie-baking grandmothers in Anastasia's old storybooks, but Anastasia was beginning to think that was just fine. Wiggy was brave and fierce. She was a *hero*.

The admiration brimming in Anastasia's eyes fizzled away as she slid her attention to a picture of Ludowiga, bewigged and beauty-marked, nostrils arched in their trademark sniff. Beside Ludowiga, a rococo-framed likeness of Saskia simpered: porcelain-skinned, silver-golden-haired, clasping a rose to her lacy bodice. Saskia looked every inch the princess. Anastasia scowled.

Then she shifted her gaze to the next portrait: Fred McCrumpet, slightly ridiculous in a frilly collar the likes of which he had of course never worn in Mooselick. He didn't look fierce like Baldwin, or noble like Wiggy, or clever like Penny, or imperious like Ludowiga, or beautiful like Saskia. He was plain and little, and his mustache drooped. But the artist had captured Fred's gentle, kind expression.

A dull ache throbbed through Anastasia's chest.

"That's my dad," she said.

"Prrrrp." Pippistrella snugged Anastasia's ear in a batty hug.

"He looks really nice," Gus said softly. "He looks like you."

Anastasia bit her lip. Where did she, Anastasia, fit into

this Merrymoon gallery? She couldn't visualize herself among the frills and armor.

"What's this?" Quentin crossed to an alcove wherein hung a curtain of black velveteen. He plucked the corner of the shroud between forefinger and thumb and peeled it upward. "Oh! It's Nicodemus!"

"It's the painting in our *Cavelands History* textbook!" Gus said.

"Why do you suppose Nicodemus is covered up with a curtain?" Ollie asked.

"Maybe it makes Wiggy too sad to see him," Anastasia pondered.

"I think it's sadder still to cover him up," Quentin said.

Anastasia leaned closer, examining the compass tattoo gilding Nicodemus's hand. A shivery thrill limned her veins. Could this cluster of circles and stars really guide her to Fred? What if Calixto's magic had gone sour, and the compass instead pointed the Dreadfuls to a random hot dog stand on Coney Island?

Still, the compass was her best bet of finding her father. Anastasia let the velveteen fall and checked her pocket watch. "It's half past three," she said. "Baldy and Aunt Penny said we'd leave for Dinkledorf around four o'clock."

Venturing from the gallery, Anastasia found that she'd lost all sense of direction. The Dreadfuls muddled through the labyrinth of palace corridors until they emerged in a great hallway filled with snow globes. In the gloomy realm of shadow and candle glow, the spheres shimmered like miniature moons.

"I recognize *this*," Anastasia panted. "We're in the Hall of Snow Globes—the dining room is at the end."

"The queen's snow globes!" Ollie said. "Pretty! Ooooh—this one has a little Cavepearl Palace inside it!"

Gus peered into one of the snow-sprinkled little worlds. "This one is snowing all on its own!"

Sure enough, artificial snowflakes whirled within the rondure as though stirred by their own private wind.

"How does that work?" Gus asked, amazed. "We didn't even touch it! Do you suppose—"

"Ludowiga! *Really!*" Penny's protest drifted from the dining hall. "Anastasia is a *child*!"

The Dreadfuls exchanged wide-eyed glances and then shuffled closer to the door.

"Oh, Penny," Ludowiga sneered. "Your holier-than-thou attitude isn't serving Anastasia here. The princess needs to know about Caveland politics."

"Sweet mother of teacup, Loodie!" Baldwin bellowed. "Anastasia's only eleven."

"Ah," Ludowiga said. "But she won't be eleven forever,

Baldwin. And, unfortunately for us all, she's the firstborn of the firstborn. Even if you two are content to let her while away her days gobbling pizza and reading cheap mystery novels, *I* am *not*. She must prepare for her duties as queen."

"Duties as queen!" Gus whispered, eyeing Anastasia.

Her stomach wambled. *Queen?*

"Stop pretending you have Anastasia's best interests at heart," Baldwin said.

"I have *this family's* best interests at heart," Ludowiga hissed. "If anything happens to Wiggy, Anastasia is next in succession."

"Unless Fred is here," Penny said.

"He won't be," Ludowiga said. "Fred is long gone. He's dead, or maybe he ran away again. And if Anastasia is queen, don't you want her to have a strong army? Or would you rather roll out a welcome mat and toss confetti at the witches as they storm the castle?"

"Penny and I will always safeguard Anastasia," Baldwin said. "If anything happens to Her Mommyness before Anastasia's ready to rule, we'll just take her abovecaves. We'll go hide out in the Arctic Circle, if that's what it takes! Then *you* can have the throne. That's what you *really* want, isn't it?"

"It's what I *deserve*," Ludowiga cried. "Fredmund is a *lump*, and he always has been. He's only two minutes older than me—two minutes! Do you really think *two lousy minutes* better equips him than me for the throne?"

"No," Penny said. "I think Fred's *heart* better equips him."

"His *heart*?" Ludowiga raged.

"Fred's heart is wide and warm and good," Baldwin said. "He's kind and compassionate. Whereas you, Ludowiga, *aren't.*"

"Let's consider the rest of Fred's anatomy, shall we?" Ludowiga's voice trembled with rage. "He's *lily-livered.* He's *gutless.* He's *spineless*! He turned his *back* on this family—and our subjects—to marry a human and hole up in some dinky town halfway across the world. And now he's gone missing *yet again* and left us with a Halfling heir apparent. So forgive me if I don't care about Fred's mushy, gushy heart—when he's proven to be the Crown's *Achilles' heel*!"

The *clickity-click* of high-heeled slippers punctuated this diatribe. Ludowiga had quit the dining hall, Anastasia gathered, and Penny's and Baldwin's murmurs faded away as they, too, departed. Anastasia turned from the doorway, shaking.

"Anastasia," Gus said, his eyes round, "you're not just a princess. You're the *crown* princess. *You're next in line for the throne.*"

❧ 9 ❧
The Sordid Truth

BACK IN THE library, the Dreadfuls gathered around Anastasia.

"Did you have any idea?" Gus asked.

The Halfling heir apparent stared at him in a daze. "No. I knew Dad and Ludowiga were twins . . . but for some reason, I thought she was older. She *seems* older."

"Your dad has been out of the Cavelands for years," Gus said slowly. "I've only heard Ludowiga mentioned as the heir. I think everyone sort of assumed Fred abdicated his right of succession, and that Ludowiga was next in line."

"I don't *want* to be queen." Anastasia's voice wobbled. "Did you hear what Ludowiga said about witches storming the castle?"

"We won't let anything happen to you," Ollie declared, giving her a fierce hug. "We'd run away first!"

"Peep!" Pippistrella agreed.

"We won't need to," Gus said firmly. "Because we're going to find Nicodemus and your dad, Anastasia. Even if something happens to your grandmother, you won't have to be queen for a long time."

Anastasia nodded, but a ghastly chill had settled deep inside her chest. What if Ludowiga was right? What if Fred was *dead*?

"Oh, here you are!" Penny said. Her voice was bright, but her eyes were red and puffy behind her glasses.

"Are you ready for our abovecaves frolics?" Baldwin dumped a jumble of hats and mittens and scarves onto one of the library tables. "It's supposed to be a full moon tonight!"

Anastasia dragged her thoughts from crowns and thrones and her father. She wanted to find out whether the moon sozzled her bones the way it sozzled other Morfolk's bones. "Yes," she said. "We're ready."

"Goody," Baldwin said. "And we should have time to visit the cuckoo clock shop, too. I'm simply dying for a new cuckoo."

Penny rolled her eyes. "Boys, your parents know you're coming abovecaves with us, right?"

The boys all nodded. Gus nodded especially vigorously.

"They're not worried?" Penny said.

The boys all shook their heads. Gus shook his head especially vigorously.

"We've been to Dinkledorf lots of times," Ollie said. "Our dad takes us up on snow globe runs."

"Ah yes," Baldwin said. "For his music boxes. I've been meaning to drop by your shop and get a present for a certain lady friend."

"For Penny?" Anastasia asked.

Baldwin crimsoned. "Ah—no. A different kind of lady friend. Of course," he added, "we could just drop by Celestina Wata's workshop and get a snow globe there. Besides, I'm sure Gus would like to visit his aunt."

"O-o-oh," Gus stammered. "You know, I can see Aunt Teeny anytime. And I'd much rather see that cuckoo clock shop. I'm—er—curious to know how cuckoo clocks work."

"Good for you!" Penny said. "I'm rather peckish for a little lesson in mechanical engineering myself!" She snugged a knit cap over Gus's head. "Now, keep this on the entire time we're in Dinkledorf. You don't want anyone up there seeing your snakes."

"And we're off!" Baldwin declared. "The game's afoot!"

"What *game*?" Ollie asked.

"Why," Baldwin puzzled, "general fun and tomfoolery, I suppose."

A jaunt in the royal gondola took them to a pier on

the outskirts of Nowhere Special, and thence the sledding party hiked up a steep, ninety-nine-step stairwell to Dinkledorf. To be precise, they hiked ninety-nine stairs to a little cavern jam-packed with cheese. This petite cave was the cellar of the Merry Mouse, Dinkledorf's premier cheese shop.

"Ah!" Penny cried, savoring the bouquet of one hundred ripe wheels of stinky cheese. "Delicious!"

They scaled a second flight of stairs, arriving in a cramped chalet chockablock with even more cheese. An elderly lady, pink-cheeked and white-aproned, was busy adjusting jars of jam on one of the wooden shelves. Upon spying her new visitors, she launched herself at Penny with a hug. "Ah! Penelope, *liebe*!"

"*Guten Tag*, Gisela," Penny mumbled into the cheesemonger's collar. "Oh, it's good to see you!"

"And here is the good Baldwin, strapping and handsome as ever." Gisela beamed. "But who are these little ones?"

Penny introduced the Dreadfuls. "And this," she said, "is Fräulein Dinkle. Her family invented the recipe for Merry Mouse Gruyère over three hundred years ago, and Dinkledorf is named after them."

"My *son* invented Merry Mouse Gruyère," Gisela clarified. "He was history's greatest cheesemonger." Her eyes twinkled, and she dabbed them with the edge of her apron.

"Stolen from us far too young," Baldwin snuffled,

clasping Gisela's shoulder. "When Klaus left us, the world lost a true cheese genius."

"And Penelope and I lost more than that." Gisela smiled sadly at Penny.

"He's clog-stomping in the great hereafter," Baldwin eulogized.

"I like to think so." Gisela sniffled. "Ah, well, we mustn't dwell on sorrows of yesteryear. Won't you stay for a nice fondue? I have a delicious new Stinking Bishop—"

"Perhaps next time, Gisela," Penny said. "We've promised to take the children sledding."

"Well, enjoy yourselves, *liebchens*," Gisela said. "And, Penny, you must come round for dinner sometime soon. It—it does my heart good to see you. Even if Klaus is gone, I still think of you as a daughter."

The sledding party clamored through the front door of the cheese shop and out into Dinkledorf's snow-bespangled backwoods.

It was Anastasia's first time abovecaves in months. She inhaled deeply, and thousands of pine-tree-scented molecules flooded her nostrils and jozzled her lungs. Gus and Ollie and Quentin and Pippistrella whuffled in tandem beside her.

"Fresh air!" Quentin sighed.

"And I smell fresh *pastry*!" Ollie cried.

"Ah! Well sniffed, my lad!" Baldwin praised. "That'll be

the illustrious Zucker Weg or, in English, *Sugar Way*. It's the pastry district of Dinkledorf!"

Ollie gripped Anastasia's arm in a swoon of delight. She smiled at him, and then she turned to see Gus. He was hunkered in a pillow of snow, scooping up handfuls of flakes and peering at them with the intensity of a jeweler examining diamonds. He lifted his shining eyes to Anastasia's.

"Snow is *beautiful*," he said.

"Lucky for you, there's plenty of it around here." Baldwin galumphed down the cheese shop's snow-laden stoop. "Onward ho, troops! To Zucker Weg!"

Even though the Merry Mouse nestled on the outmost fringe of Dinkledorf, the village was so itty-bitty that tromping to the village heart would take no more than fifteen minutes. Baldwin and Ollie and Quentin frolicked through the frosty drifts, and Pippistrella wheeled between pine boughs, and Gus stumbled along with his face tilted toward the sky. Anastasia fell into step beside her aunt.

"Aunt Penny," Anastasia said quietly, "why would Gisela think of you as a *daughter*?"

Penny blushed. "Klaus and I were engaged, you see."

"You were *engaged*?" Anastasia exclaimed.

"Yes," Penny said. "He was a wonderful man. A brilliant cheesemonger, and clever and sweet. And *brave*. Perhaps a bit *too* brave. He died in the first battles of the Perpetual War."

Anastasia stared at her, astonished. "Oh, Aunt Penny! I'm so sorry. I shouldn't have asked—"

"No, dear, it's fine," Penny said. "Perhaps, one day, someone will tell you, 'It's better to have loved and lost, than never to have loved at all.' Perhaps *I* am telling you, now. And it is true." She reached out to tug the end of Anastasia's scarf. "Nonetheless, losing love is a horrible thing. It's the most horrible thing in the world. That's why I'm so protective of *you*."

"But you're letting me come abovecaves today," Anastasia said.

"Yes." Penny smiled. "There's another wise saying: 'A life lived in fear is a life half-lived.' And I don't want you to spend your entire childhood feeling like a fugitive and missing out on pleasures like sledding and sunshine and starlight. That said," she added, "we still have to be careful." She let out a low whistle, drawing Pippistrella from her loop-the-loops. "We'd better get you undercover, Lady Bat. We're getting close to the village proper."

Pippistrella squeaked and dived to burrow in the hood of Anastasia's coat.

The pine trees petered out into snowcapped cottages

trimmed with lacy shingles and candy-colored shutters. As the little troop of Morfolk neared downtown Dinkledorf, the cottages clustered closer and closer together until they were squeezed eave to eave, cheek to cheek. It reminded Anastasia of a song her father used to sing (off-key and botching the lyrics), sweeping her into his flour-dusted arms and waltzing around the McCrumpet kitchen:

Heaven! I'm in heaven . . .
When we're out together dancing cheek to cheek.

Anastasia wondered, now, about her mother. Anastasia had grown up with a horrid woman who lay about in bed all day and complained of headaches and tummy aches and toothaches and shin splints. She had never said a kind word to Anastasia or to Fred, and Fred had certainly never danced cheek to cheek with her. That woman had been Anastasia's stepmother, and she had run away with a podiatrist after Prim and Prude snatched Anastasia and Fred disappeared. Anastasia did not spend much time thinking about Trixie McCrumpet. She did, however, think about her mother, who had died shortly after Anastasia's birth. Anastasia did not even know her name. No one in the Merrymoon family did except for Fred.

Had Fred waltzed cheek to cheek with Anastasia's mother? Or at least clog-stomped with her? How had they met? Why hadn't Fred ever told Anastasia anything about her? Anastasia wished she could ask her father about her never-known mom. If—*when*—she found him, she vowed, she *would*.

Tromping through the winding Dinkledorfian alleys, the sledding party passed a toy shop and a bookstore and a florist's. The perfume of piping-hot pastry grew stronger and stronger with every snow-upholstered step, until at last they turned down a lane lined with steamy windows chock-full of pastries. Strudel! Plump turnovers oozing hot applesauce! Donuts and éclairs and cupcakes! Linzer tortes and butter tarts! Sweet buns and sticky buns and cinnamon buns and hot cross buns!

"Remember," Baldwin cautioned them, "pace yourself. This isn't a sprint; it's a marathon." He swung open the nearest door, and a cloud of warm, sugary steam puffed without as though tootled from a sweet-toothed dragon within.

The merry band of Morfolk chomped their way through the confections of Zucker Weg until even Ollie hesitated outside the last bakery in the row, clutching his stomach. "Give me half an hour," he groaned. "I'm sure I could eat another piece of cake in half an hour."

"Amateurs," Baldwin chuckled. He checked his pocket watch. "Oh, splendid! We're right on time to pop into Die Kuckucksnest as the clocks strike six!"

"*Kuckucks* . . . what?" Anastasia echoed.

"Cuckoo's Nest," Baldwin said. "The most illustrious,

marvelous, gobsmackingly glorious cuckoo clock shop in the world. And it's right around the corner . . . see?"

Penny smiled. "Dinkledorf is so small, *everything's* right around the corner."

"Look at this!" Gus cried, dashing up to the clock shop's mullioned windows.

"Ah, yes," Baldwin rhapsodized. "The cuckoos within that hallowed nest are—"

"No," Gus said. "Look at this icy stuff on the window! It's like fancy, squished snowflakes." He bent close to peer. "This is frost, isn't it? I read about frost in a book."

Anastasia sidled up beside Gus, her mind flashing to a puzzle left over from St. Agony's: she had—or she *thought* she had—breathed frosty pictures onto various glassy bits and bobs around the chilly asylum. After stumbling upon the Morfo branches of her family tree, she had wondered whether frost breath was a Morfolky peculiarity. Penny and Baldwin assured her that it was not. They hypothesized Anastasia had, in her lonely distress, *imagined* the frost pictures. And Anastasia had been unable to prove otherwise: ever since escaping the drafty, gloomy, silver-crammed asylum, she had not breathed a single glimmer of frost.

Anastasia narrowed her eyes, thinking about the silver in the asylum. Silver, as you know, affected Morfolk badly. It sapped their strength. It made them sick. Anastasia wondered now whether spending so much time amidst Prim and

Prude's silver forks and spoons and candlesticks and jewelry and other doodads might have affected her mind. Had all that silver made her hallucinate?

It was an unpleasant idea. Anastasia now puffed experimentally upon the window, but her balmy breath simply fogged against and melted part of the icy patterning.

"Quickly, now," Baldwin urged them. "It's nearly six!"

An entire village-worth of cuckoo cottages wallpapered the narrow shop. Some were big as steamer trunks and others were no larger than matchboxes. A clock clucked at the heart of each cuckoo chalet: *tick tick tick tick tick.*

"Gosh, it's noisy in here," Gus observed.

"Just wait till the clocks strike the hour!" Baldwin said. "Oh, what a sublime rumpus that shall be! It's different in here than back at the palace, you understand. Our clocks in the library are spread out over a great long cavern. The cuckoos in here are packed together tight as sardines, and so are we. Their singing will rattle you silly."

"It's almost six now!" Ollie shouted.

"Prepare yourselves!" Baldwin yelled, grabbing Anastasia's and Gus's hands. "It'll be like a bomb going off!"

Cuckoo! Cuckoo! The shop erupted in a cacophony of metallic twangs and piping hoots. Little wooden shutters beneath the eaves of each cottage snapped open to release carved cuckoo birds. *Cuckoo!* Miniature peasants twirled;

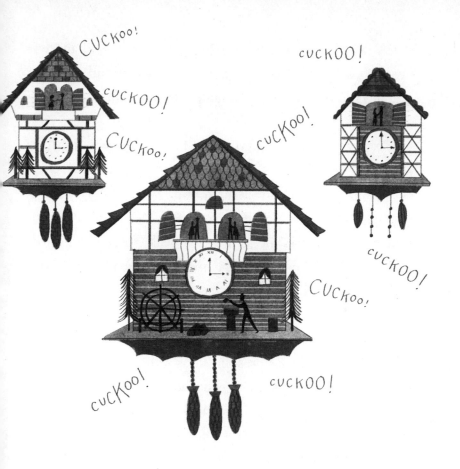

waterwheels spun; Lilliputian woodcutters snapped their axes toward wee tree trunks. *Cuckoo! Cuckoo!*

And then, with a clockwork hiccup, the cuckoos retreated. The shutters clicked closed, and the clocks fell back into ticking.

"Egads!" Baldwin said. "That was transcendent! My eardrums are properly *cuckooed*!"

A door at the back of the shop thwacked open, and out bustled a roly-poly fellow with yellow whiskers and a nose as red and round as a cherry lollipop. "Is that *Baldwin Merrymoon* I hear?"

"Franz!" Baldwin cried. "Oh, Franz, you're a sight for sore eyes! No offense to the rest of you," he added quickly.

"None taken," Penny assured him.

"Children, this is the great Franz Winkler," Baldwin said, reaching across the counter to tweak one side of Franz's bow tie. "You'll never find a finer clock than a Winkler cuckoo. His family practically has a monopoly on the cuckoo market!"

Franz beamed. "My father and grandfather were two of the original Black Forest cuckoosmiths. Ah! You should have seen our village then! The houses of Winterwalzen were so crammed with cuckoo clocks, we had to start hanging them from trees! There were more wooden birds in that forest than real ones."

"It sounds like heaven," Baldwin breathed.

"It was." The cheer faded from Franz's round face. "Alas, we had to flee Germany after the Red Riding Hood scandal."

"You mean *Little* Red Riding Hood?" Ollie exclaimed. "Like the fairy tale?"

"Indeed," Franz said. "But those Grimm bumblers got the story wrong. Little Red was no cute moppet delivering sweetmeats to her sick *oma*. She was a teenage hoodlum and a common burglar, to boot!"

Ollie gasped, and Franz nodded gloomily.

"Heidi Honigbär was her real name," Franz said. "The Honigbärs were competing cuckoosmiths. They were after our trade secrets, you see. And Heidi broke into our home in the hopes of sneaking a peek into our workshop. But she instead wandered into one of our bedrooms, where Granny Winkler was taking a nap. After one look at Granny, that meddlesome snoop started shrieking her fool head off."

"Why?" Anastasia asked.

"Because Granny liked to snooze in wolf form." Franz heaved a deep sigh. "Perhaps we could have convinced the Winterwalzers that a wild wolf got into our house, except Granny fell asleep with her spectacles on. And her nightcap. And she talked in her sleep."

"Crumbs!" Anastasia said.

"*Croombs*, indeed," Franz agreed. "After Heidi Honigbär went screaming into town with stories of witchcraft and werewolves, we Winklers had to flee Winterwalzen at once."

"How terrible," Penny murmured.

"It was." Franz removed his spectacles and wiped at his eyes. "Anyway, over time, the story somehow got twisted into the Red Riding Hood hooey you've heard. Ach." He shook his head. "Now, what can I do for you? Are you in the market for a new cuckoo, Baldy, or is this just a friendly visit?"

"Both," Baldwin declared. "Always both. Do I see a new specimen over there—?"

As Baldwin darted to examine a model in the corner, Gus leaned across the counter. "Why does that clock have *rocks* hanging from it?"

"Ah!" Franz said. "This is the modern cuckoo's ancestor, so to speak." He lifted the timepiece from its hook and swiveled it to display the exposed wooden cogs. A chain snaked through the gadgetry to hang down about twenty inches on either side, like skinny brass braids on a clockwork head, and attached to each end of this chain was a rock. One of the rocks was bigger than an orange, and the other was the size of a hen's egg.

"This is how you wind it." Franz jerked the smaller stone, pulling the chain through the mechanism. *Gzzzzt!* Now the big rock dangled only a few inches from the gizmo's base, and the little rock hung down perhaps three feet.

"Over the course of the day, the big rock falls," Franz said, replacing the clock on the wall. "But it falls very, very slowly. It pulls the chain through the clockwork, driving the movement for twelve hours until it falls to the end of its length. Then you have to wind it again." He smiled. "New cuckoos operate on the same principle. That's why they all have weights." He tapped the metal pinecone of one of the fancier ticktockers.

"Ingenious!" Penny enthused.

"You think that's ingenious? Look at *this*!" Baldwin crowed, dancing a jig before a timepiece in the corner. "This clockwork man drinks beer every hour, on the hour! Oh, Franz, I *must* have it!"

"Speaking of beer, Baldy, we'll have to pop into the pub soon." Franz winked. "It's been far too long since we've shared a pint. In the meantime, I'll wrap up this clock and have it delivered down to the palace."

"Goodbye, Franz," Penny said. "It was lovely to see you."

"Farewell!" Franz cried. "Farewell! Down with Little Red Riding Hood!"

"Down with Little Red Riding Hood!" Baldwin whooped, pushing the door open for Penny and the Dreadfuls and ushering them out into the snow and twilight.

"Is that story about Franz's wolf-granny really true?" Ollie asked. "Was Little Red Riding Hood a *spy*?"

"You better believe it," Baldwin said. "Ah, children! You wouldn't believe the sordid truth behind most fairy-tales-as-you-know-'em. But enough about scurvy little red-riding-hooded snoops. Night is nigh and the moon doth rise and the sledding hour is upon us."

10

Witch Lights

THE SUN SETS quickity-quick in winter, and it slinks out of sight especially fast in places surrounded by tall mountains. The sky shook off its lavender dusk and its mantle of clouds to reveal night, ink-black and star-freckled. From halfway up Mount Dinkle's hip, the lights of Dinkledorf looked like a smattering of fallen stars. The Dreadfuls pressed against the funicular window, watching as the miniature galaxy receded into the distance.

A funicular is a bit like a funny little train. Funiculars travel up sheer mountainsides, so imagine a cable car with a base slanted to fit snugly against a track as steep as a steep staircase. The benches inside are graded to fit this crooked floor, much like the bleachers at a sports stadium, or the seats at a top-notch movie theater. The Dinkledorf funicular moved slowly indeed, creaking and groaning as it went.

"This funicular dates from 1860," Penny said. "Then, as now, it was primarily used to carry cheese."

"Cheese?" Anastasia echoed.

"It's dicey getting in and out of Dinkledorf in the winter," Baldwin explained. "The roads are too snowy—cars nowadays can't even manage it. Imagine how rough it would be for a horse-drawn carriage!"

"Too rough," Penny agreed. "And much of Dinkledorf's income comes from cheese, you know. The cheesemongers needed a way to get cheese up the mountainside even in the snowiest months of the year. They used to have dogsleds carry out cheese, but the invention of the funicular made things much easier for everyone."

"Especially for the dogs," Baldwin said.

"I think I might throw up," Gus reported, swooning against the window.

"Oh dear," Penny said. "All those pastries made you sick, I'm afraid."

"Nonsense!" Baldwin said. "Pastry never made anyone sick. The lad has a touch of vertigo, that's all. Close your eyes and you'll be sound as a pound in no time."

Ollie edged as far away from Gus as was possible in the cramped cable car. "Vomiting in a funicular seems *precarious*," he said. "Do these windows open?"

"Ollie," Gus muttered, "you aren't helping."

"You'll be fine," Baldwin reassured him, but he scooted over, too, and everyone disembarked in a jiffy when the funicular finally clattered to the top of its track.

The moon was round and white as a scoop of celestial vanilla ice cream, and just as delicious, too. How, you might ask, could the moon be *delicious*? You and I, human Reader, cannot taste the moon. We might gaze upon it and think it beautiful. We might acknowledge that the moon commands the earth's oceans. We might even use it to navigate at night. But we cannot *taste* it, or smell it. Morfolk, on the other hand, *can*.

Anastasia, you will remember, had been deep in the Cavelands for several months, untouched by moonbeam since before her eleventh birthday. Age eleven is very special for Morflings, because the eleventh birthday is like an alarm clock waking up the wonders and powers sleeping in a Morfo's blood.

Beneath the moon now for the first time since turning eleven, Anastasia felt the moon as surely as you would feel velvet on your skin. She smelled it: a smell of cinnamon and vanilla and honey and fresh, fresh milk; the loveliest, freshest milk you can imagine. And she *tasted* it, not with her tongue but with her *bones*. Her bones guzzled the moonlight and converted it into pure effervescence. She laughed! She jumped! She spun and she spun and she spun beneath the sublime, splendiferous, spellbinding moon.

"That's the spirit!" Baldwin cried. He rounded his mouth and let out a howling yodel that echoed and shivered across the valley below. *"AWOOOO! AWOOOO! AWOOOOOOOO!"*

"Baldy," Penny said, "mind your howling, dear. You don't want to start another werewolf rumor down in Dinkledorf."

"I'm sorry," he said. "This moon brings out the wolf in me, you know."

"And the shadow in *me*," Ollie said. "I'm just twitching to umbrate. But I'm not going to, because I want to sled, too."

"And sled we shall," Baldwin said. He turned back to the funicular and began heaving out their sleds: sturdy, old-timey wooden beauties borrowed from a Morfo family who lived at the base of Mount Dinkle.

Each member of the sledding crew pulled a sled across the shivery ground and to the top of a snow-packed trail, marble-smooth and glowing silver-white beneath the full moon's blaze.

"Does this go all the way back down the mountain?" Gus asked, eyeing the slippery chute a bit dubiously.

"It surely does," Penny said. "It curves and crooks around, though. It's not a straight up-and-down shot like the funicular."

"The whole shebang takes seven minutes," Baldwin said.

"Sit down on your sled and lean back a bit," Penny instructed them. "Hold tight to your reins. Put your feet on the outside of the runners, like so—"

"And try not to crash into a tree," Baldwin said, giving Penny a great push. Off she slid down the mountain, letting out a soft librarian huzzah. Next Quentin, then Ollie, then Gus, then Anastasia launched into the wild snowy yonder; and Baldwin brought up the rear.

The jaunt down Mount Dinkle indeed lasted seven minutes, and, oh, what a seven minutes it was! Anastasia forgot about Pettifog Academy. She forgot about Ludowiga. She forgot all about crowns and thrones and witches and CRUD. For seven minutes, the twin stones of worry and loss—hanging constantly at Anastasia's heart like the weights on a cuckoo clock—lifted. Featherlight she felt, helium-hearted, zinging shooting-star-like through the night with Pip-pistrella clinging to one of her braids. The yelps and cheers of the sledding party rang out and sang out and shivered upon the crisp frosty air. It was one of those gorgeous occasions when, despite all evidence to the contrary, everything in the world was right and good and lovely.

Whump! Whump-whump-whump-whump-whump! The six sleds disgorged their Morfo cargo into a thick snowbank at the base of Mount Dinkle. Everyone was wheeze-laughing and wobbly-legged, blurry-eyed with tears jiggled loose by the cold.

Then Gus pointed at the sky. "Look!"

Anastasia rubbed her peepers. A smear of color coated the starry vault from the celestial North Pole to the horizon, pale green and delicate pink, gossamer-sheer and scintillating. It reminded Anastasia of the oil rainbows that sometimes slick parking lot puddles, but on a gobsmackingly grand scale. And Anastasia *was* gobsmacked. Her jaw dropped and she boggled.

"The aurora borealis," Baldwin whispered.

"Crumbs," Anastasia breathed. "I've never seen anything so pretty!"

"It *is* pretty," Penny said, but a tremor rippled through her voice.

Baldwin's mustache bristled. "As much as I hate to forgo a trip to the S'mores Chalet, I think we should go to ground."

"Go to ground!" Anastasia protested. "Can't we sled down the mountain just one more time? *Please?*"

"I promise not to throw up in the funicular," Gus added.

"Not tonight," Penny said. "Quickly now, children. Leave your sleds here." She was using her No-Nonsense, Brook-No-Argument librarian tone, and she and Baldwin had already begun marching through the snowdrifts heaping the edge of Dinkledorf. Anastasia exchanged a bewildered glance with the boys, and then they scrambled to follow.

The elder Merrymoons didn't offer a word of explanation until they were safely squished back into the royal gondola, sailing posthaste for Cavepearl Palace.

"There's probably nothing to worry about," Penny said. "The northern lights are, in most cases, an entirely natural phenomenon."

"In most cases?" Gus echoed.

"Sometimes the aurora borealis shows up when witches are near," Baldwin said.

"You mean a witch might have cooked up that—that *boory-alice*—with a *magic spell*?" Ollie squeaked.

Penny shook her head. "Not exactly. It's very rare, but certain witches influence their surroundings just by *being*. The magic brimming inside them somehow affects the atmosphere, even if they don't try to. Even if they try *not* to."

"We used to know a witch who couldn't go near a harpsichord without ruining its pitch," Baldwin said. "She was banned from the symphony, actually."

"How horrible!" Quentin cried.

"And some witches interfere with clockwork," Penny said. "Not all of them, but some. Franz's brother, Hansel, owns a watch shop in Dark-o'-the-Moon Common—actually, he's the queen's official timekeeper—and he forbade witches from entering his showroom."

"Anyway," Baldwin said, "back when witches lived in Nowhere Special, the aurora borealis popped up around Dinkledorf more nights than it didn't! I'll wager Calixto Swift triggered 'em. His great-granddaddy was a Lapland wizard, after all."

"Lapland?" Gus crinkled his brow. "You mean that place in Finland?"

Baldwin nodded. "They used to brew powerful strange magic up in Lapland. The wizards there slopped the sky with their Witch Lights, and they worked all kinds of spells with snow."

"Calixto used to say snow-magic ran in his blood," Penny murmured.

"Well," Baldwin said grimly, "he was certainly *cold-blooded*."

Anastasia paled. "Does this mean there's a witch up in Dinkledorf now?"

Penny hesitated. "Probably not. The world is full of all kinds of marvels and strangeness, and most of it has nothing to do with witch magic. But it *is* unusual to see the northern lights as far south as Switzerland nowadays—and we're better safe than sorry." She removed her glasses and rubbed away the last twinkling bits of frost. "I just hope the news of this aurora sighting doesn't send Nowhere Special into a tizzy. Morfolk tend to panic at the mere mention of the northern lights."

Anastasia felt a little panicked herself. The prospect of witches lurking in cozy Dinkledorf sent shivers down her spine.

"Oh, don't look so perturbed, my girl." Baldwin tweaked Anastasia's braid. "Once we get back to the palace, we'll roast s'mores in the library fireplace. How does that sound?"

Anastasia managed a weak smile. However, Reader, there are woes in life that even the most delicious of s'mores cannot sweeten, and Anastasia suspected her new batch of witchy worries was lamentably s'mores-proof.

❧ 11 ❧
En Garde

WHENEVER ANASTASIA IMAGINED a city in the throes of panic, she pictured people running in circles and tearing at their hair and hollering. She had gotten such notions from television movies depicting earthquakes and alien invasions and the like, and she wondered whether Nowhere Special would spiral into that kind of ruckus once the Cavelanders heard about the borealis in Dinkledorf. However, it did not. Everyone went about their normal business of drinking tea and wearing wigs and going to work, and things seemed normal enough.

But whispers rustled through the Cavelands: *witch . . . witch . . . witch.* Morfolk whispered about witches in their homes and at the beauty parlor and the coffee shop. *Witch . . .*

witch . . . witch. Morflings whispered about witches at school. *Witch . . . witch . . .*

"Stop whispering!" Marm Pettifog scolded. "You may not speak in class unless spoken to!"

"But, Marm Pettifog, we're scared!" Taffline said. "What if there's a witch in Nowhere Special?"

"Then you best prepare yourself by studying hard for your Practical Survival exams," Marm Pettifog said. "Speaking of which, it's time for your first fencing lesson—" Her rebuke dissolved into a fit of coughing.

"Marm Pettifog, are you sick?" Jasper asked eagerly. "Maybe you should stay home tomorrow."

"Jasper's right," Ollie piped up. "Your bellowing is rather *raspy* today."

"Nonsense," the schoolmistress croaked. "Illness is for the weak-willed. Now, go meet Sir Foxglove in the gymnasium! And I recommend you all behave for him: Sir Foxglove used to be a cutthroat pirate captain, and he doesn't take kindly to back talk. It reminds him of mutinies." Her evil smile convulsed into a sneeze, and she waved the children away.

"A pirate captain!" Jasper thrilled as the fifth graders clambered downstairs. "Do you suppose he'll have a parrot? And a peg leg?"

"What if he has a hook instead of a hand?" Ollie squealed.

A man stood at the front of the gym cave, watching the approaching Pettifoggers with bright-eyed interest, and they stared back at him. He was neat and trim and no taller than most of the fifth graders. He wore a pin-striped suit and a bowler hat, and no diabolical hook curved from either of his crisp white cuffs. He was holding a teacup in one hand and a saucer in the other. A closed umbrella dangled from the crook of his right arm. He resembled any smart businessman you might see in a coffee shop abovecaves, sipping tea before heading off to catch his morning train.

"Are *you* Sir Foxglove?" Jasper blurted out. "You don't *look* like a pirate."

"The golden days of piracy ended many years ago, my dear lad," Sir Foxglove replied in polished tones. "And with them went the pirate traditions of yore."

"So you don't have a parrot?" Jasper persisted.

"Certainly not," Sir Foxglove said. "I never understood the appeal. My colleague One-Eyed Greenbeard had a big African gray, and went about with his shoulder absolutely *coated* in bird droppings. *Most* unhygienic." Sir Foxglove drained the last of his tea. "But you aren't here to learn about pirates. You're here to learn how to defend yourselves in the event of a witch attack."

Sir Foxglove flung up teacup and saucer and umbrella. With his right hand he grabbed the umbrella handle, and with the left he yanked off the nylon canopy, revealing a long,

metal skewer. *Slash! Whiz!* The spike sliced back and forth, smashing the teacup and saucer to bits midair. *CRASH! Tinkle!* Before the stunned Pettifoggers could even blink, the broken bits of china pattered to the gymnasium floor, and the sharp red tip of Sir Foxglove's foil hovered a mere inch away from Ollie's lapel. A foil is a type of thin, pointed sword. The Pettifoggers now stared at the red-tinged tip of Sir Foxglove's foil.

"Witches could strike at any moment," Sir Foxglove said. "They won't send a telegram asking whether it would be convenient to strike after tea next Friday. Witches are most impolite!"

He pressed the foil ever closer to Ollie, urging the

Shadowboy backward. The Pettifoggers followed its crimson point with their eyes, hypnotized.

"That's why you must be ready for a witch invasion at any moment. No matter if you're taking tea or watching the ballet or sitting in the loo. If witches sneak down to the Cavelands, what will you do?"

"My daddy and grandfather say witches will never return to the Cavelands," Ophelia Dellacava declared. "And *they* should know."

"My nanny says witches will attack within the year. She says she can *feel it in her bones*," countered Rupert. "That's why the queen needs more money for the army."

"I bet your nanny's never even seen a witch," Ophelia scoffed.

"If *I* saw a witch, I'd run away!" Taffline cried. "I'd run home and my mother would protect me!"

"But sometimes you *can't* run," Sir Foxglove said. "Sometimes a witch will back you into a corner."

Indeed, Ollie's shoulders were now firmly pressed against the gymnasium wall. Sir Foxglove did not lower his sword, and he did not remove his gaze from Ollie's lapel. "Some witches will get you with magic. If you come up against an older witch who knows plenty of spells, you're a goner."

Anastasia gulped.

"But most younger witches don't fight that way," Sir Foxglove went on. "No, they'll try to stab you with a silver weapon. They'll try to run you through the heart with one of these, except coated with silver."

A collective shudder went up at the mention of *silver.*

"Abovecaves now, tens of thousands of witchlings are learning how to fence with foils like this one. A foil is nice and light and even children can carry them around," Sir Foxglove said. "And older witches like foils, too. If a witch has drained all her magic for the day, she might switch to her foil. Some witches even sharpen their silver wands at the end, so they can stab you if their spell doesn't do the trick. Do you know what a witch calls her sword?"

"No, Sir Foxglove," the Pettifoggers chorused.

"A Morfolk sticker." Sir Foxglove paused a moment, letting the grim implication sink into the minds of the twenty fifth graders. "A witch wants to stick you. She wants to stick you with a silver blade, right in your Morfolk heart." Sir Foxglove returned his sword to its umbrella sheath. "So you'd best learn how to fight. Suit up in the locker rooms, and we'll begin."

As it turned out, the red at the tip of Sir Foxglove's foil was no more than chalk dust. Sir Foxglove now passed around bits of red chalk to all the students, and they rubbed the chalk on their own foils.

"If you leave a red mark on your opponent's jacket, you've

scored a *touch*," Sir Foxglove said. "Your goal is to leave your rival's jacket *crimson*."

Anastasia glanced down at her white fencing uniform, wondering how long it would be before she looked like a walking tic-tac-toe grid. After forty minutes of stumbling through footwork drills and learning how to handle a foil, she had concluded that she would quickly bite the dust in any real sword fight.

"Time for your first bout," Sir Foxglove announced. "Get into position, two per mat!"

Ten long, narrow rubber mats stretched side by side on the gymnasium floor. Anastasia took her place on one of these mats, careful to stay behind the *en garde* line scored about six feet from the center. She bent her legs slightly, as Sir Foxglove had taught them, and looked across the mat at her opponent. Because everyone was wearing identical white fencing costumes and metal masks, it was impossible to tell who faced her. Gus? Jasper Cummerbund?

"Try to score as many touches as possible without being touched yourself," Sir Foxglove said. "You move forward and backward along the mat using the footwork we just reviewed. If you step off the mat, you lose. Try to drive your opponent off the end of their mat."

Anastasia eyed her partner's foil. Even though she knew the sword was blunted with a safety tip, she still didn't much like the sight of someone standing opposite her with a weapon.

"*En garde!*" Sir Foxglove commanded, and the twenty Pettifoggers began to shuffle across the mats. *Clink! CLANK!* Swords clashed. Anastasia hesitated. Her fencing partner's sword was raised, but the figure in white didn't move. He—or she—was still as a statue.

"Cleave 'em to the brisket, you scurvy scalawag!" Sir Foxglove hollered, quite losing his posh accent in all the excitement. "Give 'em no quarter! Blow the man down, I say!"

Anastasia shambled forth. She thrust her foil toward her partner's jacket.

CLUNK! Her opponent sprang to life, deflecting the flimsy attack. Anastasia's sword juddered to the left. "Oops!"

Now her rival was full of ginger, leaping and twirling and lunging. The foil zinged at Anastasia again and again. Pippistrella, observing from a nearby stalactite, squeaked and chirped in distress as her mistress stumbled backward, trying to evade the blade. *CLINK! CLUNK!* Anastasia toppled off the mat, catching her right heel on her left shin and sprawling to the hard gymnasium floor. "*Oof!*" All the wind puffed from her lungs, and the adversary stood over her for one final blow, jabbing the point of their sword into Anastasia's chest.

"Shiver me timbers!" Sir Foxglove cried. "Er—that is to

say, jolly good! Your technique is *superb*! I've never seen anything quite like it—why, you were practically *dancing*!"

"I expect it's all my ballet training," oozed a muffled drawl from behind the metal visor.

"Saskia!" Anastasia wheezed.

The Loondorfer princess pulled off her mask with a flourish.

"I tip my hat to you, young lady!" Sir Foxglove congratulated her. "You would make a *splendid* pirate."

"I've been taking fencing lessons since I was five." Saskia shrugged. "I'm a *royal*, after all. I need to know how to protect myself." She sneered down at Anastasia. "You'd better hope Congress gives Wiggy her extra soldiers, because if you ever have to defend *yourself* in a witch attack, you'll be mincemeat. *Halfling mincemeat.*" She skipped away as Ollie and Gus hurried to Anastasia's side.

"That was brutal," Gus panted, helping up his fallen Dreadful. "I'll never learn to—Anastasia, look at your jacket!"

She peered down. Chalk marks scarred the pale fabric, and betwixt these slashes and dots, a swirly scarlet *S* emblazoned the spot directly above her heart.

"Crumbs, Anastasia!" Ollie yelped. "Saskia just gave you *the Zorro treatment*!"

☙ 12 ❧

The Cuckoo's Secret

ANASTASIA MAY HAVE been a lousy athlete, but she was plenty good at other things: she could draw, and she could sleuth. The first meeting of the Pettifog Art Club would provide Anastasia with opportunity to flex both these talents, and she was looking forward to shining in a Saskia-free zone.

However, Anastasia's happy little glow dwindled as Miss Ramachandra ushered the art-clubbers into the theater auditorium. A waltz tootled up from the orchestra pit, propelling a troupe of ballerinas onstage through leaps and gambols. Smack-dab in the center of these frolics twirled Saskia, her golden hair gleaming star-bright beneath the spotlight.

"I didn't know the Twinkle Toe Ballet would be practicing here," Anastasia muttered to Ollie and Gus as the art-clubbers clumped stage-ward down the aisle. The melody tweedled to its finale, and the ballerinas froze in place.

"Well done, Saskia!" shouted a tiny lady standing off to the side. "Those were some bang-up pirouettes!"

"Thank you, Madame Pamplemousse." Saskia preened.

"The rest of you are lumps!" the instructor howled. "Saskia, take five. You others, give me a hundred pliés!"

The ballerinas began bobbing like manic jack-in-the-boxes. Saskia's gaze lit on Anastasia, and she pranced to the edge of the stage. "What are *you* doing here?"

"We're going to help paint sets," Anastasia muttered.

"Really? You joined *art club*?" Saskia smirked. "How *cute*. But *do* try not to muss anything up—it all has to be *perfect* for my Triumphant Debut."

"Anastasia is a *brilliant* artist," Ollie huffed, but Saskia was already pirouetting back into the gaggle of dancers, her giggles spiraling up into the stalactites.

"Goodness!" Miss Ramachandra exclaimed. "Imagine, one of your classmates starring in *Sugarplum Bat*! You must all be so excited!"

"Ugh." Ollie mimed vomiting. Anastasia nodded, but her cheeks prickled pink as Ludowiga's sneers sniped her memory: *Saskia's triumphs bring glory to the royal family.* She stared wistfully at her ballerina cousin, dainty and fair as a little tutu'd figurine spinning inside a jewelry box. Anastasia's heart panged.

But only for a moment. She balled her hand into a fist and thumped her sternum, drumming the schmaltz up her windpipe and releasing it in a hiccup. She didn't care about bringing *glory* to the royal family. She cared about bringing home its missing members—Fred and Nicodemus. That's what *mattered*.

A portly man in a paint-spattered jacket and breeches emerged onstage, pushing through the huffing Twinkle Toes to descend a staircase adjoining the proscenium. "Miss Ramachandra, I presume?"

"Oh my gracious! Oh my golly!" Miss Ramachandra twittered. "Signor Mezzaluna, I studied your work at university. It's such an honor to *meet* you!"

"I know," the man agreed. "I'm delighted to give you the opportunity." He clasped Miss Ramachandra's hand in greeting, then frowned. "Madam, you're *sticky*."

"Oh! *Glue!*" Miss Ramachandra said. "My kindergartners were making macaroni mosaics this afternoon."

Signor Mezzaluna extracted a lace-edged handkerchief from his waistcoat and scrubbed at his palm. "Macaroni is the *scourge* of pastas. I never *eat* it, let alone use it in my *work!*"

"I *like* macaroni," Jasper piped up.

"*You* are not an artistic genius. *I* am." The great *signor* returned the hanky to his blotchy vest. "Under normal circumstances, I would *never* agree to let schoolchildren muck around with my sets, but we're over budget and behind schedule. *Sugarplum Bat* opens in May! Do you know how long Michelangelo and his flunkies spent shellacking the Sistine Chapel ceiling? *Four years!* I have less than *two months* to whip up a fake fairyland for this blasted ballet."

"Well," Miss Ramachandra flustered, "we're ever so pleased to help you."

Signor Mezzaluna sniffed. "I just hope you lot know how to handle a paintbrush."

He led them up the little staircase and past Madame Pamplemousse's leaping troupe, veering through the wings and into the backstage fug of turpentine and sawdust. Carpenters hammered at the wooden skeletons of half-finished platforms. Painters hunkered over props, daubing gilt and sprinkling glitter.

"There are eight of you? You two"—Signor Mezzaluna gestured at Ophelia and Jasper—"will help varnish these fake lollipops. You three"—he indicated Anastasia and Gus and Ollie—"will stencil snowflakes on the winter forest backdrop. And the rest of you will polka-dot these papier-mâché Dalmatians. We keep the supplies over here. . . ."

Armed with pots of silvery lacquer, the Dreadfuls weaved through the obstacle course of paint cans and jumbo lollies and scurrying stagehands, halting by a canvas panel ashimmer with a pale forest scene. They set to their stenciling. *Dunk, dab, dab. Dunk, dab, dab.*

"When should we sneak off?" Ollie asked, craning his neck around the tarp to peer toward the Dreadfuls' secret egress. "I hope the way to Sickle Alley hasn't been blocked. There's stuff piled *everywhere.*"

"Ollie!" Gus said. "You're dripping paint on my shoes!"

"Oh!" Ollie jerked his errant paintbrush, flicking a wave of silver flecks over Anastasia's cheeks and hair. Pippistrella squealed and launched from her mistress's braid, alighting on the leg of a capsized chair.

Anastasia wiped her face with the back of her hand, smearing glitter across her freckles. "Ollie, try using less paint."

"I told you I'm not an artist," Ollie huffed.

"Oh, but of *course* you are!" Miss Ramachandra cried, swooping in like a scatterbrained fairy godmother. "Your soul is *sopping full* of creative juice, Oliver!"

"Do you really think so?"

"I'm sure of it! You just need a little help with your technique." Miss Ramachandra took the brush from him and swiped it lightly over the canvas. "Think of it like glazing a pastry. See? Thin layers."

"Well, I *am* good at glazes. You should see my plum Danishes." Ollie dabbed paint through the stencil, then lifted it to behold a neatly formed snowflake.

"Magnificent!" Miss Ramachandra praised. "Keep up the good work! Oh—Parveen—on that Dalmatian, strive for *dots*, not *spots*. . . ." She drifted away.

Ollie glared at his single silvery hexagon. "This is going to take forever! This canvas is *huge*! How many snowflakes have you made, Anastasia?"

"Twelve."

"I don't think—Q!"

Quentin edged around a downed chandelier and stooped. "I told Maestro that I had a stomachache and had to go home early. Do you think anyone would notice if you ducked out now?"

Anastasia scanned the backstage activity. Miss Ramachandra was helping Jasper mop up a puddle of spilled paint, and Signor Mezzaluna was arguing loudly with two apprentices about the dimensions of a cluster of papier-mâché clouds.

"Let's go," Anastasia whispered.

The Dreadfuls set down their paintbrushes and edged deeper into the jumble of props, all the way to the crawlway hidden in the cavern's farthermost corner. Mrs. Honeysop's parlor was just a hop, skip, and jump down Sickle Alley, but the Dreadfuls neither hopped nor skipped nor jumped. They ran the entire way.

As Anastasia and Quentin unscrewed the bolts fastening the metal screen in front of the fire, Ollie riffled through the old witch's tattered cookbook.

"I thought there might be weird recipes in here," he commented. "But there isn't any eye of newt or tongue of dragon or silver powder. These ingredients look completely normal . . . but, my gosh! Putting cinnamon in the batter . . . ingenious!" He looked up. "Hey, Gus! Why are you so interested in that old clock?"

Gus rattled the wooden cuckoo chalet. "I'm interested in it because it doesn't make sense. Why would there be a cuckoo clock *here*?"

"Even witches have to tell time," Anastasia reasoned.

"Sure," Gus said. "But remember what Franz said about the cuckoo mechanism? The *weights* drive the clock movement. But in here, without gravity"—he touched one of the buoyant metal pinecones—"there *is* no weight. So the clock can't work."

Ollie shrugged. "Maybe Calixto or Mrs. Honeysop charmed it to run on its own."

"Or maybe it was just a decoration," Quentin suggested. "Cuckoo clocks are *terribly* attractive. I wouldn't mind having one in my room, actually."

Gus twitched open the cuckoo's door. "There isn't even a bird in here. Anastasia, would you pass me that screwdriver?"

With a few twists of the wrist, Gus removed the cuckoo's back panel. "Not a single cog inside! It's empty—except for *this*." He pulled out a small scroll of paper tied with a narrow black ribbon.

The Dreadfuls swam toward him. "Unroll it," Anastasia urged.

Gus undid the ribbon and unfurled the scroll. There, in Calixto Swift's unmistakable, sprawling cursive, was a note:

January 2, 1756

A—

If something should happen to me, follow my M.O. to Stinking Crumpet. Tell no one.

Through this doorway clear and crystal
Whisk me on a whirlwind trip!
Take me where your whirlwind twinkles
Make me a globe-trotting witch.

—C

"Who's *A*?" Ollie asked.

"Mrs. Honeysop?" Gus asked. "The clock was in *her* house, after all. Calixto must have left the note for her."

"I wonder what *A* stands for," Quentin mused. "Amelia? Agnes?"

"Aggie!" Anastasia said. "It stands for *Aggie*!"

"Why *Aggie*?" Gus asked.

"That was his witch-nanny," Anastasia said. "I read it in one of the Calixto Swift biographies from Cavepearl Library. Mrs. Honeysop must have been Calixto's nanny!"

"Why on earth would a grown warlock need a nanny?" Ollie demanded.

"She was his nanny when he was a *little boy*, Ollie," Anastasia said. "But they must have kept in touch. She taught him nursery rhymes."

"So is *this* a nursery rhyme?" Ollie tapped the couplet about twinkling doorways and globe-trotting witches.

"I don't think so," Gus said slowly. "Might it be the spell

to get through Calixto's magic doors? *Whisk me on a whirl-wind trip?* Wasn't that a line from his travel journal?"

"Yes!" Anastasia cried. "It was!"

"Clear and crystal," Quentin murmured. "Maybe the magic doors are made out of *glass!*"

"Like the revolving doors at the bank?" Ollie asked. "I always like going through those."

"But what do you suppose the M.O. might be?" Gus quizzed. "And who—or where—is Stinking Crumpet?"

"I don't know about the M.O., but look at the date!" Anastasia exclaimed. *"January second, 1756!* Calixto Swift wrote this note *the day of the Dastardly Deed."*

13

The Art of Keeping Secrets

A THOUGHT FLASHED INTO Anastasia's cranium, bright as a thunderbolt and twice as shocking. "I bet Stinking Crumpet is where Calixto hid the Silver Chest!"

The Dreadfuls' eyes glittered as though someone had shoved sparklers right up their nostrils. If she had not been floating midair, Anastasia would have danced a little jig right then and there. "What an incredible clue!"

"Hear, hear!" Ollie cheered. "Do you reckon that spell might work on the cabinet, too? After all, *it's* clear and crystal. Maybe Calixto had one all-purpose getting-through-glass spell."

"It's worth a try," Anastasia breathed.

Up in the warlock's study, Quentin cleared his throat and intoned:

"Through this doorway clear and crystal
Whisk me on a whirlwind trip!
Take me where your whirlwind twinkles
Make me a globe-trotting witch."

No doorway clear and crystal appeared upon the cabinet's breast. Gus and Anastasia ran their palms over its flanks to check for invisible-to-the-Morfling-eye seams or hinges, but the glass was still entirely unblemished.

"Nope," Anastasia sighed. "No magic door. Maybe that spell doesn't work for non-witches."

"Or maybe it's the wrong spell entirely," Gus said.

"But you *sounded* good, Q," Ollie said. "That sounded wonderful! You should narrate audiobooks! Your denunciation is spot-on."

"I think you mean *enunciation*, Pudding," Quentin said. "But thank you."

Gus gave the cabinet a frustrated little kick. "So it's back to the books."

"Cheer up!" Quentin said. "That note is a spiffing discovery! And now we know to look for glass doors."

"And once we find the magic door to Stinking Crumpet, we'll know how to go through it," Anastasia added.

"Do you think the cuckoo clock was a sort of—er— *mailbox* for Calixto and Mrs. Honeysop?" Gus asked. "So they could secretly leave messages for each other? They could just shove the note through the cuckoo's door."

"I bet it was!" Ollie said. "But for some reason, Mrs. Honeysop never got that letter."

The Dreadfuls fell into uneasy silence. If Calixto had written the note on the day of the Dastardly Deed, Mrs. Honeysop might not have had any opportunity to open the cuckoo clock mailbox. Morfolk had stormed Dark-o'-the-Moon Common and killed Calixto in the middle of a puppet show, and then the Perpetual War erupted. Had Mrs. Honeysop remained in the Cavelands to fight? Had Morfolk dragged her from her house? Or did she escape to one of the secret witch towns abovecaves?

"Speaking of clocks, we should probably get back to the theater," Gus said. "Miss Ramachandra won't notice we're gone, but Ophelia Dellacava might, and she's a *tattletale*."

"All right," Anastasia agreed reluctantly. "Let's see . . . which books should I borrow from Calixto's library today?" She selected a few leather-bound journals from the floating archives, and Gus and Quentin slid some teensy ledgers into their vests. Ollie hesitated, and then he handed Mrs. Honeysop's cookbook to Anastasia. "Would you put this in your satchel for me? I don't want to get caught with witch things."

"Ollie!" Quentin protested. "How is a cookbook going to help us?"

"We need snacks while we're on our great mission, don't we?" Ollie asked. "And there's a *brilliant* recipe for gingerbread in here."

"Well," Quentin pondered, "I do *like* gingerbread."

"I know you do." Ollie beamed. "Anastasia, can you copy out the recipes for me on normal, non-witchy notebook paper?"

"Sure." Anastasia buttoned the pilfered books into her satchel.

"Come on, before anyone notices we're missing," Gus urged.

As they retraced their path to the theater's backstage, Anastasia's mind jumbled with words plucked from Calixto Swift's cursive: *Doorway clear and crystal. Globe-trotting witch. Stinking Crumpet.* Perhaps they didn't yet know how to open the glass cabinet and retrieve the Silver Hammer, but she felt they were on the right path to tracking down the Silver Chest. And that meant they were getting closer to rescuing Nicodemus and his Fred-finding compass! Her heart skipped a happy little hopscotch. What if—

"Look!" Ollie gasped.

Glistering snowflakes sprinkled the length and width of the entire snowscape. Snowflakes trimmed the painted pine trees. Snowflakes glimmered against the pale silver sky in swirling curlicues. There were thousands of them. Anastasia gazed at the diadems in wonderment. "Someone stenciled all the snow in while we were gone!"

"*How?*" Gus asked. "It would take *hours and hours* to paint all those snowflakes, even with a dozen people working!"

Anastasia wheeled her gaze across the cavern. Whether sawing or gilding or polka-dotting, every drudge backstage seemed to be deeply absorbed in a task. Claudio Mezzaluna caught her eye and weaved through the bustle of activity to stare at the snow-spangled backdrop.

"*Santo cielo!*" he cried. "This—this is dazzling! It's *magnifico*! You children know your stencils, after all! But how in caves did you paint this so quickly?"

The Dreadfuls exchanged a perplexed glance.

"Ah! So you won't share your tricks of the trade?" Mezzaluna chuckled. "Secretive as Venetian glassblowers, the lot of you!"

Ollie furrowed his brow. "What does *blowing glass* have to do with keeping secrets?"

"Venetian glassblowers of yore were *quite* a cloak-and-dagger bunch!" Mezzaluna said. "They guarded their glass-making techniques very fiercely. In fact, blabbing professional secrets was punishable by death!"

"Crumbs and biscuits!" Anastasia squeaked.

"Gus's aunt is a glassblower." Ollie elbowed the gorgon. "Did Celestina live in Venice?"

"*Celestina?*" Mezzaluna exclaimed. "You don't mean to say *Celestina Wata* is your *aunt*? *Allora*, there you have it! *She* schooled you in the art of keeping secrets, didn't she?" Mezzaluna wagged his finger, eyes twinkling. "Celestina Wata is *renowned* for her secrecy. She holds on to a secret tighter than an oyster does its pearl!"

"She *does*?" Gus said.

"Ah, but I'm sure you already know that." Mezzaluna winked at them.

"I guess Aunt Teeny *is* pretty quiet," Gus admitted.

"*Quiet?* That woman was *born* with zipped lips!" Mezzaluna said. "I met her once, and she wouldn't even tell me what

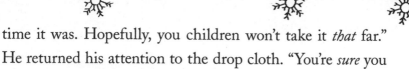

time it was. Hopefully, you children won't take it *that* far."
He returned his attention to the drop cloth. "You're *sure* you
won't tell me how you finished this snowscape so quickly?"

"But we didn't—" Anastasia faltered.

"Tut-tut! No false modesty, here." Mezzaluna clapped.
"Attenzione! Attenzione, prego!"

The crowd of stagehands and artisans and Pettifoggers
swiveled their faces toward the painted screen.

"Look at this ravishing winter scene," Mezzaluna commanded. "Less than one hour ago, the screen was dull as
ditchwater. It did not sparkle. It did not shine. These
schoolchildren"—he leveled a scornful glare at his apprentices, who hung their heads—"transformed it! Let this be an
example to you all. Henceforth, I will not accept excuses for
shoddy, slow work."

Anastasia waited for someone to leap forth and claim credit
for the beautified snowscape. Nobody did. The woebegone
helpers resumed their various chores, and Signor Mezzaluna
dashed off to chastise the Dalmatian polka-dotters.

"But who stenciled the screen?" Gus whispered.

"I don't know," Anastasia said, tracing one of the frosty
whorls with the tip of her index finger. "I guess they know
the art of keeping secrets, too."

May 30, 1751

Today was young Penny's twelfth birthday. 'Tis strange to imagine she's already twelve . . . wondrous-strange, how children grow. I've oft pondered, it's the most magical thing under the moon.

Nico and I staged a shadow spectacle for her, for which I made twelve new puppets. Beautiful as they are, Nico himself is really more ingenious: when he umbrates he can create the most wonderful shapes. Oh, how the children laughed and laughed, to see their Shadowfather skulking about as a tiger!

I admit, in the midst of our jollification, I found my heart tinged with sadness. At times I do sorely feel my lack of a family. But it does no good to dwell on what one doesn't have—far better to count one's blessings. I am most grateful for my nieces and nephews, and the Merrymoon children (with the exception of Ludowiga—although I'd never tell Nico that!) are much like family to me. And my apprentice, Dagfinn, is becoming like a son to me. He's a clever lad, curious and full of potential, although I do worry he tries to rush his craft. It takes time for magic to reveal its secrets, and dark things happen to those who hasten.

Anastasia surfaced from the chronicle, her thoughts in a dander. For all Calixto's hearts and flowers about the

Merrymoons, he certainly hadn't balked at sealing Nico into a poisonous silver box! Fink! Traitor! Double-crosser! It angered Anastasia, and it perplexed her, too. She again wondered why Calixto had turned against her family. Was it just the wicked nature of witches?

She struggled through the warlock's cursive to read about a trip to the ice creamery, a quibble with Dagfinn, and woes about thinning hair. None of it seemed relevant to the Dreadfuls' great mission. Anastasia sighed and picked up the second volume pilfered from Calixto's office.

It proved to be a diary, too, albeit from a later period in the warlock's life. Anastasia muddled through a few rambling entries about shadow puppets and a witch fondue party, the script blurring beneath her sleepy peepers. Her eyelids were just drooping shut when her gaze snagged on the word *glass*.

Jozzled awake, Anastasia returned to the beginning of the section.

February 28, 1755

Oh, how I crave an ice lolly! Today I spent hours in the Glass Lady's workshop, and her ovens burn hotter than a thousand dragon sneezes. In exchange for her work on my doors, I helped the Lady craft a pair of magic lenses. They are to be a gift for her father; although shut away from the sky, the old man still likes to build telescopes.

A telescope's power, of course, dwells in its lenses. And no lenses in the world could compete with the ones the Lady and I cooked up today—they are charmed to peer through solid rock! The old astronomer will be able to stargaze even beneath the stalactites! Ingenious, if I may say so myself. And I'm doubly pleased with today's work, because it gave me a most marvelous idea. . . .

Anastasia stared at the page in shock. An idea was starting to take shape in her brainbox, and she didn't like it. Not one little bit.

She scanned ahead to find any further mention of glass embedded in the warlock's sprawling cursive. The next one came months later, in Calixto's final journal entry.

December 1, 1755

My experiments with my magnum opus have gone well—too well, I fear. There are times when magic outwits the warlock and starts growing in strange and unexpected ways. Now I know too much; yes, more than I ever wanted to know.

Knowledge is the fire that lights the world—and sometimes it burns. In the wrong hands, the magnum opus could consume us all. It is too powerful; too dangerous. And yet I cannot bring myself to destroy it—for it could be used for good. I must hide my magnum opus, and hide it well. I especially fear Dagfinn finding it—he who demands knowledge without work and time. Knowledge is not the same thing as wisdom, have not I oft told him? But I fear my words dissolve in his ears like smoke. Yes, I must hide the magnum opus.

To that end, I visited two artisans today with secret commissions. First I went to the silversmith Zebedee. He shall forge me a silver trunk to stow the opus, and eight nails to seal its lid, and a hammer with which to bind the nails. Of course, I will be the one to enchant the silver sledge and pins: enchantment upon enchantment, lock upon lock. When the last nail drives home, the Silver Chest will vanish to a secret place, and the Hammer will away to my secret study at the top of old Aggie's chimney—to the special glass strongbox I commissioned from the Glass Lady.

Neither the Lady nor Zebedee knows the dark need behind my requests—only Aggie knows about the magnum opus. I do trust the Lady—her time in Murano engrained secrecy into her very marrow—but I don't trust those around her.

Aggie! So addressee *A* of the cuckoo clock note *was* Calixto's old witch-nanny. And, Anastasia thought, the identity of the Glass Lady was—even through Calixto's scrawl of scrambled handwriting—now crystalline clear.

And that Glass Lady had fashioned the glass chest stashed in Calixto's secret lair.

But what was this mysterious *magnum opus*? Anastasia was too weary to go back and untangle the warlock's cursive to find out that night; she resolved to do so the next day. She did, however, reread the final diary log. Thrice. After her third review, she slumped back into her pillows and gazed at the roses stitched on her canopy, speculations tumbling through her addled wits.

What could have happened during that fateful December to twist Calixto's intentions from hiding a magical doohickey in the Silver Chest to instead locking up Nicodemus Merrymoon? And, since Nicodemus was now in the sterling strongbox . . . *where was the dangerous magnum opus that threatened to consume the world?*

❧ 14 ❧

Ambivalence

AMBIVALENCE, DEAR READER, is a fancy word that means you feel two different and opposite ways about the same thing. Anastasia was ambivalent indeed about her discoveries in the warlock's diaries. On the one hand, she itched to report her findings to her fellow Dreadfuls. She itched to tell the league about the magnum opus and the two chests designed to hide it. She itched to tell them about the Glass Lady.

On the other hand, she wasn't itchy at all to divulge certain of the new details gleaned from Calixto's memoirs—at least, not to *Gus*. Anastasia was 99 percent positive, you understand, that the Glass Lady was Celestina Wata. How would Gus react to the notion that his aunt Teeny had been chummy with Calixto Swift, villain extraordinaire? It would rattle him. And Anastasia had no desire to rattle one of her best friends.

At the same time, Calixto had noted the Glass Lady knew plenty of his witchy secrets—more secrets, even, than his apprentice, Dagfinn. If Celestina Wata was, in fact, Calixto's glass-crafting pal, then she could have oodles of crackerjack clues stashed up her sleeve. She might even know how to open the glass cabinet!

Anastasia kept her suspicions bottled up all that morning through her breakfast pancakes and the gondola ride to school. But where were her classmates? The pier lay abandoned. She glanced at her pocket watch and confirmed: yes, it had stopped *again*.

"Crumbs!" Anastasia grabbed her satchel and scrambled to the dock. "I'm late! Marm Pettifog will probably lock me in the academy basement for the rest of fifth grade!"

However, Marm Pettifog was not stationed behind her lectern as Anastasia scurried into class. *Miss Ramachandra* was.

"Good morning!" The art teacher beamed at her over the edge of Francie Dewdrop thriller number eighty-four, *The Clue in the Lapis Lazuli*. "Oh, you're just in time! You wouldn't want to miss a minute of Storybook Tuesday, would you?"

"Storybook Tuesday?" Anastasia echoed.

"That's what we do *every* Tuesday, dummy," Saskia called from her desk. *"Remember?"*

The twenty-odd fifth graders stared at Anastasia with

scorching intensity, and through that special mischief-telepathy particular to children of school age, they communicated this message to her without uttering a word: *Smile and nod and just go along and for Pete's sake don't ruin this for everyone, you nitwit!*

"Oh, right," Anastasia said, taking her seat. "Storybook Tuesday. Er—where's Marm Pettifog?"

"Out sick, I'm afraid!" Miss Ramachandra lamented. "She's stuck in bed with some kind of flu."

"Do you think it's fatal?" Jasper asked hopefully.

"Oh *no*," Miss Ramachandra cried. "You mustn't worry about that, dear! Marm Pettifog will be right as rain in a few days or so."

"I *wasn't* worried," Jasper grumbled.

"In the meantime, I'll be your substitute," Miss Ramachandra went on. "I know you'll miss Marm Pettifog, but we'll do our best to soldier on without her. And, of course, we'll be visiting the Dinkledorf Yodeling Museum tomorrow! That should cheer you up!"

Anastasia wheeled her gaze across the cavern, noting her classmates' high jinks:

Ollie—brazenly eating toffees
Saskia and Taffline—giggling over an origami
    fortune-teller
Jasper—launching spitballs at the stalactites

And so forth. Through it all, Miss Ramachandra dutifully warbled the tale of Francie Dewdrop's run-ins with a murderous jeweler.

Under normal circumstances, Anastasia would savor every delicious moment of a read-aloud, but she had her own mystery to think about. The secrets bottled up in her brain threatened to fizz out her nostrils like soda. The Dreadfuls had scarcely settled down for lunch in the caveteria before she burbled forth the clues collected from Calixto's diaries.

"Magnum opus!" Ollie echoed in bewilderment. "What's that?"

"A masterpiece," Gus said.

"And Calixto Swift's magnum opus *could destroy the world*," Anastasia whispered. "What do you think it was?"

"Calixto Swift was pretty powerful," Gus said nervously. "He warped gravity in Mrs. Honeysop's cave, after all." He started. "Do you suppose the magnum opus is the *M.O.* Calixto planned to hide in Stinking Crumpet?"

"It must be!" Anastasia gasped. "He said in his diary that only Aggie knew about the magnum opus!"

"And now we're planning a trip to Stinking Crumpet," Ollie quavered.

"We don't know whether the M.O. ever got there," Anastasia said. "Besides, we need to figure out the glass cabinet and Calixto's magic doors before we make any trips." She looked at Gus.

"Aunt Teeny isn't the only glass smith in the world, you know." Perturbed, Gus picked at his sandwich.

"But she was probably one of the only glass smiths in Nowhere Special back when Calixto Swift lived here," Anastasia said. "And it makes sense that she would give her dad a telescope. How many glass smiths have astronomer dads?"

"And she's secretive," Ollie said. "She's *renowned* for her secrecy!"

"So were all the other Venetian glassblowers," Gus argued, his eyes flashing. "My aunt isn't a witch-sympathizer!"

"Lots of Morfolk were friends with witches before the Perpetual War," Anastasia said softly. "My *grandfather* was friends with Calixto Swift. My entire family was! Calixto fooled lots of people."

"Sure," Gus said, "but lots of people didn't make glass chests for Calixto to stash away his witchy tools. If Celestina helped Calixto Swift stow the Silver Hammer, it would make her an accomplice to the Dastardly Deed! It would make her guilty of *treason*!"

"No, it wouldn't," Anastasia reassured him. "Calixto said in his journal that the Glass Lady didn't know what he planned to do with the cabinet." She reached out and squeezed Gus's arm. "We have to at least *ask* her. If Celestina knows how to open the glass cabinet, we can get *the Silver Hammer*. We'd be closer to freeing Nicodemus and finding my dad."

"And Celestina might know what Calixto's magical doors look like, too," Ollie suggested. "She might even remember which one leads to the Silver Chest!"

Gus sighed. "Well, even *if* Aunt Teeny really is the Glass Lady, and even *if* she knows anything helpful, do you really think she'll tell *us* any witch secrets? I can't imagine her spilling the beans just because we *asked*."

"Maybe if we tell her about our Mission of Life-and-Death Importance . . . ," Ollie suggested.

Anastasia shook her head. "No! We can't tell anyone

we're looking for my dad and grandpa. If Penny and Baldwin find out, they'll try to stop us. They think messing around with magic is too dangerous."

"How can we get a secret out of an expert secret-keeper?" Ollie pondered.

"First you'll have to figure out a way to see her," Gus grumped. "Aunt Teeny hardly comes down to the Cavelands."

"Couldn't you invite her over for tea?" Anastasia asked hopefully. "In Francie Dewdrop books, people always let secrets slip during teatime."

"My dad and grandpa would be around," Gus said. "Celestina certainly isn't going to chitchat about witch glass in front of them!"

"Maybe *we* could visit *her* instead," Ollie suggested. "Maybe Prince Baldwin and Princess Penelope could take us up to Dinkledorf again. You know Baldwin would jump at the chance to go clock shopping!"

"He'd jump at the chance to go snow globe shopping, too," Anastasia groaned. "We wouldn't be able to ask Celestina anything about Calixto. Besides, Celestina knows Gus isn't allowed abovecaves. She might tell Mr. Wata."

"But Celestina's great at keeping secrets!" Ollie nudged Gus. "You don't think she'd tattle, do you?"

Gus lapsed into thought. "No," he admitted, "I guess not. She's not really the *meddling* type."

"So . . . should we just sneak into Dinkledorf by ourselves?" Anastasia asked.

Ollie shook his head. "Too risky."

"Because of CRUD?" Gus asked.

"I wasn't even thinking about *them*." Ollie dismissed the murderous minions of CRUD with a wave of his fork. "Even if we manage to escape our families for an afternoon, Morfolk own businesses with all the secret doors leading into Dinkledorf. They would wonder why four Morflings were abovecaves without their parents."

"They might even recognize Anastasia from her photograph in the newspaper," Gus reasoned. "Remember? The *Nowhere Special Echo* printed photos when she arrived in the Cavelands."

Anastasia sagged against her seat. What a quandary! The Dreadfuls couldn't visit Celestina with adults in tow, and they couldn't risk sneaking into Dinkledorf alone. Unless—

She smiled. She smiled the smile of someone who has hit upon the answer to a particularly difficult crossword puzzle. "I know how we can see Celestina. We'll just have to break a few rules. . . ."

❧ 15 ❧
Clouds

"**ALL RIGHT, CHILDREN!**" Miss Ramachandra called. "Does everyone have coats? It's going to be chilly up in Dinkledorf! Into the boats, now! Grayson—no shoving! We'll row to Bumbershoot Square—you all know the way, right? That was one of your Applied Navigation assignments?"

"Yes, Miss Ramachandra," the Pettifoggers chorused.

"Super! We'll row to Bumbershoot Square and from there head up to our great Dinkledorf adventure!"

"Here, Miss Ramachandra." Gus flourished a permission slip. "I forgot to give this to Marm Pettifog."

"Oh!" Miss Ramachandra accepted the slip and shoved it into her pocket. "Better late than never, dear. You'll hide your snakes under a hat? Good. What seems to be the problem, Jennifer? You forgot your gloves? Tsk! Let's find you something from the cloakroom—" Miss Ramachandra hurried off to mitten a few unprepared students.

"Come on," Gus said. "Before I lose my nerve."

The Dreadfuls rummaged paddles from the bin and hurried to the pier. A train of pink Pettifog rowboats was already snaking from Old Crescent Lagoon and into the canal system.

"Miss Ramachandra didn't even look at our great forgery," Ollie grumped as the Dreadfuls hopped into their own craft.

"It was *Anastasia's* forgery," Gus pointed out. "And we're lucky Miss Ramachandra is so absentminded. I heard that Marm Pettifog actually examines the signatures on permission slips with a jeweler's loupe." He scrooched down in the belly of the boat. "If you don't mind, I'm not going to help row. I'm going to hide."

"Lazy," Ollie complained.

Gus grinned up at him. "What if my dad is out running errands today? I can't risk being seen."

Anastasia and Ollie churned their oars, propelling their boat toward the Pettifog flotilla ahead. They rowed through the Spelunker Straits, and under Gardyloo Bridge, and angled down Gypsum Alley. Anastasia swiveled her head, collecting mental bread crumbs for the Applied Navigation exam. There! The pickle shop at the corner of Gypsum Alley and Bumbershoot Gutter was a distinctive waypost. She stared at the shop window, letting the view of rubbery green fruits imprint her memory. Then the Pettifoggers turned toward Bumbershoot Square, where they awaited the last stragglers. Anastasia danced from galosh to galosh, impatient to get up to Dinkledorf. Finally Miss Ramachandra's boat glided up to the pier.

"All right!" she cried, clambering to the dock. "To Penumbra Alley! Er—it's to the left, right?"

"No, Miss Ramachandra," piped up Jasper Cummerbund. "It's to the right."

"Of course! Silly me. This way, children!" Miss Ramachandra waved them down a side tunnel. "Now, if you'll give me just a smidgen of help . . . is this the way up to Die Zuckerhutte?" She hesitated by a stone stairwell curving up between a calligrapher's and a pharmacy.

"*Yes,*" Saskia snickered. "*Obviously.* Look at the sign."

"Oh!" Miss Ramachandra blinked at a wooden plaque reading TO DIE ZUCKERHUTTE/GREATER DINKLEDORF. "Excellent!"

"What's dee—dee zookerhooty?" Anastasia asked as they puffed up the stone flight.

"Chocolate shop," Ollie said. "Whenever we go on a school field trip, we come up through its back closet. Nobody's surprised to see a bunch of kids suddenly hanging around a candy store. I wonder if Miss Ramachandra will let us buy some sweets? Marm Pettifog never does."

As they neared the stairwell's zenith, Gus pulled his knit hat tightly over his snakes, and Anastasia flipped her hood over her braids to hide the snoozing Pippistrella. Miss Ramachandra paused at the wooden door leading to the chocolatier's and withdrew a letter from her pocket. "Marm Pettifog sent me a note to read to you," she announced.

The students groaned.

"I know you're anxious to get to the Yodeling Museum, but this will only take a second. Ahem." Miss Ramachandra rustled the letter. "'Students: I trust you will all be on your best behavior (as shabby as that may be) for Miss Ramachandra. Stay close together—no dawdling, no lollygagging, and absolutely *no* wandering away from the group. If any of you misbehaves, Miss Ramachandra will see that you *all* return to Pettifog Academy *immediately,* where you will spend the rest of the day scrubbing mildew from the gym lockers.'"

The Dreadfuls exchanged furtive glances. Despite Marm Pettifog's threats, wandering away from the group topped their list of things to do in Dinkledorf. They planned to wander all the way to Celestina Wata's workshop, where they would try to ferret out whether the artisan knew the secrets of Calixto's glass cabinet and magic doors. But if they got caught sneaking off, they'd ruin the field trip for everyone.

"'Remember: do not talk about Nowhere Special,'" Miss

Ramachandra continued. "'Do not mention Morfolk, or witches, or the Cavelands. Many of the Dinkledorfers are Morfolk, but many are not, and we mustn't draw attention to ourselves. If you defy these orders, my wrath shall be great and nasty and extremely scary. P.S.: Poormina, don't you *dare* let those rotten little gluttons try to talk you into letting them buy chocolate at the candy shop'—oh dear!" Miss Ramachandra stopped, flustered. "I don't think I was supposed to read that postscript out loud."

"It's all right, Miss Ramachandra," Jasper said cheerfully. "We already know Marm Pettifog thinks we're rotten."

"Well, you *aren't*," Miss Ramachandra said. "I try not to contradict Marm Pettifog, but I certainly disagree with her on that point. She is right, however, that we need to be on our best behavior." She paused. "Including *me*. I don't want detention again." With a little shudder, she pushed open the door leading to Die Zuckerhutte.

The chocolate shop was a blur of bonbons and truffles; dutiful Miss Ramachandra ushered the students out without so much as a nibble.

"But, Miss Ramachandra, I'm *hungry*," wailed Parveen.

"We'll get lunch after the museum, dear," Miss Ramachandra promised. "You only need to wait until eleven-thirty."

As they tumbled outside and into the snow of Dinkledorf, Ollie clasped his mitten over his face.

"Cold?" Anastasia asked.

Ollie shook his head. "No. I'm trying to bottle up the good smell."

"Clouds!" Gus's gaze was riveted to the heavens. Anastasia grabbed his hand and tugged him after the Pettifog group.

"Watch your feet!" she cautioned. "It's icy."

"What's that sound?" Gus asked.

"That," Ollie muttered, "is the Yodeling Museum."

Perhaps, Reader, you have visited a fanciful museum in your hometown or upon a family holiday. Perhaps you have visited enormous institutions chock-full of magnificent displays of fabulous Egyptian artifacts, or entire dinosaur skeletons, or rare works of art. The Yodeling Museum was no such sleek and sprawling treasure hold. Like the other shops and houses of Dinkledorf, the museum resembled an overgrown dollhouse. Carved gingerbread frilled its snow-capped eaves, and pretty pink shutters flanked its windows. A wooden figure of a man in green lederhosen stood sentry by the museum's front door, its lower jaw jabbering and juddering like the maw on a Christmas nutcracker. Yodels tootled from his wooden windpipe.

"Isn't that *charming*!" Miss Ramachandra said.

The school group shuffled into the museum, stamping snow from their boots.

"Odelay-hee-hoo!" cried the woman behind the ticket

counter. "Welcome to the world-famous Dinkledorf Yodeling Museum!"

"Is this place really world-famous?" Anastasia whispered to Ollie.

He shook his head. "How could it be? Hardly anyone's even heard of Dinkledorf!"

Miss Ramachandra clapped her hands. "Children! Go on ahead into the museum. Explore! Discover! We'll meet in the Singing Gallery at ten-thirty for the yodeling demonstration." She rustled in her purse, spilling a flood of purple tickets onto the floor, and the museum greeter bent to help the art teacher pick them up. Amidst the chaos of flurrying tickets and stampeding Pettifoggers, another band of backpacked children—presumably visiting from a nearby Swiss school—arrived. Anastasia brightened. The more crowded the museum, the better the Dreadfuls' chances of slinking away unnoticed.

As they headed toward the exhibits, Ollie nudged Anastasia and pointed down a hallway. Past the bathrooms lay a wooden door, its glass window revealing Dinkledorf beyond.

"That'll be our escape route," Ollie whispered. Anastasia nodded.

The first gallery contained a number of displays under dusty glass cases. Ollie heaved an enormous sigh. "This place is *so* boring."

"Well, at least *pretend* to be interested," Gus muttered.

"Once Miss Ramachandra goes into the next room, we can make a run for it."

"Fine." Ollie turned his gaze to the nearest vitrine. "What's this?"

Gus glanced at the card below. "The lederhosen worn by Zelig Immergluck at the Dinkledorf Yodeling Championship in 1850."

"Fascinating." Ollie removed a lump of taffy from his jacket and began champing it.

"'Yodeling began in the Alps as a form of communication hollered, peak to peak, by chatty cowherds,'" Anastasia read aloud from another placard. She lowered her voice. "Has Miss Ramachandra wandered off yet?"

Gus's gaze darted from a display of alpenhorns and into the next gallery. "Yup, and it looks like she's trying to get gum out of Jasper's hair."

"That'll keep her busy for a while," Ollie predicted.

"Let's go," Anastasia urged.

They slipped from the room to sidle down the empty hallway. Hinges creaked as they pushed open the door, but a volley of yodeling between museum docents camouflaged the noise. Once they were standing outside, Ollie swung the door so it was almost shut, and then he removed the taffy from his mouth. This he squished between door and jamb. "Now it won't lock us out."

"Smart," Gus complimented him.

"Are you sure you know the way to Celestina's shop?" Anastasia fretted as their steps took them farther and farther from the museum and deeper and deeper into the maze of winding Dinkledorfian lanes.

"It'll be easy to find," Ollie said. "Piece of cake—literally! Der Glasforst is at the end of Sugar Way."

Anastasia frowned. "I wish we had a map."

"We don't need a map." Ollie grinned. "I have this." He tapped his nose, and then he inhaled deeply. "Hmm." He darted down a side alley. *Sniff! Sniff!* "This way!"

"I can't smell anything," Gus protested.

"You will soon," Ollie promised. *Sniff!* "Let's go down here. . . ."

"Mmmm!" Anastasia murmured. "I smell cake!"

"Me too!" Gus said.

"See?" Ollie pointed to a sign bolted to the side of a lop-sided bakery. "Zucker Weg."

The lovely perfume of hundreds of cakes wafted from the lane to greet their nostrils. "Do you think we could stop in for a nibble?" Ollie begged. "Just one tiny little nibble of one teeny, tiny crumb? Look at that Bundt!"

"We don't have time for sweets," Anastasia said.

"That, Anastasia, is the most depressing thing you have ever said." Ollie scowled.

"Oh, Ollie! We only have about an hour before the yodeling demonstration is over," Anastasia said. "Miss

Ramachandra told Parveen that we're eating lunch at eleven-thirty."

They drifted down Sugar Way, through the warm and fragrant air, betwixt shop windows fogged with sugary steam and crammed with luscious confections, until at the very end of their snowy, cookie-scented trek Ollie pulled them around a corner. There, cushioned by deep snowdrifts, hunkered a cabin with a sign reading DER GLASFORST.

"Ready?" Ollie asked.

"I guess," Gus grumbled. "But we're wasting our time. I *know* Aunt Teeny isn't mixed up in the Dastardly Deed. She's not a witch-sympathizer—she's *sweet*. She takes me for ice cream every year on my birthday, and she's always sending me funny cards." His gaze dropped, but not before Anastasia glimpsed the doubt swimming in his eyes. *He thinks Celestina is the Glass Lady, too,* she realized. *He just won't admit it, because he's worried.*

Anastasia's conscience prickled like a hedgehog, but she *had* to talk to Celestina. Her family's fate could very well hang upon whatever secrets the glass smith hoarded. "Well," she said softly, "*whoever* the Glass Lady is, I don't blame her for what happened to my grandpa. Not one little bit."

As the Dreadfuls neared the window, they beheld an entire magical world of delicate glass: glass ballerinas and ice skaters and swans and polar bears perched on the minute lake of a frosted mirror. Glass deer and foxes and unicorns wandered a forest of miniature glass trees. Glass snowflakes dangled from clouds of lovely, lacy spun glass.

"Beautiful!" she breathed.

The depths of Der Glasforst proved just as enchanting as the shop window. Illuminated shelves lined the walls, and shining on those shelves were hundreds of magnificent snow globes. Anastasia leaned close to peer at the maker's mark tattooed near the base of one: CW with a star.

A tiny woman rounded a display of glass unicorns. "Gus! What on earth are you doing here?"

"Hi, Aunt Teeny," Gus mumbled.

"Where's Mercurio? Does he know you're aboveca—" Celestina cut herself off, glancing around the shop. They were alone. *"Abovecaves?"*

"We're on a field trip," Gus said quickly.

Celestina gawped. "Mercurio actually let you go on a field trip?"

"Not exactly," Gus admitted. "But I'm tired of staying behind at school every year."

"So you *sneaked* up, did you?" Celestina laughed. "Don't worry. Your secret is safe with me." She winked. "I do love a good secret."

Ollie jabbed Anastasia's ribs.

"Where are your classmates?" Celestina asked.

"Back at the Yodeling Museum," Gus said. "I just—I

really wanted to come visit you. I've never seen your shop, you know."

Celestina's face softened. "I know." She pulled Gus into a hug and then patted his lumpy woolen hat. An irritated hiss sounded beneath the pompon. "Be careful to keep these fellows hidden, eh?"

Gus nodded and tugged the edges of his hat down around his ears.

"My goodness," Celestina said. "I knew this was an important day when I woke up—I could feel it deep inside my bones. Something strange and special will happen today, I thought to myself, and so it has! My nephew's first visit to my shop!" She danced to the front window and flipped the OPEN/CLOSED sign so the CLOSED side would face out to the street. "There! We'll have the place all for ourselves."

Gus beamed.

"Now, who are these other field trip fugitives?" Celestina asked, grinning.

"Ollie and Anastasia," Gus answered.

"*Princess* Anastasia," Ollie emphasized, and Anastasia blushed.

"Oh my!" Celestina said. "That's right. Mercurio mentioned in one of his letters that you arrived in the Cavelands several months ago. How do you like it here? You live in the palace, don't you?"

Anastasia nodded. "Yes. My grandmother has a collection of your snow globes, you know."

"Your grandmother? The *queen*?" Celestina puzzled. "She must have received them as gifts. Queen Wiggy has never commissioned globes from me."

"How do you make them snow?" Anastasia asked.

"Just as you would with any snow globe—you shake it!"

Anastasia shook her head. "No. Sometimes the snow whirls around all on its own."

Celestina frowned. "You must have imagined it, dear. Perhaps you bumped into the globe?"

"I didn't," Anastasia said. "And it isn't just one globe. Wiggy has an entire hallway of snow globes, and they all snow at once."

Something flickered over Celestina's face. It was only there a moment. If Anastasia had blinked, she would have missed it. But she didn't blink, and she recognized the expression at once: *fear*. For some reason, the glass smith was afraid.

"I don't know anything about automatic snow globes," Celestina said with a brittle smile. "The queen must have gotten them from a different workshop. But I have something else that might interest you. . . ."

She steered the Dreadfuls, and the conversation, over to a case in the corner. "I just finished this glass cello yesterday.

Listen—it really works." She plucked up a bow and swiped it across the cello's breast, dredging forth a glassine sigh.

"Quentin would love that!" Ollie marveled.

"What other sorts of things do you make?" Anastasia asked in her best I Am Very Innocent and Not Digging for Information voice. "Do you make furniture?"

"I once made a set of little glass chairs for a duchess's dollhouse," Celestina said. "Spun glass; very nice."

"What about a glass cabinet? Did you ever make a glass cabinet without doors?" Anastasia quizzed.

CRASH! Tinkle! The crystalline cello bow smashed on the floor, splintering into smithereens. Eyes saucer-round, Celestina stared at Anastasia. "A cabinet without doors?" she echoed hoarsely. "No! I've never made anything like that. Never!"

"Aunt Teeny—" Gus faltered, touching her arm.

"Why would you ask me that, Princess?" Celestina demanded. "Did you see something like that in the palace?"

"N-no," Anastasia stammered.

"Aunt Teeny, you're stepping on broken glass!" Gus said.

Celestina stiffened and looked down. "Oh. Oh dear. I'd better clean that up."

"I'll help you," Gus offered hastily. "Where's your broom?"

"No, dear. It's time for you to run along." Celestina ushered the trio toward the shop entrance. "Thanks so much for visiting, children. Gus, I'll see you at your parents' anniversary party next month."

And with a hug and three shoves, the Dreadfuls were back out in the snowy lane.

"Odelay-hee . . . odelay-hay . . . odelay-HEE-HOO!"

The yodeler finished with a flourish, and the museum-goers launched into polite applause right as the Dreadfuls sidled into the Singing Gallery.

"Bravo! Bravo!" Miss Ramachandra cheered. "That was marvelous! All right, children. Let's head over to the Fondue Haus and get your lunch."

As the school group tromped through the snowy Dinkle-dorfian lanes, the Dreadfuls huddled close and whispered about their secret visit.

"Celestina practically threw us out on our noses!" Ollie said.

"She did act a little strange," Gus admitted. "But she probably—um—just had to get back to work."

"As soon as we mentioned glass cabinets, she got nutty as a fruitcake!" Ollie pressed. "Obviously she knows about Calixto's chest. She's the Glass Lady, Gus—I'm sure of it!"

"Me too," Anastasia said quietly.

Gus heaved a sigh and tilted his gaze toward the sky. "Hey! Look at that cloud!"

"Don't change the subject, Gus," Ollie said. "You know your aunt—"

"*Look!*" Gus had stopped in his tracks, and his mouth was ajar. "My gosh, that cumulus looks just like a ballerina!"

Anastasia wheeled her eyes skyward. "Oh, it's pretty!"

"Do clouds always make pictures?" Gus puzzled.

"Well—sometimes they *resemble* things—bunnies or rabbits or lambs—but I've never seen one quite like that," Anastasia said. "It looks almost—er—sculpted."

A few of their schoolmates were now staring at the wild white yonder. "Look! Miss Ramachandra, look!"

Now the entire class studied the cloud ballerina. She moved, as clouds buffeted by high winds do. However, instead of lumping into another shape or stretching like cloud taffy into cirrus clouds or fizzling out altogether, the ballerina cloud *danced*. She raised her arms and lifted her legs into a leap. She brought her heels back together into first position. From the swirls of a nearby cloud the shape of another ballerina formed. Then another. Standing in a row, the ballerina clouds danced in tandem. They moved slowly, as though they danced underwater, but they *danced*.

"*Magical!*" Miss Ramachandra thrilled.

"Magic?" cried Taffline. "Do you think it *is*, Miss Ramachandra?"

"I—oh no, dear, I didn't mean—you see, clouds often resemble—"

"Do you think there's a *witch* nearby?" asked Parveen, whirling her gaze around the charming buildings of Dinkledorf.

"Parveen!" hissed Tommy. "Shut up! We aren't supposed to talk about the W-word up here, remember?"

"Miss Ramachandra! Tommy told me to shut up!"

"Now, Tommy, that isn't nice—"

"I've seen plenty of clouds before, and none of them act like that." Saskia's voice trembled. "It must be witchcraft."

"They certainly are strange," Miss Ramachandra said. "Perhaps we should go back to school, children."

One or two protests punctuated the air, but most of the Pettifoggers nodded in frightened agreement. Miss Ramachandra pulled out her map, peered at it in utter befuddlement, and rotated it 180 degrees. "How do we get back to the chocolate shop?"

"Miss Ramachandra—" piped up Rupert.

"Just a moment, Rupert." Miss Ramachandra swiveled the map again. "I'm trying to sort out this map—it seems to have been printed upside down!"

"But, Miss Ramachandra—"

"Hold on, dear."

"But, Miss Ramachandra!" Rupert shrilled, now tugging her arm. "Where's Jasper?"

As it turned out, none of the students could spot Jasper Cummerbund. Nor could the panic-stricken Miss Ramachandra. The class-turned-search-party roved the snowy lanes and checked the museum lavatories and peered into every bakery on Zucker Weg and asked at every toy shop and even at a shoe store and an insurance agency. A sweep of gray clouds upholstered the sky, blotting out the ballerinas and shivering snowflakes down to Dinkledorf, and nowhere, nowhere was the boy to be found.

Jasper Cummerbund was gone.

16

Witch or Watcher?

CRUD WATCHERS HAD snatched Jasper. Or maybe witches took him! Or might he have wandered off into the woods and the clutches of a hungry bear?

Theories multiplied in Nowhere Special. Some of them were reasonable, and some of them were far-fetched, but they were all of them grim. One thing was certain: Jasper Cummerbund had vanished without a trace. None of the Morfo search parties sent up in the days following the disastrous Yodeling Museum excursion found a single clue as to Jasper's whereabouts.

"And some of those searchers are shifted *wolves*," Ollie said glumly, slopping varnish on Signor Mezzaluna's papier-mâché clouds. "If anyone could track down Jasper, it's them."

Anastasia nodded. "Baldy's spent every night this week sniffing around Dinkledorf. He says Jasper's scent leads from the chocolate shop to the museum, and then it just ends— like he disappeared into thin air."

"Like *magic*," Ollie breathed.

Anastasia nibbled the end of one of her braids. "Speaking of magic, what do your parents think about those clouds?"

The *Echo* had printed an account of the entire ill-fated field trip, from the Pettifoggers' boat ride to Bumbershoot Square to Miss Ramachandra attempting to tweeze gum from Jasper's head at the Yodeling Museum to the mysterious clouds gamboling above Dinkledorf. Opinion regarding the Cloud Phenomenon was divided: half of Nowhere Special feared witch magic had whipped the sky into a magical ballet, and half did not.

The half that *did* marched outside the Senate Cave, waving signs reading MORE SOLDIERS, MORE SPIES, MORE SAFETY! SAY "YEA" TO THE MERRYMOON MILITIA BILL!

Their opponents tacked up posters blazing KEEP OUR PURSES AND OUR PEOPLE SAFE . . . FROM ABSOLUTE MONARCHY! VOTE "HECK NO" ON MMB!

"Mom and Dad don't think it's a coincidence that we saw those clouds right when Jasper went missing," Gus said. "They say it's witch-work, and they wrote a letter to Senator Dellacava telling him to vote yes on the Merrymoon Militia Bill. How about your folks, Ollie?"

"Undecided." Ollie hunched over the pot of varnish. "What does the royal family think?"

"Ludowiga is screaming witches. Penny and Baldy think it was a CRUD snatching. And Wiggy—I'm not sure about Wiggy. She's worried, though." Anastasia bit her lip. She, Anastasia, was also worried. The threat of villains creeping about the sweet Swiss village, directly above Nowhere Special, sent flurries of fear swirling through her belly.

"CRUD is bad, but witches would be worse," Gus said.

"They're both awful," Anastasia agreed.

"You know what else is awful?" Ollie said. "Having Marm Pettifog back."

Once news of the snatching scandal had trickled to Marm Pettifog, the old dictator had struggled from her sickbed to return to her academy. She had exiled Miss Ramachandra back to the art cave. Three different students had caught the distraught art teacher weeping into glue pots that week, and she now sobbed noisily over the polka-dotted Dalmatians in the Cavepearl Theater backstage.

"I feel sorry for Miss Ramachandra," Anastasia said. "A lot of people are blaming her for Jasper's disappearance, but it wasn't her fault. Witches and Watchers are *tricky*. Whether it was CRUD or the witches, I don't think Miss Ramachandra could have stopped them."

"If it was CRUD, why didn't they snatch *us*?" Ollie wondered aloud.

"What do you mean?" Gus asked.

"Well, CRUD knows what Anastasia and I look like. They know we're Morflings. And we were walking through the streets of Nowhere Special by ourselves. It would have been easy for someone to grab us." Ollie shivered.

"Duncan! You, there! Help me with this mirror for the ice waltz," Mezzaluna shouted at a hapless stagehand.

"Speaking of mirrors . . ." Gus leaned forward. "I've been thinking about Calixto's glass doors, and we already know of at least *one* piece of witch glass in the palace."

"We do?" Ollie said.

Anastasia gasped. "Yes, Ollie, *we do*—the Glimmerglass!"

"That mirror is *definitely* magical," Gus said. "Your reflection *talked* to you, for crumb's sake. Aisatsana even *argued* with you."

Anastasia wrinkled her nose. Her mirror-twin, Aisatsana (*Anastasia* backward), had proved to be an extremely unpleasant little girl. Aisatsana was rude. She was sour and snooty. She was even, I am sorry to say, a bit of a *blackmailer*. Anastasia found it vexing indeed to know that Aisatsana spied upon her from any nearby polished spoon or limpid puddle or looking glass—just as your mirror-twin watches *you*, gentle Reader.

Of course, our reflections do not speak to us from ordinary mirrors. They *can't*. Aisatsana could only sass Anastasia from Calixto Swift's enchanted Glimmerglass, stashed in Wiggy's chambers.

"Maybe the Glimmerglass is a magic door!" Ollie said. "Maybe it's a portal to mirrors in other countries!"

For one thrilling moment, Anastasia's snoop instincts perked like a bloodhound scenting prey. Then she remembered a detail from her confabs with Aisatsana, and down again her instincts drooped. "Aisatsana told me I couldn't step through the mirror."

Gus made an impatient noise. "She could have been *lying*. Aisatsana is a complete *pill*, remember?"

"But I tried to reach inside, and my hand just bumped against the glass."

"Yes, but you didn't have Calixto's twinkly nursery rhyme spell!" Ollie said.

"And even if the Glimmerglass isn't a magical portal, Aisatsana might have heard something about glass doors from one of her reflection friends," Gus mused. "Some of those old mirror folk have been around for hundreds of years! They've peeked into places all over the world, and they've been spying on everyone in the Cavelands for centuries. They probably know *everyone's* secrets."

Anastasia's breath snagged against her molars. "You know who would definitely know about Calixto's glass doors? And probably the glass cabinet, too?"

"Squeak?" Pippistrella demanded.

"*Celestina's mirror-twin.* Whenever Celestina works with glass, her reflection must show up, right? Glass is *shiny*."

Ollie let out a soft huzzah. "Anastasia, that's brilliant!"

Gus frowned. "Even if Celestina is the Glass Lady—"

"She *is*," Ollie interrupted. "Face facts, Gus."

"Even if she *is*, what makes you think her mirror-twin would tell you anything?" Gus demanded. "If Ani—er—Anitselec is anything like my aunt, she'll clam right up as soon as you start asking questions about Calixto."

"But Anitselec *won't* be like Celestina," Anastasia said. "Aisatsana is the *opposite* of me, remember? I like mystery stories and Aisatsana hates them. I like floating in Mrs. Honeysop's cavern, so Aisatsana doesn't!"

"Celestina is secretive, so Anit—Ani—good ol' What's-Her-Name will be a blabbermouth!" Ollie grinned. "Anastasia, you've *got* to visit Aisatsana right away!"

A grim realization capsized Anastasia's smile. "But I can't get into Grandwiggy's cavern. Remember the guard bat?"

Ollie groaned. "If only the queen hadn't taken away that photo of Mrs. Wata!"

Photographs of lady gorgons were illegal, because a single glimpse would send the seer into a deep snooze. A lady gorgon's picture was powerful indeed. It was stronger than sleeping pills. It was stronger than *knockout gas*. And, as an accessory for missions of stealth and trespass, a lady gorgon's photograph was very, very handy.

Armed with a gold locket loaded with Mrs. Wata's potent photo, Anastasia had sleepified the guard bat stationed outside the queen's private chambers, and past this snoring guard the Dreadfuls had tiptoed to discover the Glimmerglass and other forbidden wonders.

"Do you have any other pictures of your mom, Gus?" Anastasia asked.

"Nope."

"I wish you *did*," Ollie said wistfully. "I wish—"

"Krrrp-peepity squeak!" Pippistrella chirruped from beneath Anastasia's braid.

"Scrrr-prrp!"

Perhaps Anastasia's hard work in Echolalia class was finally yielding results, or perhaps metamorphosing had tuned her eardrums to a finer frequency. Whatever the reason, she understood every peep and squeak of her bat-in-waiting's suggestion.

"Pippistrella, you batty little genius!" she exclaimed. "And we're supposed to visit them after school tomorrow, anyway! We can—"

"It's almost four-thirty, children," Miss Ramachandra interrupted, dabbing her eyes as she shuffled up. "You can go home, and I'll finish those"—her voice cracked—"clouds."

"Miss Ramachandra, do *you* think those ballerina clouds in Dinkledorf were witch magic?" Ollie asked.

The art teacher hesitated, folding and unfolding her

tearstained handkerchief. "I don't know," she finally said. "But I'm frightened. Yes, I'm *frightened.* I moved to Nowhere Special because I thought I'd feel safe here, surrounded by Morfolk, but now . . ." She eyed the papier-mâché clouds. "Run along home, children, and stick close to your parents. It's a dangerous world—even more dangerous than we dared imagine."

❦ 17 ❦
Metamorphosis

*P*A-RUM-PA-DUM! TWEET! TWEEEEEDLE! *BLAAAAAT!*
Anastasia was not in the Pettifog orchestra, and she felt very glad about it. Watching her schoolmates pummel their drums and tootle their flutes and torture their tubas, she flashed back to a haunting episode from fourth grade. Here's a little life lesson for you, prudent Reader: dinging the triangle in a junior marching band may *seem* all harmless fun and games, but it *isn't*. It's deadly dangerous. Anastasia learned this the hard way, after knocking over an entire line of cornet players. They had toppled, she remembered, like dominoes: *thump-thump-thump-thud-HONK.*

Much, much better to observe performances from the safety of the audience—especially on the date of Superintendent Sternum's long-awaited visit. Stationed in the front row, the ancient sage solemnly beheld the school concert through gold-rimmed pince-nez, which are fussy little spectacles that perch on the bridge of one's nose.

"Great Bundt cake, I'm bored!" Ollie mumbled into Anastasia's ear, dusting her cheek with white powder. Here's a second life lesson for your files: if you plan to sneak sweets into school, avoid messy treats like sugar-dusted donuts. Anastasia was surprised that a seasoned sneak like Ollie would breach this basic tenet of sugarplum-smuggling.

Gus elbowed him. "How can you be bored, Ollie? Quentin is performing!"

Ollie's gaze flicked to the stage, where his brother wheedled a strange melody from his musical saw. "Oh, I hear Q play that thing day and night."

"And now," announced the music teacher, "for the last piece of our performance, 'Waltz of the One-Legged Flamingo.'"

"Finally," Ollie grumbled.

Anastasia also yearned for the concert to end. She had a Great and Exciting Errand to run after school. Most errands, as you know, are not particularly exciting. They're dull as ditchwater, and that's why we invented the Fine Art of Putting Things Off. But Anastasia's errand included no trek to the Laundromat, or the post office, or the pickle-monger. Our princess had plans to visit three very peculiar ladies, and from these ladies obtain—so she hoped—a way into Wiggy's private caverns.

"Why is that chair empty?" Gus asked, staring at a vacant seat in the middle of the brass section.

"Jasper is second chair trumpet," Ollie said sadly.

Anastasia bit her lip, wondering what had happened to Jasper. As the attentive Reader will recall, Anastasia had suffered at the hands of two diabolical CRUD kidnappers. Had the same nasty fate befallen Jasper? Just thinking about Primrose and Prudence made Anastasia's skin crawl. Or maybe the auditorium was stuffy; either way, sweat prickled her brow. She fanned herself with a program. The violins howled; the flutes shrilled. A cymbal clanged, the brassy crash detonating a nuclear headache inside Anastasia's skull. She dropped the program and clapped her hands over her ears.

"Don't you like 'Waltz of the One-Legged Flamingo'?" Ollie said beside her.

"I—I don't feel so good." She swallowed. Her heart felt like a popcorn kernel on the verge of exploding.

And then it happened.

A great firework of pain, and her bones suddenly felt too big for her body, and a strange and horrifying sensation of being tossed into a trash compactor and sucked down a drain and thrown into a pitch-dark sack all at once. The world went black, and Anastasia screamed.

"SQUEEEEEAK!"

"Anastasia!" Ollie said. Anastasia's eardrums rustled, and then bright light dazzled her eyeballs. She blinked.

Ollie's face loomed over her, an enormous round cloud. A grin swifted across his face. "Anastasia! You've turned into a bat!"

He disentangled Anastasia from her rumpled school uniform. He held her cupped in his hands, and he gazed into her blinky little black eyes. Anastasia rattled her wings, peeping.

"Calm down," Gus urged. "Think happy thoughts!"

But Anastasia's addled bat brain couldn't dredge up notions of whiskery kittens or rain-speckled roses. Panic drop-kicked her heart into a hypersonic jig, and every single molecule of her tiny new body blazed with the need to flee. So flee she did.

She thrashed from the sugar-dusted cradle of Ollie's palms and reeled up, up, into a lurching flight above the audience, somewhere over Ollie's and Gus's cries of dismay. This maiden voyage was no graceful sally into greatness. The princess-bat careened like a punch-drunk airplane, trailing commotion in her wake. Hoots and giggles percolated the auditorium as Anastasia torpedoed by. Marm Pettifog's eyes snapped to the audience.

"Who is that?" she sputtered, her gaze latching onto the wayward bat. "Metamorphosing at school is strictly forbidden! Land *at once!*"

But Anastasia was, quite simply, out of control. The world rushed by in a crazy, dizzy, nauseating blur, and she flapped her wings even harder, knowing that if she stopped moving she would fall.

"Oh *no,*" Gus groaned. "She just knocked off Superintendent Sternum's glasses!"

"Egad! Egad, I say!" the superintendent bleated.

"She's flying into the orchestra!" Ollie exclaimed.

Anastasia zigzagged between slashing violin bows like a skier hurtling through a terrifying slalom race. Sheet music twirled into the air as she whiffled through the woodwind section.

"Keep playing!" Mr. Dirgecomb commanded, a brave general exhorting his troops in the face of grave adversity. "The show must go on!"

But Anastasia's wing grazed the edge of a rickety music stand, sending it crashing against the back of a bass player. "Hey!" He staggered, capsizing his enormous instrument. The melody dwindled as musicians hesitated and rubbernecked and dropped notes.

Marm Pettifog let out a hoarse scream of undiluted rage. "STOP! STOP IT RIGHT THIS INSTANT!"

And Anastasia did, but not because she chose to. She swerved into the side of a bass drum. *Crash!* Right through its side she tore, and then she sprawled in its curved belly, panting and dazed. Her ears were ringing—no, that was the tenacious xylophone player, still soldiering on with "Waltz of the One-Legged Flamingo."

"Oh, for pity's sake, *shut up!*" Marm Pettifog snapped, and the final chimes died away.

The auditorium was now silent; absolutely, utterly, breathlessly, ominously silent. Anastasia's eyes were closed, but everyone else's gaze was riveted to the headmistress. When Marm Pettifog was *annoyed,* she screamed. She stamped her tiny foot. But when Marm Pettifog was *really* angry, she went statue-still, with the exception of a twitch at the corner of her eye. Her eyelid was twitching now.

And then Anastasia morphed back into her normal, freckled, girl-shaped self. If she had to be anywhere in the auditorium, she was glad indeed to be crunched inside the drum. She was in her birthday suit, you understand. She shifted to peek through the bat-size tear in the cylinder's flank.

"Anastasia Merrymoon," Marm Pettifog rasped, "remove yourself from that drum immediately. That instrument is property of Pettifog Academy."

"I'm sorry, Marm Pettifog," Anastasia faltered, "but I can't. I don't have any clothes."

Snickers erupted across the cavern.

"Shocking!" Superintendent Sternum cried. "Absolutely shocking! Marm Pettifog, I am *appalled* by the lack of discipline at this institution. Students morphing during school hours? Children coming to classes

without clothes? Why, your orchestra didn't even have the discipline to finish a simple waltz!"

"Pettifog Academy isn't the problem," Marm Pettifog retorted. "It's that rotten little wretch! She's nothing but trouble!"

Superintendent Sternum creaked to his feet, fidgeting his pince-nez back to his nose. "Madam, the school board shall hear about this." And he stormed from the auditorium.

Ollie grabbed Anastasia's discarded school uniform and stood, and he squished past the knees of ten fifth graders to make his way to the aisle. Marm Pettifog snatched the bundle from his arms with a swift, tigerlike movement. "This concert is *over!*"

"What do you think will happen to Anastasia?" Ollie asked Gus as they shuffled into the lobby amidst dozens of buzzing Pettifog students.

"I don't know," Gus said nervously, "but it's not going to be good."

"It wasn't her fault," Ollie said. "She's new at morphing."

"Do you think that makes any difference to Marm Pettifog?" Gus pointed out.

Indeed, it did not. Sitting in Marm Pettifog's office ten minutes later, Anastasia stared at her girl-again hands. Her entire body ached. Each and every one of her teeth buzzed with their own private misery. At least, she consoled herself, this metamorphosis hadn't left her with bits of batty fluff clinging to her upper lip. Perhaps that was a sign of personal growth.

"Your crimes," Marm Pettifog said, "include the following: Transmogrifying in school. Disrupting a school performance. Destroying school property."

Anastasia cringed. She *had* ruined the bass drum upon exiting it; she had smashed through its side to collect her clothes from Marm Pettifog.

"You're no better than a common *vandal*," the schoolmistress said.

"It was an accident," Anastasia mumbled.

"Really?" Marm Pettifog drew the word out. "I find that very difficult to believe."

"I was *scared*," Anastasia said. "It's only my second morph, Marm Pettifog. And I didn't mean to shift! I started feeling really sick, and then suddenly I was a bat."

"Pettifog Academy has been educating Morflings for three hundred years, Anastasia," Marm Pettifog said. "I have personally witnessed hundreds of Morfo children grow up. And while the occasional whippersnapper has shifted by accident, no one has ever wreaked the havoc you wreaked today. No, Princess, I think you intended every bit of your great performance this afternoon."

"It wasn't a *performance*!" Anastasia protested. "I couldn't help it! I've never flown before, Marm Pettifog. I was flapping all over—"

"Yes," Marm Pettifog said icily. "I saw. And I have never seen anything like it. A Morfling's first shifts may be awkward, but no one crashes about like a deranged demolition ball. Don't try to fool me, little girl. I'm older than you and smarter than you." She adjusted the small bust of Machiavelli adorning her desktop.

Anastasia clamped her mouth over her response. Fighting with Marm Pettifog wouldn't achieve anything.

The schoolmistress eyed a clock in the corner. "It's nearly three. Are your guardians picking you up this afternoon?"

Anastasia swallowed. "My uncle Baldy is."

"Baldwin!" Marm Pettifog huffed. *"Baldwin* won't take this seriously! He doesn't take *anything* seriously. You and he are two delinquent peas in a pod." She grasped a quill from her desk and jabbed it into an ink bottle. "I'm going to send a note home with you, and you're to give it to Penelope." And she scratched out a full page of angry cursive before flinging the stylus down.

"While we wait for that ink to dry, I shall tell you a little bit about the contents of that note," she said. *"Introduction:* Dear Merrymoons, et cetera, I write in barely contained fury to inform you of Anastasia's latest mischief. *Body:* Today she—well, you already know what you did; suffice it to say the summary is plenty long. *Conclusion:* Anastasia is forbidden from participation in the Pettifog Academy Art Club for the next month, as are Oliver Drybread and Gus Wata."

"But, Marm Pettifog!" Anastasia spluttered. "Why would you keep Ollie and Gus from going to art club because of something *I* did? It isn't fair!"

"Fairness?" Marm Pettifog said. "I don't give a fig about *fairness!* I'm interested in *results.* And plenty of able tyrants have enjoyed great success controlling their underlings with distributed punishment. If you don't believe me, just pick up a history book!" She smiled an evil smile. "Remember that when you're considering your next prank, Anastasia: I'm happy to dole out punishments, and you'll be sharing with your friends."

"It *wasn't* a prank!" Anastasia said.

"So you've already said; and I've already told you I don't believe you. *You're officially on my naughty list,* Princess. Ah. The ink is dry." Marm Pettifog folded the grim memorandum, inserted it into an envelope, and handed it over to Anastasia. "Now remove yourself from my office."

Reader, have you ever heard the expression "run the gauntlet"? It's a saying derived from an old punishment. In the jolly days of yore, a wretch running the gauntlet jogged between two rows of soldiers who whacked and walloped and clobbered him with cudgels. Gauntlets nowadays feature fewer cudgels and more public criticism. Anastasia ran the gauntlet all the way back to her classroom, all the way through the mob of students jumbling to leave school. Titters and whispers swept around her as she scurried.

Saskia hovered in the doorway. "Congratulations, cousin. Your very first flight was a *crashing* success."

"Shut up, Saskia." Anastasia pushed past her.

"I can't wait to share the exciting news with Mumsy," Saskia called after her. "And won't Grandwiggy be proud?"

Ollie rushed to hug Anastasia. "Are you okay?"

She shook her head and told them Marm Pettifog's decree.

"She banished us from art club?" Ollie cried. *"All* of us?"

"But—but how are we going to sneak into Calixto's study?" Gus asked.

"I don't know," Anastasia snuffled, grabbing a few books from her desk and stuffing them into her satchel.

Quentin poked his head into the classroom. "Salutations!" he said. "That was a heck of a concert, wasn't it?"

"I'm so sorry I spoiled it, Quentin," Anastasia said. "I didn't mean—"

"Oh, it's okay. I've seen worse." He waved her apology away, grinning. "So you finally flew! Well done, you!"

"But it *wasn't* well done," Anastasia said, her eyes welling with tears. "I couldn't control it. And I wouldn't even know how to shift again on *purpose*."

"It'll come to you in time," Quentin said.

"When *I* first started umbrating, I would squish my eyes shut and concentrate very hard until I felt hot all over," Ollie said. "I would concentrate and imagine myself as a shadow, and then suddenly I'd *be* one."

"That might help," Quentin said. "You should try it, Anastasia."

"Maybe." Anastasia shut her desk with a thump. "But I don't want to metamorphose again for a very, very long time."

18

Wishes for Your Heart's Every Desire (Almost)

"CHEER UP, MY girl," Baldwin said, clapping Anastasia's shoulder as Belfry angled the gondola away from the academy. "You mustn't worry too much about Marm Pettifog."

"She said I'm on her *naughty list*," Anastasia whimpered.

"You and everyone else in Nowhere Special," Baldwin chuckled. "Including yours truly. And who does she think she is, anyway? Only Santa Claus gets to make *naughty* and *nice* lists, and I'm sure he'll put you on the latter. I'll put in a good word for you."

"It's not just the naughty list," Anastasia moped. "I'm *terrible* at metamorphosing, Baldy. I'm afraid I'll never get it right."

"Oh, come now." Baldwin gave her braid a gentle tug. "You haven't given yourself very much time, have you?

Sometimes we just have to wait and let nature work her wonderful ways. I didn't even morph until I was fifteen, and now I make a *smashing* wolf."

Anastasia managed a wobbly smile. "Yes, you do."

"Darn tootin'! So stop stewing and turn that frown upside down and let's go have a little fun. We're here."

Dark-o'-the-Moon Common was a wide, cobblestoned plaza at the very heart of Nowhere Special. Morfolk bustled through the town center, carrying about their business in the little cave shops that lined the square, sipping coffee in murky cavern cafés sibilant with the *shhhhh* of monstrous espresso makers. It was a busy, jolly, crowded place, full of chatter and life. But as Anastasia followed Baldwin across the plaza toward the Wish Hags' home, she trod the cobbles with trepidation. Despite the merry everydayness of Dark-o'-the-Moon, a sinister episode lurked within its history. Calixto Swift had been staging a puppet show in the common when Morfolk learned of the Dastardly Deed, and the pantomime had ended with the warlock's death.

It was strange, Anastasia thought, that Calixto had bothered with children's puppet plays—especially on the very day he sealed Nicodemus into the Silver Chest. Surely he would have realized the Morfolk would seek revenge as soon as they discovered his crime. She shivered, wondering where, exactly, Calixto had kicked the bucket.

Reminders of a more recent misadventure papered the

common, too: Jasper Cummerbund's face gazed from the MISSING MORFLING posters plastering stalagmites and shop fronts and even the side of the maggot vendor's cart. And as Anastasia ventured deeper into the plaza, her keen Morfling ears picked up whispers amidst the espresso machines' hisses: *witch . . . witch . . . witch.* Everyone in Nowhere Special was still on edge, wondering whether witches lurked in Dinkledorf. Anastasia trained her eardrums on the conversations of passersby.

"All I'm saying is, a little tax raise is worth it. We need

MISSING
Have you seen me?

JASPER CUMMERBUND

AGE : 11

HEIGHT : 4'9"

WEIGHT : 107 LBS

JASPER WAS LAST SEEN AT THE YODELING MUSEUM IN DINKLEDORF.
IF FOUND, PLEASE BRING BACK TO NOWHERE SPECIAL.

to keep the Cavelands safe from those magic-mongers," declared a woman emerging from Winkler's Watch Emporium. "And you'd think so, too, Chester, if you weren't such a miser."

"Oh, Lydia!" her husband grumped. "You eat up that Merrymoon propaganda like it's *candy*. Everyone knows the queen just wants to line her coffers."

"Really?" Lydia gestured at one of the MISSING MORFLING notices. "Mark my words, Chester, *witches* snatched that boy! Witches are at our doorstep, and it'll be another horrible battle if they come back to the Cavelands! They'll kill us all!"

"Now, Lyddie, you know how you overreact—"

The couple's quarrel faded as they passed out of earshot.

"Merrymoon propaganda!" Baldwin huffed. "How do you like that?"

Anastasia nibbled her lip. "Do you think the bill will pass, Baldy?"

He stroked his mustache. "I hope so. But it'll be a close call, even with Senator Cummerbund's support. He switched sides after Jasper disappeared." He shrugged and smiled. "Let's forget about politics for the afternoon. Should we get a sundae at the Soda Straw before we head to the well?"

Tempting as a trip to the Cavelands ice creamery was, Anastasia shook her head. She was on a mission. "No. We're almost there."

The Be-Careful-What-You-Wish-For Well was on the far side of the common, outside a haberdashery and an antique bookshop. A lady with bright red hair now stood beside the well, and she cupped her hands around her mouth and hollered:

"Wishes! Wishes! Come and get 'em! Wishes for what ails ye! Wishes big and wishes small, guaranteed to charm and thrill!"

Anastasia turned a quizzical glance to Baldwin.

"The hags just reopened their wishery," Baldwin said. "And *that* lovely lass is Sonia Elbow, although I'm not sure why she's whooping outside the well. See how muscular her arms are? She used to be a trapeze artiste in the circus. Zounds, she's fetching!" He raised his voice. "Hellooo, Miss Elbow!"

"Well, hello, Prince Baldwin," Sonia said. "And this must be the princess Anastasia." She smiled, revealing glittering white teeth. She really *was* pretty. "The hags hired me to operate their new pulley system."

Anastasia peered at the contraption dangling in the well. Wells normally have a pulley system of joists and rods and a rope to lower a bucket down to fetch water. The Be-Careful-What-You-Wish-For Well had such a system, but *two* ropes dangled from the rod, and hitched to these ropes was a carved wooden seat upholstered in green velveteen.

"Business has been booming ever since the hags reopened

shop," Sonia explained. "But the first customers found it a bit awkward to get down the well, so they rigged up this elevator chair. Now anybody looking to buy a wish may ride down in comfort and style—I just crank the pulley for them."

"Ingenious!" Baldwin declared. "And might I say you're *perfect* for the job? My goodness, your arms are *herculean*! I think you could wrestle an alligator without batting an eyelash!"

Sonia giggled, batting her eyelashes now. "Oh, you! Now, are you two in the market for a wish? Big or small, they charm and thrill!"

"I'm sure they do, but this is a social call," Baldwin said. "My niece is friends with the hags, you see."

Sonia grasped Anastasia beneath the armpits and hefted her into the seat. "Are you visiting the old dears, too, Prince Baldwin?"

"I think I'll stay up here," Baldwin said. "I have loads of questions about the circus, and you're just the artiste to answer them! Those trained bears, for example. Are any of them metamorphosed Morfolk? Er, do you mind going down alone, Anastasia?"

Anastasia shook her head. It worked to her advantage if Baldwin stayed behind to flirt with Sonia Elbow. She didn't want him to hear her wish order.

Sonia twirled the crank, and the chair creaked downward. Candles guttered along the well's curved stone walls, illuminating hand-drawn posters. OONA, MAUDE, AND TWYLA, THE FOREMOST EXPERTS IN WISH-BREW SINCE 1599. WISHES FOR YOUR HEART'S EVERY DESIRE (ALMOST). WISHES GRANTED SUBJECT TO HAGS' APPROVAL. WE OFFER PAYMENT PLANS.

The last time Anastasia had glimpsed the Be-Careful-What-You-Wish-For Well, a heap of coins and a plashet of clammy water had camouflaged the secret trapdoor at its base. Now the coins and puddle were gone, and the trapdoor yawned open. The pulley seat creaked down through the hatch, coming to a stop in the Wish Hags' parlor.

Anastasia hopped from the chairlift, her galoshes splooshing through the shallow pond flooding the hags' weird house. A tumble of loopy fur and big paws leapt off a soggy sofa and dashed across the parlor to greet her.

"Borg!" Anastasia cried, patting the dreamdoodle's ears. A dreamdoodle is a bit like an anteater-labradoodle hybrid, but instead of snuffling insects or fire hydrants, these wonderful creatures snuffle *dreams*. Borg now snuffled Anastasia in great excitement, his long nose making adorable kazoo noises.

"Who goes there?" rasped an ancient woman, straightening up from a cauldron burbling in the corner.

"Anastasia Merrymoon."

"Oh, Maude! Oona!" the hag cried. "The princess is here!"

The Wish Hags' chain mail tunics clinked as they flurried over to welcome her. "My dear girl!" said Oona, crunching Anastasia in a metallic hug. "We're so very glad to see you!"

Of course, the hags couldn't really *see* Anastasia. The hags were troglodytes. In case you don't know, a troglodyte is a kind of eyeless cave creature.

The hags ushered Anastasia over to a mildewed love seat. "Would you like a cookie, dear? We baked cookies."

Maude thrust forth a platter of bumpy oatmeal cookies.

"Thanks." Anastasia took one of the unpleasant lumps,

but she did not eat it. Instead she thrust it into the pocket of her Pettifog jacket. "Yum!"

"Oh, I'm so glad you like them!" Maude beamed. "Would you believe I'm just now learning how to bake? Six hundred years old, and this is only my third batch of cookies!"

"Normally we just brew a wish for sweets," said Twyla.

"Ollie likes to bake," Anastasia said. "He's going to be a pastry chef when he grows up."

"Oh, dear little Ollie!" Maude twittered, settling into a chair. "Perhaps he can offer me some culinary tips."

"Now, tell us, Princess," Oona said, "did your birthday wish come true?"

"Yes, it did," Anastasia said. "Thank you."

"Rather an odd wish," Twyla mused. "Most eleven-year-olds wish for ponies or fancy robots or that sort of thing. But, of course, we were glad to grant your wish."

"We've been brewing all sorts of wishes these past few weeks!" Maude said. "We're backed up on wish orders until *next year*!"

"Next year?" Anastasia cried.

"Oh, *everyone* has a wish," Oona said. "And we do our best to help everyone—"

"Everyone who *pays*," Twyla interjected with a little chuckle.

"But you wouldn't believe some of the things people ask of us," Maude confided.

"Like what?"

"We're not supposed to talk about wish requests," Oona said. "People won't come to us with their hearts' secret desires if they worry we blab."

"We only have to keep secrets if we *grant* the wishes," Twyla pointed out. "There's no secrecy clause if we refuse the order."

"So you sometimes tell people no?" Anastasia asked.

"Indeed we do!" Twyla huffed. "Just yesterday we told Senator Dellacava we would *not* interfere with Caveland politics! No, sir! And kindly remove yourself from our parlor *and don't come back*!"

Anastasia stiffened. "Senator Dellacava came down here?"

"He was *most* impolite," Twyla said. "He carried on like a colicky infant when we told him no."

"Twyla, hush," Oona said. "It's bad form to gossip about our customers."

"Oh, Oona, don't be such a stick-in-the-mud," Twyla retorted. "Princess Anastasia isn't going to tell anyone about Senator Dellacava's wish! And besides, Senator Dellacava *isn't* our customer, remember?"

"What did he wish for?" Anastasia asked.

"It had to do with some bill Congress is reviewing," Twyla said. "To be honest, dear, we don't follow politics very closely."

"But we wouldn't go against the queen," Maude said. "We're very grateful to Queen Wiggy for signing our diplomatic treaty. And we're grateful to *you* for your part in it."

"But I didn't do anything," Anastasia said.

"You most certainly did!" Maude said. "Perhaps you didn't *mean* to, but you and your friends got us out of this well and back into *life*. Fate has many agents, dear, in all shapes and sizes."

"And you're one of them!" Oona reached over to squeeze Anastasia's hand.

Anastasia grinned. She liked to imagine herself as an agent of fate. It sounded important.

"Now, tell us," Oona said, "is there a special wish pit-a-patting within your heart *today*?"

"We'll put your wish to the front of the list," Twyla promised. "Perhaps you'd like to spruce up your wig? We have wish-shampoo that'll make your wig grow three inches per night!"

"You might wish for another batch of my cookies," Maude said hopefully. "We wouldn't even need wish-brew for that."

"We could plague your worst enemy with dandruff! We have *vats* of dandruff brew!"

"Those things all sound very nice," Anastasia said politely, although they did not. "But I have a certain wish in mind, actually." And she told them what it was.

"Oh, Princess," Oona protested. "I don't think—"

"If you want to go into your grandmother's private chambers, why don't you just *ask* her?" Maude queried.

"Er—because I don't want to ruin the surprise," Anastasia said. "I . . . um . . . embroidered a pillowcase for Grandwiggy, and I want to leave it on her bed, but no one can enter without her orders. So the Royal Guard Bat won't let me through the door."

Of course, the only thing Anastasia had recently embroidered was this excuse to get inside Wiggy's caverns. However, the trusting hags bought it hook, line, and sinker.

"What a thoughtful girl!" Oona exclaimed. "Why, of *course* we'll help with that."

The hags set down their teacups and creaked from their chairs to rummage through the bottles swimming in the water flooding their floor. Anastasia wondered how the hags could tell the vials apart. The bottles were labeled, but the hags, as you know, had no eyes with which to read them. "Mandrake root . . . mandrake root . . . now, where can that mandrake be?" Twyla muttered.

"It's in your hair, dearie," Maude said.

"Oh yes." Twyla fumbled a vial of mandrake from her long tangles. "Do you have the mermaid's locks?"

"Hmm. I can't find it."

"I think it might be on one of the spice racks," Oona

said. "Princess, would you mind taking a peeksy? Look for a bottle labeled MERMAID'S LOCKS."

"Mermaid's locks?" Anastasia nudged Borg off her lap and trudged across the parlor. Hundreds of bottles cluttered the hags' floor-to-ceiling spice racks: bottles brimming with inky black sludge and golden glimmers and cloudy wisps, and bottles rattly full of glowing little pebbles, and bottles crammed with withered violets and forget-me-nots. An entire row of bottles bore glowering skulls and crossbones.

"Are some of these things *poisonous*?" Anastasia called to the hags.

"Yes indeed, my dear." Maude chuckled. "Our wishes often call for rather potent ingredients."

CYANIDE. ARSENIC. DEADLY NIGHTSHADE. SHADOW TEARS. Anastasia's gaze latched to a canister encasing a lock of faded green hair tied with a pink ribbon. "Did this *really* come from a mermaid?"

"Yes, and it's very rare," Oona said. "So please be careful handling that bottle."

"Mermaids are *real*?"

"They *were*. They're extinct now, I'm afraid."

After adding a single green strand to their brew, the hags chanted and murmured and crooned. Anastasia poked around the poison bottles. She wondered whether she should tell Penny and Baldwin that Caesar Dellacava had visited the hags. Obviously his wish had involved the Merrymoon Militia Bill.

"All done!" the hags chorused.

Anastasia turned. Oona held between her thumb and forefinger a slender vial of thick green ooze. "This will give you seven minutes in the queen's chambers—plenty of time to stuff a pillow into your embroidered case! When you want to visit, just crush the bottle," she said. "The goop will evaporate immediately, so don't worry about stains."

"Oh, I *never* worry about stains," Anastasia assured her, accepting the potion. "Thank you."

"It's our pleasure!" Maude beamed. "We do hope the queen likes her pillowcase!"

"We wish we could chat all afternoon, but unfortunately we need to tend to our work," Oona said. "A Wish Hag's work is never done!"

Twyla crushed Anastasia in a farewell hug. "Please do come again soon!"

"Shall we send some cookies home with you, too, dear?" Maude asked.

"Oh no," Anastasia said hastily. "I'm full."

"Too full for cookies?" Maude giggled. "My goodness, you *are* a strange child!"

❈ 19 ❈

The Glimmerglass

BACK IN HER bedchamber that evening, Anastasia carried her candle into the loo and regarded her reflection in the gloomy mirror. She took a deep breath.

"Aisatsana, I need your help. Remember how you told me you visit other places in the mirror-realm when you aren't reflecting me?"

Aisatsana stared back, mum. She couldn't reply from an ordinary looking glass, of course. Only through the Glimmerglass could the girls carry on a proper two-way conversation.

"I need you to go to Celestina Wata's glass shop and bring her reflection to the Glimmerglass tomorrow morning," Anastasia continued. "It's really important. She might be able to help me find my dad. You see and hear everything

I do, so you know I'm looking for him. You know he's been missing for months."

Anastasia leaned close to the glass, searching her mirror-twin's face for a response. Aisatsana simply mimed Anastasia, crinkling her forehead and squinting. It was like a maddening game of follow-the-leader.

"Isn't my dad's reflection—Derf, I guess—*your* father?" Anastasia asked. "Derf's been cooking waffles for you and hugging you and telling you bedtime stories all this time, right? And if something happens to my dad—if he's hurt or . . . or *killed*—wouldn't that happen to Derf, too? Would Derf just disappear?"

Aisatsana's eyes glittered, but they were just reflecting Anastasia's tears.

"I'm going to come visit you tomorrow morning after Wiggy leaves for the Senate Cave. And if you can convince Celestina's reflection—" Her words snagged against her tonsils as an idea dazzled her cranium. "Wait! Have you seen Derf? Would Derf know where my dad is?"

Why hadn't she thought of it before? *Derf* could tell them where Fred Merrymoon was!

"Aisatsana, please, *please* try to find Derf. If you can help me find my dad, I'll do anything you want. I'll have Ollie bake more peanut butter s'mores cupcakes, and you can eat the reflections. Or I'll wear whatever you want to wear. Even if it's really uncomfortable."

Anastasia reached out and touched the mirror-girl's shoulder, just for a second. "Please, Aisatsana."

Then she turned her back to the looking glass, reluctant to let her silvery twin watch her cry any longer.

Entry to Wiggy's chamber was forbidden to anyone lacking a royal summons, and Anastasia didn't have a royal summons. She did, however, possess a nice little vial of fresh wish-goop. Sometimes, Anastasia thought, wishes were better than a queen's decree.

The elder Merrymoons were off screaming about the Militia Bill at a special Saturday Senate meeting, so Anastasia knew she could pop into Wiggy's private caverns without any danger of running into the queen. She just hoped a helpful chambermaid wasn't busy fluffing the queen's pillows.

"I'll be back in seven minutes, Peeps," she informed Pippistrella, and then she threw the vial on the floor. *Tinkle!* The bottle smashed, the wish came true, and Anastasia was in the queen's quartz-crusted cavern.

"I was wondering when you'd show up," piped a voice from the far end of the chamber.

Woozy on wish-goop, heart swollen with hope, Anastasia reeled toward the splotchy mirror crowning the queen's vanity table. "Did you find Derf? Did you look?"

Aisatsana scowled, hugging herself as though she had

a tummy ache. "Of course I looked! I've been looking for *months*! I knew our dads were missing before *you* did."

"Really?" Anastasia yelped.

"Really." Aisatsana smirked. "Maybe *you* believed those silly lies Prim and Prude told you about Fred and your sickly stepmom dying in a freak vacuum accident, but *I* didn't."

"Why not?"

"I could visit the reflection of our old house, couldn't I?" Aisatsana said. "And I saw dear old Trixie lying around swigging cough syrup. Straight from the bottle," she added.

Anastasia's eyebrows crinkled. "So you've been hunting for Derf all this time, and you *haven't* found him?"

"As a matter of fact, I have," Aisatsana said. "I found him last night." The mirror-girl reached into her jacket and pulled out a fluffy brown guinea pig.

Anastasia gawped. It was the first time she had seen her father in guinea pig form. Of course, it wasn't her father, exactly.

"That's Derf?"

"Yep." Aisatsana scratched Derf's head. "And you can see he's very much alive, which means Fred is, too."

Anastasia's heart cartwheeled with joy, and she gave a little whoop. "Does Derf know where my dad is?"

"I'm sure he does," Aisatsana said. "Unfortunately, he can't tell us. He can only squeak, and I don't speak guinea pig."

"Can't he shift back into a man?" Anastasia demanded.

"Not until Fred does." Aisatsana swallowed. "Derf once told me Fred *went pig* whenever he was frightened. So your dad is *scared*, wherever he is."

Anastasia bit her lip, toying anxiously with the jewelry scattered on Wiggy's vanity. It was awful to imagine her father holed up somewhere as a small, hapless rodent. Surely he wouldn't have morphed into a guinea pig to look for her. Did that mean he was in CRUD's dastardly clutches? If so, why was he still alive?

Cradling Derf in one arm, Aisatsana dug in her jacket pocket. "I hope you remembered to wind our watch today? Hmm, five past ten. I wonder if Anitselec is coming."

"So you invited her?" Anastasia asked. "Were you—um—polite?"

"I can be *very* polite when I want to be," Aisatsana sniffed. "See? Here she comes now."

Celestina Wata's mirror image edged onto the looking glass. "The queen's bedchamber!" she cried. "Just look at it! So fancy! Wait'll I tell the girls about *this*!" She peered at Anastasia. "And *you're* the princess. I saw you when you visited Celestina's shop, of course. Speaking of royalty, my friend Elle once saw Marie Antoinette! Imagine! Not nearly so pretty as her portraits, Elle said. And—"

"I need to ask you something about Celestina," Anastasia interrupted. "Did you ever see her make a glass cabinet?"

"Indeed I did," Anitselec said, unruffled by this abrupt change in topic. "A cabinet without a door. She gave it to that warlock, Calixto Swift! Imagine! Of course, they were good friends. He was *always* hanging around."

Anastasia sucked in a breath. Just as she'd suspected! "Do you know how to open it?"

"The cabinet? I'm afraid not, dear." The mirror-woman clucked her tongue. "Celestina never found out. Believe me, she *asked* Calixto about it! But he'd only answer in riddles. That man could drive you crazy with all his puzzles—he was *such* a jokester. Personally, I've never cared for puzzles, not even the crossword. Why would anyone—"

"Riddles?" Anastasia asked. "Do you remember what he said?"

"Oh, let's see." Anitselec tilted her head, thinking. "*I'll never breathe that secret, Celestina, except to the cabinet itself.* Those were his exact words. I have an *excellent* memory, you know. Why, I still remember the dress Celestina wore to her third birthday party—"

"He told his secret to the *cabinet*?" Anastasia demanded.

"I guess so." Anitselec shrugged. "But really, who knows? Maybe Calixto was just pulling Celestina's leg. Like I said, that witch could drive you crazy with his tricks. Just between us, I was glad when he stopped coming around to yammer about cabinets and mess around with snow globes."

"Snow globes?" Anastasia echoed.

"Very bossy, I thought," Anitselec said. "He wanted to blow the glass himself! As if Celestina couldn't do it well enough. Now, what did he say? Something about a witch's breath. . . . *It holds all kinds of power.* Something like that. Well, every spell a witch mutters is one part *sound* and one part *breath*. And that breath was brewing deep in a witch's lungs. La-di-da! Thought rather highly of himself, didn't he?" Anitselec chortled. "So Celestina prepared the tools for him, but Calixto was the one who actually blew the glass. And you know, it was the funniest thing, but I swear he actually breathed fr—"

But Anastasia didn't hear the rest of Anitselec's gossip, because she was suddenly back in her own chamber. The wish-goop had worn off! She balled her fists in frustration. What "funny thing" had Anitselec noticed about Calixto? Was it important? And Anastasia hadn't gotten a chance to try the warlock's twinkle-whirlwind spell on the Glimmer-glass!

She hadn't even gotten a final glimpse of Derf's furry face. Derf wasn't her father—not really—but he was the closest thing to Fred Merrymoon that Anastasia had.

"Cheep!" Pippistrella greeted her. "Prrp-squeak?"

"I don't know where Dad is," Anastasia said, "but he's alive, Pippistrella! He's *alive.*" She flopped to her bed, and Pippistrella snuggled against her shoulder in a batty hug.

Anastasia realized she was still clutching one of the

queen's geegaws. She uncurled her fingers, and she stared. It was Wiggy's favorite ring. The opal in this ring was gobstopper-big, girded along its circumference with golden filigree. Anastasia admired the lustrous gem for a minute, twisting it round and round and watching pale rainbows flare across its milky skin. And that, dear Reader, is how she came to spot the monogram.

Two letters twined together on the underbelly of the opal's golden mount: *CS.*

Calixto Swift.

The ring had belonged to Calixto! Anastasia goggled.

Why would Wiggy wear the warlock's ring? Had she found it among the clutter of Cavepearl Palace when the Merrymoons moved in, after the Dastardly Deed? Or had someone plucked the ring from Calixto's mitt as he lay dying in Dark-o'-the-Moon Common?

Misgivings wriggled into Anastasia's thinker. Up until that moment, she had considered it natural enough that the royal family bunked in Cavepearl Palace—Wiggy was a queen, and queens lived in castles. It was sort of spooky that Wiggy's castle had originally housed a witch, but this fact had been, to Anastasia, one more peculiarity in a peculiar place full of peculiar people.

Now, however, Anastasia envisioned Wiggy's first rambles through the palace: deciding which furniture to keep, choosing the best cavern for her bedchamber. Sliding a murdered man's ring onto her hand.

Anastasia shook her head, trying to dispel these dark fancies. Queens and kings fought wars; they claimed castles and seized treasure. That was the way of the world.

A wave of panic leapt up the back of her throat. How could she replace the ring before Wiggy noticed its absence? She didn't have another bottle of wish-goop, and she couldn't very well tell Wiggy she had been sneaking into her chamber again!

Anastasia pondered. She would have to hide the ring for now—she shoved it deep into her satchel—and later she could leave it somewhere in the palace for a servant to find. Wiggy would, she hoped, simply think it had slipped off her queenly finger and rolled beneath a chair.

Before quitting her room, Anastasia dashed into the loo and tapped the mirror. "Thank you, Aisatsana. Thank you for helping me."

Perhaps Aisatsana was Anastasia's opposite in most respects, but they were similar in one very important way: they both loved their dads, and both of their dads were in danger.

❦ 20 ❦
Globe-Trotting

YOU MAY HAVE heard the old expression, sapient Reader, that *knowledge is power.* With this in mind, the Dreadfuls were set to descend upon Cavepearl Library that morning with a Great Plan to Find Stinking Crumpet. Of all the Cavelands' book nooks and hallowed halls of learning, Cavepearl Library offered the best resources to a league intent on hunting down a mysterious locale. There were enormous globes labeled in the eighteenth century with the names of cities long forgotten by modern cartographers. Rolled-up antique maps furled within several brass umbrella stands, their secrets waiting to be discovered. And Penny had curated an astonishing collection of geography tomes, including half a dozen original journals written by great Morfo explorers.

Before they plundered Penny's charts and encyclopedias,

however, Anastasia told her fellow Dreadfuls about seeing Derf.

"Thank Bundt cake!" Ollie huzzahed. "Your dad is okay!"

"Grand!" Quentin cried. "Simply grand!"

"That's great news, Anastasia!" Gus exclaimed.

"Squeak!" Pippistrella agreed.

Anastasia's grin wobbled into a frown. "But wherever he is, he's a scared little guinea pig."

"Scared but *alive*." Gus squeezed her hand. "And we'll find him."

Anastasia squeezed back, biting her lip. "Aisatsana brought someone else to meet me, too," she admitted. And she filled them in on the rest of her Glimmerglass chitchat.

"So Celestina *is* the Glass Lady." Gus's shoulders slumped. "If the queen finds out . . ."

"Don't worry," Anastasia said. "Nobody would think your aunt is a witch-sympathizer. And besides, I won't tell Wiggy."

"Right," Ollie chimed in. "The Beastly Dreadfuls know all about the art of keeping secrets."

Gus smiled, his eyes shining a thank-you.

Quentin clapped his hands once and rubbed his palms together. "Now, let's find Stinking Crumpet! Where's the geography section, Anastasia?"

Within a half hour, the Dreadfuls were up to their armpits in books and charts.

"I didn't know Kalamazoo was a real place," Ollie said, flipping through a massive atlas.

"Yep. It's in the United States," Gus murmured, peering at a crumbly yellow map of the Bohemian Empire.

"This memoir by Mortimer Meriweather is galvanizing," Quentin reported. "He joined a pirate crew in 1712 and drank nothing but limeade for two years!"

"I like limeade, but not *that* much," Ollie said.

"*Nobody* likes limeade that much, Pudding," Quentin said. "The pirates guzzled it so they wouldn't get scurvy. They ate *heaps* of banana cream pie, too." He returned Mortimer's life story, and Ollie went back to scanning the atlas.

Anastasia tried to focus on *Ye Olde Compleat History of New World Witch Settlements,* but Anitselec's gossipy voice stuck in her mind like taffy, tugging her thoughts to Calixto and glass and magic.

"I'll be back in a second," she said, shoving the witch settlement tome off her lap and jumping to her feet.

Ollie perked up. "Are you going for a snack? All that talk about Mortimer's pirate goodies made me hungry."

"There might be a few cinnamon buns left over from breakfast," Anastasia said. "And I'm headed toward the dining hall anyway."

Anastasia and the Shadowboy zigzagged through the clammy palace passages, winding up in the corridor lined with Wiggy's snow globes. Ollie beelined to the dining hall beyond, but Anastasia lingered to study the glass rondures. She darted from globe to globe, peering at the Lilliputian world within. A cherry tree by a Shinto shrine! The turnip-shaped domes of St. Basil's Cathedral in Moscow! A miniature of the Great Sphinx of Giza!

All the places Calixto Swift had traveled to via his mysterious glass doors.

She slowed her pace as a riot of snowflakes began to churn in the nearest globe, her gaze telescoping upon a little design tattooing the glass—*CW with a star.* Celestina Wata had made these globes; Anastasia was now sure of it. But the glass smith had crafted the blizzardy spheres not for Queen Wiggy but for the original owner of Cavepearl Palace— Calixto Swift. No wonder Celestina had frozen up when Anastasia mentioned magical snow globes in the castle! Each and every globe was a piece of evidence linking the glass smith to the dastardly warlock!

"Anastasia," Ollie called from the dining hall. "There are eight cinnamon rolls. That makes two for each of us. Should I just bring the whole platter?"

Mesmerized by the frosty flakes swirling and twinkling within the globe, Anastasia didn't even hear him. She cradled the cool glass curves betwixt her bare palms, and she whispered:

"Through this doorway clear and crystal
Whisk me on a whirlwind trip!
Take me where your whirlwind twinkles
Make me a globe-trotting witch."

"Anastasia?" Ollie clumped into the corridor, hugging a domed cake platter heaped with gooey rolls to his chest. "Is it okay if—hey! Where did you go? Anastasia? Peeps?"

But Anastasia and Pippistrella were no longer in the Hall of Snow Globes. Nor, for that matter, were they anywhere in the Cavelands.

Snowflakes kissed Anastasia's cheeks.

Her eyelids stuttered, and her breath caught in her throat. Her hand darted to the ball of fluff shivering on her collar. "Peeps! Where are we?"

Pippistrella let out a frightened squeak.

Anastasia goggled. Tall pine trees surrounded them, chorusing with birdcalls; a moon-white quilt of snow spread underfoot in every direction. Anastasia took a few wobbly steps, her head reeling.

"The snow globe . . . ," she croaked.

Once she had uttered the final word in Calixto's little rhyme, a tremendous pressure had suctioned her hand to the snow globe, as though the glass were fusing to her palm. The glass had *pulled* her; pulled her so hard she felt as though she were being turned inside out, as though the snow globe were a black hole inhaling her. It had been very intense, but it had lasted only a nanosecond.

"Are we—*inside* the snow globe?" she asked Pippistrella.

"Squeak . . ." Pippistrella was just as discombobulated.

Anastasia tilted her gaze up, half-expecting to see a glass curve where the sky should have been, and perhaps Ollie's face, enormous, staring down at her. But she only saw pale, snow-clouded sky.

"Where are we?" she asked again. Her heart, still jozzled from the whirlwind journey, skidded against her ribs. Then she noticed the snow globe sitting in a cushion of snow by her feet. She picked it up and peered inside at the little village. It resembled Dinkledorf. Were they near Dinkledorf? Really, they could be in *any* snowy forest! They might be in Switzerland, but they might be in Germany, or Russia, or China! They could even be in some snowy, storybook fourth dimension! Panic welled in Anastasia's throat. How could she have been so foolish? How many times had well-intentioned, far-wiser-than-she-was souls warned her of the dangers of magic?

Then she heard singing.

It came from somewhere far away, but the ululating carried clear and lovely on the cold winter air. Anastasia turned toward the voices and started walking. *Crunch, crunch, crunch,* her galoshes mumbled with each snowy step. The pretty warbling grew louder, and louder, and louder, until it echoed around her: *Odelay—odelay—odelay—hee-hoo!*

Hope thrilled Anastasia's soul. "Peeps!" she exclaimed. "That's *yodeling*!" She yanked her galoshes into a run, and she ran through the snow until she crested a hill and saw, spread out in a valley below, a cluster of gingerbready houses with smoke trickling from their chimneys. Yodeling reverberated around the valley's snow-crusted sides. *Odelay-hee! Odelay-hee!*

Anastasia sagged in relief. All she had to do was hike to the Merry Mouse and slip down its secret stairwell to the Cavelands.

Crunch crunch crunch crunch crunch crunch. She stumbled past another clump of pines and there, lo and behold, was Dinkledorf's funicular. The little train was even at the top of the tracks, just as though it were waiting for Anastasia. She climbed inside and pulled the lever, and the funicular began its slow and perilous slide down Mount Dinkle. Anastasia hugged the snow globe, shivering. As they neared the bottom of the incline, she could see people tromping around town.

"Peeps," she said, "get under my collar. We don't want to attract attention."

Pippistrella burrowed along Anastasia's backbone.

Of course, her blue velvet Pettifog Academy uniform would stand out among parkas and sweaters and jeans. But as Anastasia ventured forth from the funicular, she saw that nobody was wearing parkas and sweaters and jeans. Pink-cheeked, lederhosen-clad Dinkledorfers tromped through the narrow streets, cheering and laughing and letting out joyful little yodels.

"Is there some kind of yodel festival today?" Anastasia whispered.

"Prrrp!" Pippistrella replied.

Clearly, some kind of celebration was underfoot. Anastasia jostled through the crowds into the main square. Two men were squishing tunes from wheezy accordions, and three ladies raised their voices in a fast, complicated melody. Anastasia only paused to watch them for a few seconds before following her nose to Zucker Weg, and thence made her way to the Merry Mouse. She cringed as a bell jangled on the door to announce her arrival in the shop, but festivalgoers crowded the cheesemonger's. Gisela, busy helping a band of cheese connoisseurs sniff samples of Stinking Bishop, didn't even glance Anastasia's way. The Morfling swerved through the aisles to the door at the back of the shop, and down she crept to the secret stone stairwell leading to Nowhere Special.

There was, of course, no gondolier waiting in Gruyère Gutter to meet her.

The canal stretched into a dark tunnel. Anastasia couldn't very well swim to the palace; the water brimmed with electric eels. Should she send Pippistrella to fetch Belfry? But then she would have to explain how she had gotten all the way to Gruyère Gutter.

Anastasia carefully stashed the snow globe in a niche in the cave wall. Perhaps she and the boys could "borrow" a palace gondola and return to fetch it. Or maybe Quentin and Ollie could beg their gondolier uncle for a ride to Gruyère Gutter. She closed her eyes and tightened her muscles and concentrated. She thought happy thoughts. She thought about fuzzy kittens, and the soft chime of sleigh bells, and her father's waffles. She imagined herself as a bat. She imagined so hard that her brain began to sizzle, and the heat spread through her body and tingled all the way into the tippity-tips of her fingers and toes. And then her feet slipped from her galoshes, and her body came loose from her school uniform, and she was midair. After a few dizzy moments of flurrying her arms, Anastasia's wings opened like two sails, and she glided. She was flying! She was flying, and oh my goodness, was it exhilarating!

Anastasia chirped aloud in sheer delight, and then she followed Pippistrella's voice through the tunnels, all the way home. She zigzagged through the corridors like a stunt plane. She did loop-the-loops and barrel rolls and climbing spins and lazy eights. And then she adjourned to her chambers and morphed back into a brave young girl and put on a pair of knickerbockers suitable for exploration. It was all entirely dignified.

No, it was better than dignified; it was *marvelous*.

An entire new realm, brimful with bright possibility, now opened up. Calixto's snow globes were, indeed, doors to the world: in the course of that whirlwind Saturday morning, the Dreadfuls traveled to no fewer than four countries on four separate continents. To return to the Cavelands, they simply used the little snow globe encapsulating the replica of Cavepearl Palace, which Anastasia carefully tucked into her satchel on every trip.

They whisked to Japan, where pale pink cherry blossoms flurried onto their heads beside a Shinto shrine as shiny red as lacquered licorice.

They found themselves in a dazzling Moroccan bazaar,

surrounded by panels of billowing silk and stacks of gleaming copper pots and pans.

They watched the sun rise over prickly pear cacti somewhere in the American Southwest.

They wandered up and down the narrow streets of Penzance, searching for the tattoo parlor Nicodemus and Calixto had visited.

"That was over two hundred years ago!" Ollie said. "Even if the shop's still there, whoever tattooed your grandpa will be long gone."

"Not if he was a Morfo," Anastasia reasoned. "He could still be alive, and he might remember Calixto. Maybe Calixto mentioned something that could help us find Stinking Crumpet."

But no tattoo parlors peppered the hilly lanes. There were, however, a number of fish 'n' chips joints opening their doors, sending delectable lunchtime smells into the lanes. Ollie dragged his feet to a standstill in front of the Cheery Chippie. "I'm *starving*! Can we *please* get something to eat?"

"We don't have any money," Gus pointed out.

"I have my allowance—four quartzes and a queenlie," Ollie persisted.

"An English chip shop isn't going to take Cavelands currency!"

"Right." Ollie sighed.

"What about the money I gave you to buy Yodel Fest

tickets?" Quentin asked. "I gave you twenty Swiss francs the morning of your field trip, remember? You were supposed to buy fest passes at the Yodeling Museum."

Ollie's eyes rounded. "Crikey! I completely forgot!" He scrounged in his jacket pockets, his fist finally emerging with a crumpled, cookie-crumb-dusted franc note. "Sorry, Q! When's the fest?"

Quentin rolled his eyes. "*Today*. But Mom and Dad wouldn't let us go up to Dinkledorf now, anyhow. And besides"—he grinned—"I'd rather be globe-trotting."

Ollie huzzahed, waving the note. "We can exchange this at the bank two streets over. I'm positive I saw one—it was by a cake shop."

Twenty minutes later, the Dreadfuls sat on a rocky bluff overlooking the sea, munching greasy cod and french fries from newspaper cones.

"Where shall we go next?" Quentin asked. "One of the globes has a couple of pyramids on a green hill. Where do you think that is?"

"Maybe Peru?" Gus suggested. "Machu Picchu?"

"There's a globe with little kangaroos inside," Ollie said. "We could go to Australia."

Anastasia fell into thought, staring at the faraway boats scudding along the horizon. Her notion of the world was rapidly expanding—and, in inverse proportion, the prospect of finding Nicodemus and her father seemed to be dwindling to a mere speck. Calixto Swift had traveled perhaps more than any other person alive in the eighteenth century. Propelled by magic, the sorcerer had explored the world's far-flung nooks and crannies. The Silver Chest could be *anywhere*. And now Anastasia realized just how vast *anywhere* was.

"You're awfully quiet, Anastasia," Ollie said.

"Traveling through the snow globes is fun," she said, "but we aren't any closer to knowing where Stinking Crumpet is. Maybe Calixto talks about it in one of his journals. Maybe he mentions visiting a palace or museum or some kind of landmark that would help us figure out which one of his snow globes leads there." She crumpled up her newspaper packet. "And we still need to figure out how to open the glass cabinet and get the Hammer."

Gus munched a french fry, pensive. "We'd better get back to Calixto's study," he mused. "But how? We can't even show our faces backstage while the Pettifog Art Club is helping with the sets, and they'll be doing that up till opening night of *Dance of the Sugarplum Bat*."

Anastasia frowned. "Then we'll have to wait," she said. "We'll wait and watch, and when the opportunity comes up—we'll snatch it."

21

The Glass Pond

HOWEVER, NO HAPPY opportunity presented itself for the snatching in the month to follow. The Dreadfuls dutifully did their schoolwork and practiced their fencing. Twice per week they churned their oars to explore the canals during Pettifog rowing sessions, but no Applied Navigation assignment ferried them anywhere near Rising Star Lagoon. Time passed, as time always does. But it passed very slowly.

The evening in which we rejoin Anastasia, however, promised to be different.

Anastasia glared at the nearest of Baldy's library cuckoos. *Ticktock ticktock tick . . . tock . . . tick . . . tick . . . tock.* Was it her imagination, or had the second hand actually juddered *backward*? Impatience jiggled her knees and fingertips. *Dance of the Sugarplum Bat* premiered at seven-thirty, and Anastasia longed to get into the Cavepearl Theater. This was not, as you might think, because she couldn't wait to observe Saskia's Triumphant Debut as Vespertina, the twinkle-toed bat. She craved another visit to Calixto's study.

Fortunately, Miss Ramachandra had given the Dreadfuls permission to watch the ballet from the wings, along with the other Pettifog art-clubbers. "Even if you've missed a few sessions, you helped this ballet happen!" the kindly lady had reassured them. "Just don't tell Marm Pettifog—she hasn't yet lifted your art club suspension."

"Oh dear." Penny rustled the evening newspaper, a fretful line creasing her forehead.

"What is it *now*, Penny?" Baldwin grumped. "What tidings of doom does the *Echo* bring us tonight?"

"There was a brawl in Dark-o'-the-Moon Common today," Penny said. "Almost a dozen Morfolk got into a fistfight, arguing over the Militia Bill."

Baldwin slumped back in his chair with a groan. "Even if this bill passes, half our citizenry is going to be mighty miffed."

"Let them be miffed."

The queen stood in the doorway, her face hard. "I'm not running a popularity contest," she said. "'Tis better to be *feared* than *loved*. I would rather the witches *fear* me than the public *love* me. We must do what's best for the Cavelands, regardless of the whims of certain fools."

Even though she was now centuries older, Wiggy looked just as fierce and resolute as her portrait hanging in the palace art gallery. "That little Cummerbund boy is *still* missing," she said. "I think about him every day; I think of him frightened and hurt—or worse. And if we fail to defend ourselves against witches and CRUD, more Morfolk shall suffer. We *all* shall."

"Both the Senators Cummerbund have pledged to vote in our favor," Penny said. "The bill *will* pass, your Mommyness."

"So it must." Wiggy sighed. "But I came here not to discuss politics. I wonder whether any of you has seen my opal ring? I can't find it anywhere."

Panic grabbled Anastasia's heart. The witchy gem was still tucked in her satchel; she had forgotten to leave it out for a servant to spy.

"Perhaps you left it with the jeweler?" Penny suggested.

"No," Wiggy replied. "I last saw it—"

"Your Mommyness!" Ludowiga shrilled, stamping into the library. "*Dance of the Sugarplum Bat* starts in less than an hour!" She glared at her siblings and niece. "Why are you lumps sitting around this blasted book nook like you've nowhere to be? Get off your derrieres and get a move on— we can't be late for Saskia's Triumphant Debut!"

"Curtain in one," the stage manager bellowed amidst the backstage commotion of scurrying stagehands and costumiers and makeup artists and ballerinas.

"Ouch!" Anastasia yelped as a dashing Twinkle Toe stamped her galosh.

"Anastasia, dear, are you all right?" Miss Ramachandra asked.

Anastasia jittered from foot to foot. "I'm okay—"

"Oh no!" Miss Ramachandra cried. "Is that dratted candelabrum shedding glitter again? Signor Mezzaluna will be *so* upset." She hurried off as zithers and tootles droned up from the orchestra pit.

"This is it," Gus muttered into Anastasia's ear. "Our big opportunity. When should we sneak to Calixto's study?"

Ollie dodged a catapulting powder puff. "How about the—"

"Trees!" Madame Pamplemousse barked at a corps of ballerinas dressed as saplings. "Trees onstage! *Vite! Vite!* Vespertina, you're on in ten . . . nine . . . eight . . ."

Saskia pranced over, every inch the ballerina princess in her sequined white tutu. She smirked and leaned close to Anastasia.

"Looks like you've finally learned your proper place— offstage, out of sight and out of mind," she whispered. "And *do* try to keep it that way. I don't want you to ruin my Triumphant Debut with one of your shifting disasters."

Anastasia opened her mouth to retort, but Madame Pamplemousse gave Saskia a little push. "Two . . . one! Vespertina, onstage!"

The harpist strummed a twinkly melody, and Saskia tiptoed forth. She leapt! She pirouetted! As the nimble ballerina drew gasps of admiration from the audience, Anastasia found herself hoping that Saskia would fall flat on her nose.

The Loondorfer princess didn't, of course. Every spin and twist and hop was perfect.

"Exquisite!" Miss Ramachandra murmured behind her. "But—do the tree costumes look *different* to you?"

Anastasia shifted her gaze to the corps of ballerinas dressed as trees, and her eyes widened. Tiny pinpricks of glow glittered, like fairy lights, among the silk leaves. Did the theater have a twinkle beetle infestation?

A murmur rumbled through the audience.

"Look at the trees!"

"They're *growing*!"

Sure enough, each tree dancer's canopy swelled and spread, unfurling leaf upon leaf. The dancers' arms trembled beneath the expanding foliage. What in caves was happening? The twinkly lights brightened. Anastasia realized the twinkles were little buds, and these buds bloomed into great, luminous flowers, just like flora in a time-lapse video.

"Magnificent!"

"Sublime!"

"Phantasmagorical!"

Praise percolated the audience. Everyone in the theater, Anastasia perceived, was staring not at Saskia in her Triumphant Debut as Vespertina but at the enchanted grove behind her. The confused trees stood a little straighter, smiles creeping onto their lips. Being a tree was suddenly special and glamorous.

A buzz throbbed within a blossom on the tree dancer nearest the wings, and then a fuzzy yellow bumble flashed across the corner of Anastasia's eye. Impossible! Had that been a—

Saskia let out a shriek and stumbled to a halt. "Ouch!"

"*Princess!*" Madame Pamplemousse hissed from beside Anastasia. "Carry on! Grand jeté! Grand jeté!"

Saskia winced, and then she hippity-hopped offstage as the music dwindled and the curtains rustled closed. Pandemonium broke out. Dancers scrambled to change into their costumes for act two. Stagehands grappled with the trappings for the Winter Forest set, unrolling the snowflake-stenciled backdrop and lowering papier-mâché clouds from the rafters. If there was any chitchat about the unruly tree costumes, Saskia's shrieks drowned it out.

"I'm telling you, a bee stung me!"

"Nonsense," Madame Pamplemousse declared. "There aren't any bees in the Cavelands. You froze up; that's all there is to it."

"Something out there stung me," Saskia retorted. "Look at this welt!"

"I wouldn't care if an alligator attacked you," Madame Pamplemousse snapped. "*True* ballerinas don't holler and stumble mid-pirouette. Why, I once broke my leg during *A Midsummer Night's Hopscotch*, and I finished my pas de deux to critical acclaim!"

"But—"

"We don't have time for a tantrum, Princess. Go change into your tutu for the Ice Waltz!"

Anastasia barely noticed the stagehands lugging props hither and thither. How had the Cavepearl Theater costumiers rigged up the sapling costumes to *blossom*? It had been— well, for lack of a better word, it had been *magical*. Anastasia squeaked as Madame Pamplemousse jostled past, hustling the ballerinas back onstage right before the curtains parted.

An enormous round mirror gleamed at the center of the proscenium. This mirror was supposed to evoke an icy pond, and the ballerinas glissaded across it with the slow swoops of ice skaters. Anastasia watched, entranced, as artificial snowflakes flurried from above. The illusion was lovely. It was lovelier than lovely.

"*Stagehands!*" Mezzaluna hissed. "No snow until the finale! Remember, Quentin Drybread's saw solo is your cue!"

"But we haven't dropped the snow yet," protested a voice from above.

Anastasia's eyes swiveled up to the catwalks, where two stagehands clutched bags of fake snow. And then she noticed—the papier-mâché clouds were *moving*. Their lumpy sides heaved like the flanks of snoring sheep, and from their swollen bellies twinkled silver-white crystals. The crystals waltzed down to alight on the ballerinas' eyelashes and shoulders and tutus.

"Stop!" Mezzaluna said. "Rodrigo! Sam! *Stop!* You won't have any snow left for Vespertina's Ice Waltz!"

"That snow isn't coming from us!" the stagehands replied.

Snowflakes blustered into the wings and onto Anastasia's face, tingling cold against her nose and cheeks. How could artificial snowflakes be *cold*?

"Look at the stage!" Gus whispered.

Ice gleamed upon the glass pond. The dancers' silk slippers skidded over the rime, sending them into hectic pirouettes.

"My gosh, this is realistic!" exclaimed a ballet-goer in the front row.

The snow was falling faster and faster, forming drifts around the fake pond. Gus's teeth chattered, and clouds of foggy breath puffed from the ballerinas' nostrils as they leapt and twirled. Saskia bravely executed a brisé volé to center stage as Quentin's saw let out a melancholy wail.

"That's our cue," said Rodrigo (or Sam), and a cascade of artificial flakes mingled with the chilly snowfall.

"Too much snow!" Mezzaluna cried.

"But you told us—"

CREEE-ACK! Saskia lurched as the mirror fractured beneath her feet. In a flash and flutter of tutu and golden hair, the Loondorfer princess plunged straight through the glass pond. Water splooshed around her upflung arms. Anastasia startled; was that part of the choreography?

"What in caves?" Mezzaluna thundered. "Did the floorboards collapse under her? And where did that water come from?"

Voices buzzed in the wings:

"Did she fall through the trapdoor?"

"That stage doesn't have a trapdoor!"

"Maybe a pipe burst!"

"There aren't any pipes down in the orchestra pit!"

"Then a canal wall must have burst!"

"Is the orchestra pit flooded?"

And yet the musicians continued to play.

"Help me!" Saskia scrabbled at the edge of the hole, sloshing water onto the glass pond. A few determined dancers continued their pirouettes only to collapse, splay-legged, on the frost-mantled mirror; others skidded offstage as snow torpedoed down from the papier-mâché clouds.

"Witchcraft!" someone hollered. "It's witchcraft! *There's a witch in the Cavepearl Theater!*"

Screams rang out as frosty gales whipped through the

theater. Morfolk scrambled from their seats to flee the blizzard-blasted auditorium, and ballerinas abandoned the stage like panicked rats jumping from a sinking ship.

"We have to help Saskia!" Anastasia shouted. She elbowed her way onstage and edged onto the mirror—but the mirror was gone completely; now it was pure ice—and inched toward the rift. Her feet slipped from beneath her, and she keeled forward and starfished onto the glacial pond.

"Help!" Saskia sputtered.

Anastasia wriggled forward, stretching out her hand. Saskia managed to lock her slick fingers around Anastasia's wrist and then, with a *CREEEEEAK,* the ice cracked and collapsed.

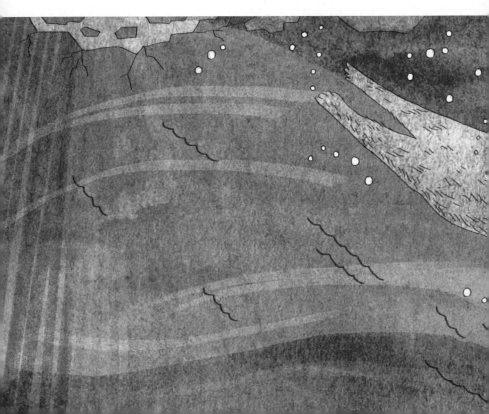

After the first shock of cold, Anastasia forced her eyelids up, expecting to find herself somewhere in the orchestra pit among swimming flautists and panicked percussionists and abandoned tubas. But Anastasia saw none of these things. Instead the cool blue glow of frigid water surrounded her, vast in all directions. Saskia's hair had come loose from its bun and streamed around her frightened face like the golden tendrils of a storybook mermaid.

Calm down, Anastasia mouthed, but her eyes widened as an enormous silhouette passed behind her cousin. What was *that*? The shadowy shape loomed closer. A dark spot turned into a nose, and two eyes materialized above it, and then two round ears above a furry white forehead. *It was a polar bear.*

As you will recall, observant Reader, Anastasia loved animals both great and small. She aspired to one day tend to their well-being as a dignified practitioner of veterinary medicine. At that moment, however, plunged into an arctic sea that had welled up from nowhere, Anastasia was none too pleased to see an enormous member of the species *Ursus maritimus* paddling her way. A scream escaped her lips in a flurry of bubbles. Saskia twisted and spotted the bear, and then, in a fresh burst of terror, latched onto Anastasia with the ferocity of an octopus in a jujitsu match. They struggled.

Many harried swimmers, in their flails of panic, drown both themselves and their would-be rescuers. Anastasia wrestled to extricate herself from Saskia's clutches. Her lungs burned. How long had she been underwater? Cold water and fear trickled down her throat; she and Saskia would both drown, and if they didn't drown, the polar bear would munch them for an intermission snack. The great beast swam closer . . . closer . . . but Anastasia was too weak to wriggle any longer. Her head lolled and her limbs went slack as the last bits of oxygen dwindled from her bloodstream. The pond went dark as the depths of a moonless midnight, and so did Anastasia's mind.

22

Witches

"ANASTASIA! ANASTASIA, WAKE up!"

Anastasia coughed and shivered. She was no longer underwater. Nor was she inside a polar bear's belly. She was sprawled upon the Cavepearl Theater stage, snow melting from her braids. Gus and Ollie and Quentin and Pippistrella and Penny and Baldwin and Wiggy and Lord Monkfish and even Claudio Mezzaluna and Miss Ramachandra and a gaggle of theater folk and a muster of Royal Guards were gathered around her, and they all let out sighs of relief as Anastasia sat up. Penny grabbed her into a hug, and Pippistrella nuzzled her ear.

"The polar bear," Anastasia croaked. "Where did he go?"

"He's stomping around backstage!" Signor Mezzaluna

wailed. "That horrid beast is chomping and bashing and clawing all our lovely handiwork!"

"Claudio!" Baldwin chided. "Show our polar visitor a little respect!"

"I thought 'our polar visitor' was going to eat me!" Anastasia said.

"On the contrary," Baldwin said. "That bear saved your life. Once he's calmed down, we'll give that bear a medal! We'll make him a peer of the realm!"

"After you fell into the pond, I couldn't even see you," Gus explained. "You sank so fast. But then the bear splashed up, and he nudged you back onstage with his nose."

"Oh." Anastasia blinked. "What about Saskia? Is she okay?"

"She is," Wiggy replied. "She's right over there."

Saskia huddled stage left, trembling beneath her mother's coat. Ludowiga knelt beside her, combing bits of ice from her soggy blond hair.

Anastasia blinked around the theater. Every last member of the audience had cleared out. Fluffy white drifts mantled the proscenium and the aisles and cushioned the velveteen theater seats, but flakes no longer gusted from above. "It's stopped snowing."

"Indeed it has, but the entire city is in an uproar," Wiggy said. "There can be no doubt about it: there's a witch in Nowhere Special."

"And that witch is going to pay for spoiling Saskia's Triumphant Debut!" Ludowiga screeched. "Who worked on these sets?"

"Why, quite a lot of people, Princess," Claudio Mezzaluna replied nervously. "Myself, and my apprentices, and Miss Ramachandra and her students."

"Miss Ramachandra?" Ludowiga echoed. "The same Miss Ramachandra who was up in Dinkledorf the day of the magical clouds? The same Miss Ramachandra who chaperoned the field trip whence Jasper Cummerbund went missing?"

"That's me," Miss Ramachandra quavered.

"So *you're* the witch!" Ludowiga leapt to her feet. "What did you do with Jasper, you rotten magic-monger? Did you arrange for one of your witchy accomplices to snatch him from the lanes of Dinkledorf, or did you simply cast a disappearing spell?"

"No!" Miss Ramachandra cried. "I would *never* have hurt Jasper. And I'm not a witch! I'm *not*!"

"Then *prove* it," Ludowiga said. "*Shift*. Whether you're a Shadow or a wolf or a bat or a blasted squirrel, shift and prove you're a Morfo."

Miss Ramachandra quailed. "I can't shift. Not anymore. The doctors say it's a psychological block—but I was a bat once, I swear—"

"Lies!" Ludowiga screamed. "Your Mommyness, have this witch locked in the dungeon!"

· 251 ·

"No!" Anastasia cried. "Miss Ramachandra *can't* be a witch!"

"Haven't you learned yet that people aren't always what they seem, you little fool?" Ludowiga snapped. "And witches are particularly devious! Posing as a bumbling art teacher was the *perfect* way for this crafty imposter to wriggle herself into the Cavelands!"

"But I *am* an art teacher!" Miss Ramachandra protested. "I'll show you! I'll show you my students' macaroni mosaics!"

"Macaroni means *nothing*," Ludowiga spat. She wheeled to Wiggy. "This was an *assassination attempt*! Witch Ramachandra must have been planning this for months—hexing the theater and cozying up to Anastasia until she had the entire royal family together where she could strike them all at once!"

Wiggy stared at Miss Ramachandra, her face grave. Then she twitched her little finger, and the Royal Guards descended upon the art teacher.

"Stop!" Anastasia shouted. "Please, Grandwiggy! She isn't a witch!"

"I'm innocent!" Miss Ramachandra howled, kicking her legs. "Help me! Someone, please help me!"

"Miss Ramachandra, you can morph if you *believe*!" Anastasia screamed. "Think happy thoughts! THINK HAPPY THOUGHTS!"

But Miss Ramachandra was, perhaps, too rattled to think happy thoughts. The guards hauled the hapless lady away in the blink of an eye, and the stunned Morfolk were now left shivering, knee-deep in witch snow. Tears brimmed Anastasia's eyes and froze her lashes.

"I'm calling an emergency Senate conclave," Wiggy said. "Miss Ramachandra may have allies nearby; we're voting on the Militia Bill *tonight*."

"After this debacle, its passage is assured, oh-mostmoonbright Queen," Lord Monkfish intoned. "I'll send out the announcement." He departed, wading through the snow.

"Come." Wiggy gestured at the elder Merrymoons. "Let's away to the Senate Cave."

"What about the girls?" Penny asked. "Anastasia and Saskia have suffered a terrible shock! We need to take them home and get them into a hot bath."

"The guards will escort the princesses home, and the royal maids can tend to their needs," Wiggy said. "Princesses, get to the palace."

"But—"

"Shhh." Penny patted Anastasia's cheek. "Go home and get warm and go to bed. Everything will seem much better tomorrow."

"Indeed it will. By tomorrow, Witch Ramachandra won't be Witch Ramachandra anymore," Ludowiga sneered. "She'll be *dead*."

You might suppose that the discovery of a witch in Nowhere Special—a witch masquerading as a Pettifog art teacher, no less—would warrant an academy closure of at least a day or so. However, just like clockwork, school resumed on Monday.

"Stiff upper lip," Marm Pettifog commanded. "We can't

cancel classes until the world is rid of witches, can we? School would be closed forever!"

"Sounds good to me," Ollie grumbled.

"I heard that, Drybread," Marm Pettifog barked. "And being a lot of ignoramuses won't help you one bit in a witch invasion. All the more reason to soldier on with today's Applied Navigation exam."

Neither huzzah nor hooray from Jasper Cummerbund punctuated this declaration, because Jasper Cummerbund was still missing. Miss Ramachandra had kept mum about his whereabouts, even after three rounds of s'mores, the Crown's weapon of choice in interrogations. As you may already know, sapient Reader, s'mores are the closest thing in existence to truth serum. Secrets are best spilled whilst eating s'mores, and Queen Wiggy had discovered centuries earlier that culprits stuffed full of s'mores couldn't resist confessing their darkest crimes.

But Miss Ramachandra maintained her innocence of Morfling-snatching schemes, cloud-and-snow-and-polar-bear hocus-pocus, and witchery in general. If she didn't spill the beans soon, the Crown would move on to non-marshmallow, far less pleasant interrogation techniques.

Anastasia shivered. Wiggy had refused Ludowiga's demands for a hasty execution—so far. How long would the Crown's inquisition last? Could Miss Ramachandra really be a *witch*? It felt *wrong*. But after a broody weekend spent kicking around the facts, Anastasia had to admit the evidence was there. Miss Ramachandra *had* been on the spot when the clouds danced above Dinkledorf. Jasper Cummerbund had gone missing under *her* watch. The *Sugarplum Bat* sets *she* worked on went haywire.

And Miss Ramachandra couldn't morph. She had given the Dreadfuls an explanation for that, but it could very well be a lie. Witches were liars, after all. Calixto Swift had seemed a friendly, fun-loving fellow, and look how *that* turned out.

"Anastasia! Pay attention!" Marm Pettifog scolded. "Now, each of your quads will be quizzed on five different destinations. Not all the destinations are the same, so don't try to cheat by following your classmates! Speaking of cheating, it's forbidden to accept help from anyone, and that includes bats." She glared at Pippistrella, lodged beneath Anastasia's braid. "No bats allowed during the exam."

Pippistrella squeaked sadly but dislodged herself from her mistress's hair and fluttered to the stalactites. Saskia's bat-in-waiting glided to join her.

Marm Pettifog swifted around the classroom, delivering five envelopes into the sweaty hands of members of the various row teams. Gus received the Dreadfuls' envelope. "Those are your first goals," Pettifog said. "The ninth-grade coxswains stationed at each checkpoint will give you a ribbon upon your arrival and reveal your team's next destination.

You must collect all five ribbons to pass your Applied Navigation exam, and you must do so within two hours."

"But what if a *witch* is lurking in one of the tunnels?" Taffline shrilled.

Marm Pettifog smiled nastily. "Which scares you more: the *possibility* of a witch, or the *reality* of flunking and contending with me?"

On this sinister note, she sent the fifth graders into the canals. The Dreadfuls had scrambled aboard their boat before Gus had even ripped open their envelope.

"Where are we supposed to go?" Anastasia panted.

"Um"—he fumbled with the page folded inside— "Bumbershoot Square!"

"Easy," Ollie scoffed. "That's where we docked before the Dinkledorf field trip, remember?"

The Dreadfuls flurried their oars, navigating their pink Pettifog vessel across Old Crescent Lagoon and into the Spelunker Straits. "Pull . . . pull . . . harder on starboard!" Ollie puffed.

"Ollie! You're a natural steersman!" Gus praised.

A grin lit up Ollie's pink face. "Well, Quentin and I *have* rowed a lot with Uncle Zed. Look, there's Gardyloo Bridge! Now we head down Bumbershoot Gutter. . . ."

"Look! It's Q!" Anastasia cried as the docks in Bumbershoot Square came into view. Quentin sat on a small chair at the edge of the pier, strumming a wobbly tune from his musical saw. He perked when he glimpsed the Dreadfuls.

"Congratulations!" He saluted them. "You've reached your first goal!" He set aside his saw and rummaged in his jacket, pulling forth a pink ribbon and a scrap of paper. "Your next destination is . . . Mudpuddle Cavern."

"Mudpuddle Cavern!" Anastasia breathed. "We'll be going right by the Cavepearl Theater!"

"We have four more checkpoints to visit," Gus protested. "We don't have time to visit Calixto's study. Not *now*."

"Besides . . . ," Ollie balked, "what if that polar bear is still stomping around?"

"She isn't," Quentin assured them. "Frosty's hibernating."

"Frosty?" Anastasia echoed.

"The bear," Quentin said. "That's what the theater director named her. Signor Mezzaluna passed by a few minutes ago on his way to the dentist"—Quentin indicated a nearby cavern garnished with a molar-shaped sign—"and said Frosty finally settled down to hibernate."

"How long do polar bears hibernate?" Gus asked.

"It could be months!" Quentin groaned. "The theater folk can't move Frosty until she's had her cubs, so they're postponing all the repair construction till then."

"Cubs?" Ollie cried. "How do they even know Frosty's a *girl*?"

"Only pregnant polar bears hibernate." Quentin heaved

a sigh. "Signor Mezzaluna told me the Bureau of Better Safe Than Sorry plans to board up the theater tomorrow."

"Why?" Anastasia exclaimed. "To trap Frosty inside?"

Quentin shook his head. "To keep people *out*. They're shutting the whole place down as a magical hazard site for the foreseeable future. And if they can't figure out how to drain that arctic lake, they might close the theater for *good*!"

"For *bad*, you mean!" Anastasia turned worried eyes onto Gus and Ollie. "This is our last chance to visit Calixto's study for who knows how long! When the Better Safe Than Sorry Bureau boards up the theater doors, we'll lose our secret way into Sickle Alley!"

"But the exam . . . ," Gus protested.

"We'll be quick," Anastasia promised. "We'll just pop in and grab a few more witch journals, and then we'll be on our way. Ollie knows all kinds of shortcuts through the canals anyway—don't you, Ollie?"

Ollie nodded uneasily. "But what if Frosty wakes up?"

"She saved my life, remember? She's a *nice* bear," Anastasia urged, even as doubt pickled her stomach. Perhaps Frosty *was* a nice bear, but she picnicked on seals and walruses. If the mood struck, Frosty probably wouldn't scruple at munching two fifth graders and polishing off a third for dessert.

However, Anastasia was prepared to take the Goldilocks path—venture into a bear's bunker, that is—in the name of her great Fred-finding mission. "I *have* to go back to Calixto's study! We still don't know how to open the glass cabinet. We still have no idea where Stinking Crumpet is, and we're all out of clues. I can go by myself. You can drop me off on your way to Mudpuddle Cavern and fetch me on the way back."

Gus set his jaw. "No. We'll go with you."

"You will?" Anastasia cried.

"We *will*?" Ollie squeaked.

"All for one, and one for all," Gus reminded them softly. "Credo of the Beastly Dreadfuls."

"Righty-o. Our credo." Ollie's brow puckered. "Okay, I'll come with you. But if Frosty mauls me, I'm going to be *very* upset."

Quentin looked worried. "*I* can't join you now. I have to stay here and hand out ribbons and tell the other quads their checkpoints."

"That's okay," Anastasia said. "We just need the key to the musicians' entrance."

The elder Drybread bit his lip but dredged the key from his pocket and pressed it into her hand. "Don't get caught," he warned. "And don't get eaten by a bear."

❧ 23 ❧
Frost

IN THE GRIM event that you must one day sneak past a six-hundred-pound polar bear, here is a neat little piece of advice to help you along: *let sleeping bears lie*. As the Dreadfuls crept through the gloomy corridor leading from the theater's side entry to the backstage, Anastasia was glad indeed for her tiptop tiptoeing skills, honed through months of snooping and gumshoeing.

Squish-squidge-sploosh.

Of course, tiptoeing through slush presents unique challenges. The thick drifts of witch snow had half-melted into chilly muck, and this muck sloshed and slopped beneath the Dreadfuls' shoes.

"*Shhhh*," Ollie hissed.

"*You're* the one making all the noise!" Gus whispered

back. "And hurry up—we'll fail our entire Applied Navigation unit if we're late getting back to Pettifog Academy!"

"But if we wake up Frosty, we'll be crunched like potato crisps!" Ollie argued.

"No, we won't," Anastasia said, but her heart lolloped like a jittery jackrabbit as they ventured into the backstage wreckage of smashed sets and capsized costume racks.

"It looks like a tornado went through here!" Gus said, kicking through a flotilla of soggy tutus.

GRRRR . . . GRRRR . . . GRRRRR . . .

Ollie gasped. "Do you hear that?"

GRRRR . . . GRRRRR . . . GRRRRR . . .

The growls sent Anastasia's jackrabbity heart hopscotching straight into her stomach.

"Frosty's *awake*." Ollie's eyes bugged, and he swiveled his gaze around the darkened backstage. "Where is she, anyway?"

"Should we play dead?" Gus gulped. "Or do we run?"

"I vote *run*," Ollie quavered.

"Wait." Anastasia grasped his sleeve. "Listen."

GRRRRR . . . GRRRRR . . . GRRRRR . . .

Anastasia grinned. "She isn't growling at us. She's just *snoring*."

GRRRRR . . . GRRRR . . .

Grumbly snorts rumbled from the farthermost corner of the cavern. Anastasia edged forth and popped her head through the tatters of a shredded canvas painted with a fairy tale forest, peering into the realm beyond.

"Oh, crumbs," she said. *"Look."*

There, beneath the branches of the artificial tree masking the Dreadfuls' secret crawlway to Sickle Alley, sprawled a good quarter ton of polar bear. Frosty lolled on her back, fuzzy tummy exposed, her great furry paws sticking up in the air.

Gus groaned. "We'll have to squeeze right by her!"

For your edification, curious Reader, here is a list of fun facts about polar bears:

Polar bears do not have eyelashes, because they
    would freeze and break off!
Polar bear claws can grow over three inches long!
Polar bears have blue tongues!

The Dreadfuls got a splendid glimpse of Frosty's tongue right as they sidled betwixt bear and wall, because she stretched her jaws into an enormous blue yawn. Ollie stared into the toothy maw, hypnotized. "It looks like she's been eating blueberry pie."

Anastasia pulled the Shadowboy's hand. "Just a few more steps—"

GRRRR . . . GRRRR . . . GRRUFF? One of Frosty's eyelashless eyelids twitched, and she twisted her damp nose toward the Dreadfuls. Then, with a great heave and groan, the bear rolled onto her stomach and rocked back onto her haunches. Even sitting, Frosty was nearly as tall as the fifth graders. She leaned forward and applied her enormous nostrils to Ollie's face. Anastasia and Gus watched in frozen horror as the bear's great whiffer whuffled down the Shadowboy's neck to his collar, and thence to his lapels. Anastasia wanted to shout at Ollie to umbrate and flit away to safety, but she was too frightened even to peep.

Frosty nuzzled Ollie's side, grumbling. She shook her head. She snorted. Her nostrils convulsed, and a pale cloud puffed from her snoot.

"Was that *frost*?" Anastasia asked.

"N-no," Ollie stammered. "It's powdered sugar." He pulled half a squished Berliner from his pocket. "Is this what you want, Frosty? Go get it!" He flung the donut back toward the downed costume racks, and the bear lumbered after it.

"*Go,*" Gus hissed, shoving Anastasia and Ollie past the tree and through the crawlway. They emerged in Sickle Alley, goose-bumpy and trembling.

"Oh," Ollie moaned. "That was *terrifying.*"

"Why didn't you umbrate, Ollie?" Anastasia asked.

"I was too scared to do *anything*," Ollie said. "Thank goodness I always keep a donut handy—otherwise, Frosty might have eaten *us* for breakfast!"

"Frosty only woke up because she smelled your donut," Gus pointed out.

"No," Ollie quibbled. "That donut *saved our lives!*"

"We don't have time to stand around arguing," Anastasia pressed. "Come on!"

Once they were floating in Calixto Swift's office, the Dreadfuls riffled madly through the various books, trying to intuit which volume might contain an inkling about Stinking Crumpet or glass-cabinet-cracking spells. Anastasia's thinker, however, lingered on Frosty's epic sneeze.

The sight of sugar blizzarding from the bear's nostrils had nudged Anastasia's neurons, jiggling loose memories of the frosty plumes she had panted within St. Agony's Asylum. She blinked, trying to scour the twinkly images from her mind's eye. Hallucinations! Mirages! Flights of fancy! Just like Penny and Baldwin said, *Morfolk didn't breathe frost.* Ridiculous, imagining her lungs piped full of miniature blizzards, like two oversize snow globes nestled within her chest. *Witches* were the ones who huffed and puffed magic.

Her thoughts snagged on this notion; stumbled; somersaulted down to her satchel.

She rummaged its jumbled belly, spilling a flotsam of pens and candy wrappers and other oddments out into the office until, finally, she clutched the Cavepearl Palace snow globe.

She peered at it. The snow looked so *real.* A new thought sent a shiver right down Anastasia's spine: what if the twinkles inside Calixto's snow globes were *real* snowflakes—snowflakes that had come not from the sky but from within the warlock's lungs?

A witch's breath carries its own special power.

Calixto descended from the Lapland wizards; his witchy blood brimmed with snow-magic. Had snow-magic sparkled deep inside his *chest,* too? Along with spells and secrets, *had Calixto Swift breathed frost?*

I'll never breathe that secret, Celestina, except to the cabinet itself.

Anastasia's eyes shifted to the cabinet, and to the warlock's Hammer stowed within. She swallowed. She sucked in an enormous, wheezing, two-lung-rattler gulp of musty cave air. She pursed her lips, and she puffed.

A twinkling corona materialized on the glass. Anastasia stared, mouth ajar, as the frosty patch swelled, sprouting before her astonished gaze into a mushroomy bulb of ice. Silvery rime radiated outward from the root of this oddball toadstool, spreading to tinsel the cabinet's breast in wintry filigree.

"Good Bundt cake!" Ollie yelped, dropping a battered weather log. "Look at the chest!"

"What's happening to it?" Gus cried.

The boys swanned across the office, joining Anastasia to gawp as the silvery rime crystallized into a distinct rectangle, buckled on one side with ornate hinges, studded in the center with the mushroomlike knob.

"It's *a door*," Gus gasped. "Why did this door suddenly appear?"

A lump formed in Anastasia's throat. *Morfolk didn't breathe frost.* Had she simply awakened magic hibernating in the witch glass? But then—what about the windows and picture frames at St. Agony's? Questions flurried her noggin: Was the asylum glass enchanted? Were Prim and Prude

witches? But didn't CRUD lump witches into the category of Unnatural Dreadfuls? Besides, the Snodgrass sisters hadn't seemed particularly *magical*. They hadn't walloped Anastasia or the Drybread boys with hocus-pocus, even in the mad chase and rumpus of the Dreadfuls' great escape. They had yelled nasty words and blasted the air with silver buckshot, which had, of course, been rather *unpleasant*, but not in the least *magical*.

But if Prim and Prude *weren't* witches, and the glass in the asylum *wasn't* ensorcelled, what explanation could possibly exist?

Anastasia could only think of one. The lump in her throat crawled down to clutch at her heart, as though a big swallow of ice cream had gone down the wrong way.

"Anastasia!" Gus touched her arm. "Did you see what happened?"

She balked. "I don't know—"

Ollie grabbed the Cavepearl Palace globe from her sweaty clasp. "Open the door before it melts, for gosh sake!"

Anastasia pushed aside her questions and twisted the chilly knob. *Creeeee—eak.* The frost hatch swung open. She stretched her arm into the cabinet, brushing aside a few branches of coral, and closed her fingers around the Silver Hammer.

❧ 24 ❧

Come Closer, My Pretties

A THRILL COURSED from Anastasia's palm and into her body, jozzling each of her hair follicles with a fizzy tingle of magic and triumph and fate.

"Sweet mother of biscuit," she whispered.

"We have it!" Ollie cheered. "We've got the Silver Hammer!"

"Don't touch it too long, Anastasia," Gus warned. "You'll get blisters!"

However, no blisters sizzled up upon Anastasia's hand. She stared at the slender silver instrument, envisioning its claw uprooting the nails binding the Silver Chest. *Tinkle. Jingle. Clunk.* She could almost hear Calixto's spellbound spikes clinking harmlessly to the ground: eight little chinkles announcing Nicodemus's freedom. A metallic drumroll proclaiming that the Dreadfuls' mission was almost at its end, that Fred was practically good as found.

"Hey!" Gus said. "Where did this come from?" He snared Wiggy's ring from the floating hodgepodge of Anastasia's junk and turned it over, examining its golden underbelly. "*S . . . C . . . Stinking Crumpet!*"

"No," Anastasia said, carefully stashing the Hammer in her satchel. "It's *CS,* for *Calixto Swift.* And . . . it's my grandmother's ring now."

The Dreadfuls bent their heads close, scrutinizing.

"The letters sort of swirl together," Ollie said. "It might be *SC.*"

Gus narrowed his eyes, tapping the opal's dainty golden girdle. "Remember that Francie Dewdrop mystery Miss Ramachandra read us—*The Clue in the Lapis Lazuli?*"

"Sure," Anastasia said slowly. "The murderer hid a pinch of cyanide in a poison ring."

A poison ring, as any Francie Dewdrop fan will know, features a hidden compartment for smuggling arsenic, or cyanide, or whatever other deadly venom its wearer might fancy. Poison rings were all the rage with la-di-da assassins of yore, and they still pop up in the odd murder nowadays.

"You think Calixto kept *poison* in that ring?" Ollie squeaked.

"No," Gus said. "I think Calixto Swift hid things in clever places." He applied his thumbnail to the golden girdle, and—hey, presto!—with one knuckle-flick, the opal's top hemisphere hinged back to expose the secret, glassy, twinkling core within.

A snow globe.

"Gus!" Anastasia jubilated. "You're a *genius*!"

The trio squinted at the bubble of glass.

"I can't see through the flakes," Ollie said.

"It's like an entire blizzard compressed into a marble," Gus agreed. "But this *must* be the magic door to Stinking Crumpet, mustn't it? Calixto didn't bother to hide any of his other snow globes."

"If it is, then we have everything we need." Anastasia plucked the ring from Gus and slid it onto her forefinger. "We have the Hammer and we have the way to Stinking Crumpet!"

Gus goggled. "You want to go *now*? But what about our Applied Navigation exam?"

"And we don't have any provisions," Ollie hedged. "Shouldn't we pack sandwiches? What if there aren't any sandwiches in Stinking Crumpet?"

"We can wait for a time when no one will notice we're

missing," Gus said. "Just like that Saturday when we went to Penzance."

Anastasia shook her head. "I can't wait a minute longer. My father has been missing for over five months, and he's *scared*. He's a helpless guinea pig—if he's still alive. And my grandfather's been cramped up in the Silver Chest for *centuries!*"

Ollie gulped. So did Gus.

"You don't have to come with me," Anastasia murmured. "It's *my* family, not yours."

"I'm not a Merrymoon," Gus said softly, "but you're practically my sister." And he pressed the pad of his index finger to the tiny snow globe.

"Well, I'm not going back to face Frosty alone!" Ollie buttoned the Cavepearl Palace snow globe into Anastasia's satchel, and then he squished his pointer down alongside Gus's. "Okay! Ready."

Anastasia cleared her throat.

"Through this doorway clear and crystal
Whisk me on a whirlwind trip!
Take me where your whirlwind twinkles
Make me a globe-trotting—"

"Witch!" The world became a dazzlement of snowflakes and pressure and then darkness.

"Where *are* we?" Gus asked.

Anastasia reached out cautiously, her fingers bumbling first into folds of damp, slick plastic (raincoats?) and then a jumble of curving wooden sticks (umbrella handles?). Her eyelids stuttered. Pinpricks of light, like faraway fireflies, brightened into candle flames, and the glow from these flames traced shrouded silhouettes. Gus grabbed her arm. She blinked again. They were in a roomful of stools and tall little tables. Green and golden bottles cluttered a wooden bar at the far end of the snug. The buzzing in Anastasia's ears subsided, and the whispers pitched into chatter. The silhouettes were people, Anastasia now saw, and they were sitting and drinking from mugs of amber liquid—apple cider? The place smelt of apples and pine and something slightly sour. Beer.

They were in a pub.

At that moment, two elderly women huddled at the nearest table swiveled their heads in tandem toward the Dreadfuls.

"Who's that?" shrilled one.

"How did you get in here?" asked the second. "No children allowed in the pub!"

The first peered over her spectacles. "I don't recognize you. You aren't from here." Her voice pitched into a shout. *"You aren't from here!"*

The pub chatter halted, and now everyone looked up

from their conversations and mugs of cider and beer and stared at the Dreadfuls.

"By the stars and the moon," murmured the barkeeper, "those are *Morflings.*"

In a synchronized, fluid, horrible motion, each and every pub-goer snaked their hand into their cloak. Each and every pub-goer withdrew from their cloak a long, sharp silver wand.

"Crumbs," Anastasia whispered. *Witches.*

In a trice, in a twinkling, in a jiffy (that is to say, very quickly), things went all squidgy.

The bespectacled witch nearest the Dreadfuls swooped forth with her wand raised. The wand traced a silver arc through the gloom and toward Anastasia.

A yellow umbrella flashed in front of Anastasia's eyes. The umbrella whacked the wand aside in a parry. In fact, the umbrella knocked the wand out of the old lady's hand entirely. The silver spike clattered to the floor.

Gus crouched, brolly aloft, *en garde.*

"Myrtle!" cried the second elderly witch, stooping to pick up the wand before planting herself stoutly between the Dreadfuls and the rest of the pub. "What's gotten into you? Attacking *children*, for goodness' sake!"

"*Children!*" Myrtle sputtered. "Nonsense—they're Morflings!"

"They most certainly are *not*," the second witch declared. "Explain how two Morflings would materialize out of thin air."

Two Morflings? Anastasia twisted her head, looking for Ollie. Where was he?

"They didn't *materialize*," a man sitting at the bar shouted scornfully. "They probably came in here as shadows or spiders or what have you and shifted back into snivel-nosed little brats."

"Fully dressed?" the witch demanded.

"Oh, Moona, what does it matter how they got here?" Myrtle squawked. "Now give me my wand and get out of the way."

Angry protests ricocheted around the tiny pub, and the crowd rustled and inched closer.

"You 'eard Myrtle," slurred a man with a round red nose. "Give 'er back the wand and let's squarsh those Merflings—I mean, Morvings—"

"You're drunk, Bill," Moona snapped. "You're *all* drunk, and you're wound up from the chili festival, and you're acting very silly. And shame on you all for scaring my wee godchildren half to death!"

"Godchildren?" echoed Myrtle. Anastasia and Gus exchanged a bewildered glance.

"Yes, *godchildren*! They're here to visit me." Moona swiveled back to glare at Anastasia and Gus. "Very naughty of you it was, sneaking into the pub! I've a good mind to send you both back home to your mother. Now march yourselves straight out of here this instant." She grabbed Anastasia's shoulders and spun her around.

Now that Anastasia's peepers had adjusted to the

gloom, she saw a silver doorknob jutting right from the middle of the wood paneling. She could not, however, discern a door.

"Go on," Moona urged.

Anastasia twisted the knob and yanked, and a section of the wall hinged inward.

"You still have my wand, Moona!" Myrtle yelled.

"And I'm not giving it back until you've sobered up!" The witch shoved Anastasia and Gus, and they tumbled out of the pub and into a thicket of green ferns. The fronds of these ferns arced above their heads, so they could not see what lay beyond.

Perhaps you have seen adventure films in which explorers must whack their way through dense jungle growth with machetes. The Dreadfuls did not have a machete, but Gus did have the yellow umbrella, and with it he whacked at the foliage. *WHACK! WHACK!* The fronds bent aside, and the two Morflings burst through the thicket and beheld, for the first time, the greater wilderness into which Calixto Swift's magic had spirited them.

Before them sprawled a forest of gargantuan trees. The trunks of these goliaths were as broad as lighthouses and seemed to stretch as tall as skyscrapers. Anastasia's gaze traveled along the moss-fuzzed bark, up some three hundred feet, all the way to the leafy canopy above. She goggled at this greeny-gray ceiling until Gus grabbed her hand to yank her into a run. However, Anastasia's feet did not patter forth into the emerald forest. Her galosh snared in a tangle of ivy, and she thudded to the wet forest floor, landing heavily on her satchel.

SMASH! Crunch-tinkle-tinkle!

"Oh no." Gus's eyes rounded in horror. "Was that—"

Anastasia shifted to her knees and unbuttoned her satchel. A swirl of snowflakes puffed out into the green-glowing light, twinkled, and evaporated. Anastasia peered down at the shards of glass spiking the satchel's belly, her heart sinking.

"Is it broken?" Gus asked.

Anastasia swallowed hard and nodded.

"Anastasia! Gus!" Ollie tripped across the carpet of vines and leaves toward them. "Am I glad to see you! I was afraid you hadn't come through! Why didn't you answer me? I've been calling and calling!"

"We didn't hear you," Gus said. "We were in that witch pub—"

"Witch pub?" Ollie interrupted. "*What* witch pub?"

"The one right there—"

But the witch pub was gone. The thicket whence Anastasia and Gus had stumbled petticoated not a pub but an enormous tree.

"It was right there!" Anastasia said. "It vanished—or it somehow turned into a tree!"

"It always was a tree," declared the witch Moona, straightening her sunny yellow raincoat as she emerged from the ferns. Spotting Ollie, she let out a sigh. "Blue blazes! Now there are *three* of you?"

"Stay back!" Gus brandished the umbrella.

Moona huffed in exasperation. "Perhaps you bested Myrtle with that bumbershoot, my dear, but she's half-blind and full of Toadstool Cider. I'm not." She whisked her silver wand from her pocket and wriggled it. The umbrella's yellow canopy sprang open, and the handle tugged free from Gus's grip. The Dreadfuls stared as the brolly floated up, up, up and disappeared into the treetops like an escaped helium balloon.

"Just like Mary Poppins's umbrella!" Ollie gasped.

"Well, sure," Moona said. "She *was* a witch, you know. But let's get down to brass tacks: it won't be too long before that lot in the pub follows us out here. If you don't want Myrtle and the rest of those drunks chasing you down and poking you full of holes or worse, you'd best behave like nice little witch godchildren and follow me."

"Witch godchildren?" Ollie exclaimed.

"Better to be three witch godchildren than three Morflings trespassing through witch woods, don't you think?" Moona said.

"Witch woods?" Ollie quailed.

Anastasia's thoughts whizzed. The Dreadfuls could not

travel through Calixto's snow globe back to Dinkledorf. They were in the middle of a strange wilderness, and that wilderness was full of witches. Should they try to flee? She could shift into a bat and fly, and Ollie could umbrate and do a Shadow flit. If they were to escape, morphing would be their best option.

However, Gus couldn't morph.

Besides, she had come here to find Nicodemus, not dash away at the first glimpse of a witch. And *this* witch, Miss Moona, had protected them in the pub. But—

"Why are you helping us?" Anastasia asked.

"Oh well, killing children isn't my cup of tea." The witch's crinkly face brightened. "Speaking of tea, it's just about tea-time! Hurry up, now. We don't want to be late." She turned and marched off into the ivy and moss.

"I'm not going anywhere with a witch," Ollie muttered. "And I'm certainly not drinking witch tea! Let's go—"

"Where?" Anastasia whispered. "The Cavepearl Palace snow globe is broken, Ollie. We're stuck here, and we don't know where *here* is—just that it's crawling with witches. Besides, we're still on a Mission of Life-and-Death Importance!"

She kicked away the leafy creeper and scrambled after the old woman. Gus and Ollie exchanged an anxious glance before hurrying to follow.

Over hill, over dale, through mist, and through ferns they footslogged, sweaty and panting and chilled, until at last the witch halted in front of one of the colossal trees.

"Well, here we are," Moona said. She grabbed a knobbly bulge in the bark and yanked it, and a round door swung out from the trunk. When closed, the door had blended perfectly into the grooved bark. It was practically invisible. But it was open now, and the witch ducked into the tree and crooked her finger into the universal hand gesture for *Come closer, my pretties.*

❧ 25 ❧

A Witchy Teatime

THE HOLLOW INSIDE the witch's tree was cool and dark and smelled of earth and . . . cake? Anastasia scrunched her eyelids, peering into the gloom. The chamber was round, of course, like a room in a tower or lighthouse. At the center of the chamber squatted a metal stove, and in the guts of this stove crackled a merry fire. The orange glow glinted off hundreds of glass jars and bottles lining the curving walls of the redwood's belly.

"Let's see," the witch said. "I think you need a nice cup of tea after that nasty scene back there. And how about cake? Would you like a smidgen of cake, my dears?" She whisked the lid from a big cake platter. The platter was bare excepting some brown crumbs and a long, wicked knife. Moona seized the knife and brandished it, glaring. Anastasia gasped. Ollie gasped. Gus gasped. So did the witch.

"I don't even have to wonder," she huffed, "who gobbled the last piece of cake and didn't even clear away the dishes! Most inconsiderate! Very bad manners!"

"Wh-who was it?" Ollie stammered, eyes glued to the knife.

"Why," the witch said, "it was *me*. I wish I wouldn't do these things. But"—she beamed at them—"I suppose nobody's perfect." She set the knife down on the table and hunkered down to rummage through a basket by the front door. "Ah!" She yanked out a pair of battered leather gloves and a spade.

"What are *those* for?" Anastasia asked, her thoughts flitting back to the little graves lining the gardens of Prim and Prudence Snodgrass.

The witch looked surprised. "I'm going to get you some cake, of course." She pulled on the gloves. "I won't be but a minute. I have a lovely chocolate cake that's been growing all week." She picked up the cake platter and bustled out the front door.

"Growing all week?" Gus echoed.

"I'm not eating witch cake, and neither should you," Ollie said stoutly. "Haven't you read *Hansel and Gretel*?"

"Do you think she's really trying to help us?" Gus asked.

Anastasia's eyebrows crinkled. "She did stop the pub witches from sticking us with their wands."

"Witches don't *help* Morfolk," Ollie hissed. "She brought us back here to murder us in private! That way, she doesn't have to share any of her nice Morfling dinner."

"But do witches really *eat* children?" Anastasia asked.

"*Hansel and Gretel,*" Ollie intoned. "*Snow White.* Remember? The evil witch queen wanted to eat Snow White's heart."

"Ollie, those are just stories," Gus protested.

"No, they aren't! Remember what Mr. Winkler told us about Little Red Riding Hood? And what that witch just said about Mary Poppins?" Ollie argued. "Fairy tales are *real,* and witches in fairy tales always try to eat children! Maybe *these* witches want to gobble our hearts—or livers—"

"Oh my goodness, no!" the witch exclaimed, stooping into the tree kitchen. On her platter trembled an enormous cake frosted thickly with chocolate and stuck all over with beautiful pink sugar roses.

"Nobody wants to eat your livers!" the witch cried, scandalized. "I can't believe you'd even *think* such a thing! Witches aren't *cannibals,* you know!" She shoved the cake into Anastasia's arms. "Of course, the witches out there *would* kill you on the spot if they knew you were Morflings.

But nobody would try to *eat* you. How repulsive! Now, take that cake upstairs to the parlor, and I'll be up with tea in two shakes of a lamb's tail." She gestured at a staircase curling along the curved wall.

Anastasia lugged the cake up to the darkened second story, and Ollie and Gus tagged after her. Two lamps with stained-glass shades beamed ruby-toned glow onto a hodge-podge of overstuffed chairs loaded with embroidered pillows. Crocheted doilies lurked like spiderwebs along the bookshelves, and framed photographs bedecked little lace-shrouded tables. It was a jumbled room, but that jumble did not seem to include a Silver Chest. Anastasia thumped the cake down onto a coffee table.

"Do you think that cake is *poisoned*?" Gus whispered.

"Why does she keep her cake pantry *outside*?" Ollie asked.

"It isn't a cake pantry, dear," Moona chuckled, wheezing up the stairs with a tea tray. Upon the tray rattled a flowered teapot and china cups and a creamer and sugar dish. "It's a cake *garden*. Like everything else, the best cakes come right from the earth."

"But doesn't the cake get all covered with dirt?" Ollie protested.

"*Tsk!* A little dirt won't hurt you," Moona replied. "Go on, now, sit down. Make yourselves comfy."

The Dreadfuls cautiously lowered their rumps onto the

witch's furniture. The cushions were so deep and squishy that the chairs nearly swallowed them whole. It *was* very comfortable, but Anastasia was again reminded of fairy tales in which witches picnicked upon children.

Moona busied herself with pouring tea and slicing cake and passing these provisions round to the Dreadfuls. "And I *didn't* poison a single thing on this tray," she reassured them. "Believe me: if I wanted to kill you, I wouldn't have to use poison. But *I don't* want to kill you, so you needn't worry, anyway. As I said, I disapprove of killing children." She looked up from the sugar bowl, and her crinkled face softened. "Oh my. Scared right out of your wits, aren't you? Poor little mites. But why on earth did you sneak into a witch pub? How did you find the Stinky Toad, anyway?"

Anastasia clamped her jaw. She wasn't about to divulge the details of the Dreadfuls' great mission to a witch!

"We—we were just exploring," Gus said.

"We were going for a hike in the woods," Ollie piped up. "And we must have taken a wrong turn."

"You must have taken quite a few 'wrong turns' to wind up in Stinking Crumpet, my boy." A wry smile flickered on the witch's lips. "We're smack-dab in the middle of nowhere. Nobody wanders around here—nobody but us witches, that is."

"Well . . . we're great explorers," Ollie floundered. "And you know how Morfolk can flit and fly."

"Bunkum! Like I said before, if you came here *that* way, you'd all be in your birthday suits," the witch said. "Where *did* you come from, anyway?"

The Dreadfuls lapsed into stubborn silence, staring down at the uneaten cake on their plates. The witch had taken care to make sure each child got a sugar rose. It seemed a strangely thoughtful gesture, coming from a witch.

"You all smell a bit like a cave," the witch mused. "But my nose must be fooling me, mustn't it? The Cavelands are halfway across the world, after all."

Halfway across the world! Anastasia's heart sank.

"And Morflings your age couldn't possibly travel so far alone. Unless . . . are your parents nearby?" Moona leaned forward, scrutinizing them.

"Yes, and they're probably looking for us right now," Anastasia said. "Probably-definitely."

"Little liar," the old lady retorted cheerfully. "Good try, though." She relaxed back into her chair and sipped at her tea. "Ooooh! Too hot!"

And then the witch did something astonishing. She rounded her lips, and she huffed a swirl of frost right into her teacup.

The Dreadfuls goggled, thunderstruck.

"You—you breathe frost?" Anastasia stuttered.

Moona shrugged. "Lapland breath. Runs in the family." She took a second chamomile swig. "Ah. That's much better."

Anastasia let out a little squeak. "Frost breath is—is *Lapland magic*?"

But a scrabbling at the wall interrupted this witchy chit-chat. Moona sighed. "Dear, would you mind opening the shutter?"

Anastasia put her cake on the table and, with an effort, struggled up from the love seat. The suspicions she had squelched in Calixto's office now bubbled up into her brain. She was wobbly-kneed and woozy.

"It's that knot over there," Moona directed. "Just give it a push."

Anastasia stumbled past Ollie and Gus. She shoved the knot snarling the wood, and out it swung to reveal a round window, much like a porthole on a ship. Twilight streamed through the window, and a small, furry blur soared into the parlor and glided to land on the witch's head.

"What's that?" Ollie cried.

"Why!" Gus said. "It's a flying squirrel!"

"Yes," the witch said. "An *insomniac* flying squirrel. Waldo here is always fussing about in the daytime, when all of his friends are sound asleep." She reached up to pat Waldo's head with her forefinger. "Are you about ready for bed, love? It's getting late."

"Does Waldo *live* here?" Gus asked.

"Waldo and about thirty of his brothers and sisters," Moona replied. "Oh! I forgot to tell you we should be quiet.

They're *sleeping*." She pointed at the doily lumps clogging the chamber's nooks and crannies. "If you hush, you'll hear them snoring."

Sure enough, once everyone shut their mouths and held still, tiny snores piped forth from the crocheted nests.

"Aw!" Ollie crooned, quite forgetting to be frightened.

Normally, a parlor full of squirrels would charm Anastasia, too. She *adored* squirrels. But dismay filled every inch of her freckled frame. If frost breath was Lapland magic—

"Ouch! *Waldo!*" The squirrel launched from Moona's head and glided on his marvelous fur-flaps to the bookcase. "Right to the fairy tales," Moona said. "He must be getting sleepy—he wants a bedtime story. As long as you're up, dear, would you fetch that big blue book? It's Waldo's favorite."

As through a fog, Anastasia crossed the tiny chamber and reached for the silver-embossed volume. Her hand froze as her gaze locked on a framed photograph perched on the shelf. Waldo chattered at her, but Anastasia barely heard him. She snatched the photo from its ledge and stared.

It was not a particularly remarkable photograph. It was the sort of picture you might spot in any household anywhere in the world. A freckled young woman with mousy-brown hair smiled up from the print. The man standing beside this young woman was smiling, too. One of his arms snugged the woman's shoulders in a hug. With his other hand he reached to touch the woman's full, round tummy. He was smiling, too. His entire mustache twitched with a big, silly, happy grin.

"Dear . . . ?" Moona said. "It's the big blue book. Right in front of you."

Still holding the photograph, Anastasia turned around. "Why," she asked in a voice so low it was nearly a whisper, "do you have a picture of my father in your parlor?"

❧ 26 ❧
Fireflies

MOONA BLINKED. SHE blinked three times; fast, like her eyes were stuttering. "Your father?"

"This is my dad." Anastasia tapped the frame's glass breastplate.

Moona smiled. She replaced her teacup to its saucer, and the saucer to the table. "You're mistaken, child," she said. "The light in here isn't very good."

Anastasia shook her head. "I can recognize my own father, for crumb's sake!" She swiveled her gaze around the parlor, as though Fred might pop up from behind a chair. "When was this picture taken? When was Dad here?"

Moona stared at her. Her eyes had stopped stuttering. They now glowed with strange light. "The man in that photograph was never *here*, child. My daughter sent that picture to me in a letter, years ago."

"Why would *your daughter* have a picture of *my dad*?" Anastasia demanded.

"Let me see it!" Ollie grabbed the picture out of Anastasia's hands. "Yep! That's Fredmund, all right. I recognize him from his portrait."

"Fredmund?" Moona cried. "As in—*Fred?*" The light in her eyes was growing brighter and brighter. She hopped from her chair and tiptoed up to Anastasia. She leaned forward, and she *peered*. She peered at Anastasia's nose and peepers and freckles. "Oh, my stars. You *are*—but you *can't* be! But— yes! You *are!*"

"I'm *what*?" Anastasia asked hoarsely.

"The young lady in that photograph is—*was*—my daughter. My Rosemary," Moona said. "And the man standing with her is my son-in-law, Fred. And the baby inside Rosie's belly . . ." The light in her eyes finally spilled out into two tears, and the tears wriggled down her crinkled cheeks. "That baby is my granddaughter, whom I've never met. All I know is her name: *Anastasia Rose.*"

Anastasia gulped. "That's *my* name."

"Yes." The witch wiped her tears away and smiled, and she grabbed Anastasia into a big, squishy hug. "Yes, I thought it might be."

Normally, family reunions swell hearts with delight and tweak vocal cords into exclamations of hooray. Anastasia's vocal cords did not vibrate into any joyful whoops, however. Her throat closed up completely, and she wrenched from the witch's embrace and staggered backward.

"Anastasia is *not* a witch!" Ollie said. "She's a Morfo!"

"Half Morfo," Moona murmured. "Half witch."

"That can't be true," Gus protested. "A Morfo wouldn't marry a witch! It's absolutely forbidden to even *talk* to a witch!"

"*You're* talking to *me*," Moona pointed out.

"It's impossible," Anastasia finally croaked. "Impossible."

But it *wasn't*; not really. Through her distress, Anastasia's keen detecting mind turned over the evidence. Hadn't she napped unscathed in Calixto Swift's Moonsilk Canopy, hexed to bedevil Morfolk with nasty dream cooties? Hadn't she breathed a door of frost upon the warlock's spellbound glass case? And had not magic followed in her wake, lo these past few months? An aurora borealis shellacked the night sky as *Anastasia* jubilated beneath the full moon. Clouds pirouetted above Dinkledorf as *she* tromped its snowy lanes. The props *she* had painted in the Cavepearl Theater transformed and rioted and created a magical hullabaloo.

Poor Miss Ramachandra, languishing in the palace dungeons, had taken the rap for it all. But to the objective observer, Anastasia was a far better suspect. She had been at the scene of each and every enchantment. The Cavelands' strangeness had started when *she* arrived in Nowhere Special.

And, of course, there was that photograph of her father hugging a witch.

Anastasia removed the portrait from Ollie's grasp and stared again at the smiley couple. Could the freckled lady *really* be her mother?

"It's a trick," Gus urged. "It's witch magic. She could have *hexed* that photograph to picture your dad, Anastasia."

"I most certainly did not," Moona said indignantly. "I'm just as surprised as you are—believe me, I never expected to find my granddaughter in a group of three wayward Morflings! I had *no idea* Fred was a Morfo! I never met him, but Rosie told me he was a plain old human." She bit her lip and squeezed Anastasia's shoulder. "It doesn't matter, dear. I don't care if you're half Morfo. You're one hundred percent my granddaughter, and that's what counts." Her eyes misted up again. "I've been wishing to meet you all these years, and finally my wish has come true."

"How did Dad meet Rosie?" Anastasia asked.

"They met in Peru," Moona said. "Rosie was a zoologist, and she was in Lima studying guinea pigs. I understand your father was on holiday down there."

Anastasia knit her brow. Fred had never mentioned any South American travels to her. Perhaps he had ventured to

Peru when he left the Cavelands for good, when he renounced his Morfolky ways after a family fight and tried to live an ordinary human life. But why would he have befriended a witch?

They must have fallen in love before realizing they were mortal foes, Anastasia mused.

"Rosie didn't tell me much about their courtship," Moona confessed. "I only found out she was married when I received a postcard from their honeymoon. Then Rosie and Fred moved away to some little town, and they wouldn't tell anyone where it was—not even *me*, and your mother and I were very close. I didn't understand it at the time, but it makes sense now: *nobody* would approve of a witch-Morfo marriage."

Anastasia's skin crept. No, they certainly wouldn't. And the fact that Fred was a Merrymoon *prince* made matters even worse! What would Wiggy think if she knew her granddaughter—the heir apparent to the Morfo throne—was half witch? Ludowiga would probably charge Anastasia with treason and try to send her to the guillotine! How would Penny and Baldy receive this news?

What did Gus and Ollie think?

The boys were staring at her, wide-eyed. Did they still consider Anastasia their friend and ally, or did her witchy blood thrust her into the ranks of the enemy? Her lower lip trembled.

"Have some tea, dear." Moona ushered Anastasia back to the love seat. "You've had a shock. You'll feel much better after some tea and cake."

Once Anastasia started eating her cake, Ollie and Gus ate theirs. They even had two slices each. It was utterly scrumptious. As they ate, Moona told Anastasia about Rosie.

Rosie had always been shy.

Rosie had adored animals.

Rosie had been a bit klutzy.

Rosie had loved Anastasia very much.

Rosie had died mysteriously just one week after Anastasia's birth.

"*Mysteriously?*" Anastasia's fork clattered to her plate. "What do you mean, *mysteriously?*"

Moona sighed and stood up and rustled in a little desk. She pulled out a faded, folded sheet of pale green paper, and she handed it to Anastasia. Anastasia smoothed it out, letting out a cry of recognition upon spying the handwriting.

Dear Moona,

I write with broken heart and the worst news in the entire world: our Rosie—our lovely, sweet, funny, darling Rosie—is dead. I took Anastasia for a stroll in her buggy, and when we returned, the house was on fire. Rosie was in the house.

The police say it was an accident, but—

I've no time to write more; we must leave this place. It isn't safe. I won't write again, Moona. Anastasia and I are going to disappear, and this time, no one will find us.

I'm so sorry.
Fred

"Dad thought Rosie was *murdered*?" Anastasia whispered.

Moona shrugged sadly. "Fred was *frightened*, that's for sure. Perhaps he worried someone realized Rosie was a witch. Humans turn into nasty little firebugs around witches, you know."

"Or maybe Fred thought CRUD was after them," Gus suggested. "If CRUD knew Fred was a Morfo, they might have thought Rosie was, too."

"I don't know exactly what ideas were rattling around Fred's brain," Moona said. She reached out and squeezed Anastasia's hand. "Your father was in shock, I'm sure, and people sometimes think strange things when they're in shock. I don't know whether there was really anything suspicious about that fire. It might have been an accident, after all." She sighed. "And I never got the chance to discuss it with Fred. I looked for you both for years, but . . . well, your father is *very* good at vanishing."

"He's missing now," Anastasia said in a wobbly voice.

"He is?" Moona's eyebrows jumped.

So Anastasia told the witch about the CRUD kidnapping. She told her that Fred had disappeared, and that nobody could find him.

"Is that what you three are doing in Stinking Crumpet?" Moona asked. "Looking for Fred?"

"Er—yes," Anastasia said. And it was true, in a roundabout way; the Dreadfuls were tracking Nicodemus Merrymoon and his Fred-finding tattoo. However, Anastasia did not want to divulge that fact—not yet. It was dangerous enough to be a Morfo (half Morfo) in the witch woods. It would be far worse to be a *Morfo princess* in the witch woods. If the other witches ferreted out that little fact, they might hold Anastasia hostage. They might try to ransom her from the Crown.

Gus and Ollie must have been pondering the same sorts of things, because neither of them piped up to ask about the Silver Chest.

"But why would you look *here*?" Moona quizzed. "There hasn't been a Morfo in Stinking Crumpet—well, *ever*."

"We took a wrong turn," Ollie said again.

"Would you be able to help me find Dad?" Anastasia asked. "Could you brew up a spell, or look in a crystal ball, or . . . ?"

The corners of Moona's mouth drooped. "I don't know, dear."

A stream of impatient chatter issued from the bookshelf.

"Oh, Waldo! I haven't forgotten your bedtime story," Moona said, standing up to fetch the blue fairy tale volume. "It's about *everyone's* bedtime now, I should think. The guest room is on the fourth floor. You'll find pajamas in the chest of drawers. Just tell it what you want and knock three times. Go on, and no arguments! I can see how sleepy your eyes are."

The Dreadfuls didn't argue. They hiked up the curving stairs to the third floor (some kind of craft room, crammed with bolts of fabric and a rainbow of spools), and thence to the fourth.

"Oh!" Ollie said in surprised delight.

Three hammocks, spun of indigo and shot through with gold, stretched across the room. Elegant crochet work tasseled the hammocks' edges, and pillows and quilts padded their silky bellies. A jar of fireflies hummed and glowed upon a narrow bureau carved of black wood. Anastasia checked the compartments of this bureau. "Empty."

"You have to tell it what you want," Gus said.

"Er." Anastasia shut the drawers and cleared her throat. "I'd like some warm jammies, please. And slippers." She rapped three times. She slid the topmost drawer out and gaped at the red plaid pj's nestled within. "Oh! And fuzzy bunny slippers—just like the ones I had in Mooselick!"

Gus and Ollie procured pajamas of their own, and after everyone had visited the (magical, self-cleaning!) chamber pot one floor above, they climbed into the hammocks. Have you ever lolled in a hammock, Reader? Hammocks as a rule are very comfortable, and the hammocks in the witch's tree house were perhaps the cushiest, cuddliest, coziest hammocks in the entire world. Snuggled amidst the pillows and quilts, the Dreadfuls listened to Moona recite a fairy tale from Waldo's favorite blue storybook. Then the witch kissed each of their foreheads.

"Now, remember: when Myrtle comes banging at my door tomorrow morning to get her wand, you're *all* witchlings," Moona cautioned. "We can't have anyone discovering there are three Morfolk children in Stinking Crumpet."

Anastasia trembled. "Do you think she'll try to stab me again?"

"No," Moona chuckled. "You mustn't mind Myrtle. She's a bit of a crab apple, to be sure, but we've been friends for ages. And she *adored* your mother, dear; in fact, Myrtle gave Rosie this book." The witch placed the blue volume in Anastasia's hands, giving her knuckles a fond little pat. "Good night, children. Be sure to let the fireflies out to play before you go to sleep."

And she padded downstairs to do whatever it is that witches do after children go to bed.

For a moment, Anastasia admired the silver design of moons and flowers tooled across the storybook's cover. Her mother's book! She wondered how many times Rosie had read it, and what her favorite story had been. Had Rosie rooted for the witches? Had she tried to mimic the magic spells?

She turned back the cover, and she gasped.

"What is it?" Gus asked.

"There's a note written on the first page," Anastasia said. "'To sweet little Rosie, may your eleventh year brim with magic. Love, Myrtle Honeysop.'"

"Honeysop!" Gus exclaimed. "Do you think that fussy witch could be related to Calixto's old nanny, Agatha Honeysop?"

Anastasia's heart pitter-pattered. "Probably! Honeysop is a pretty unusual name. Maybe we can get some clues out of Myrtle! Remember, Calixto said Agatha knew about his Silver Chest. He left that cuckoo clock note for her, telling her to come to Stinking Crumpet." She hugged the fairy tale book. "Maybe she did. Maybe she knew where the Chest was, and maybe her family's passed down the secret."

"That's a lot of *maybes*," Ollie pointed out. "And even if those *maybes* turn out to be *yeses*, why would an old witch blab the great Honeysop secret to three Morflings?"

"She wouldn't," Anastasia said. "But she might tell three *witchlings* visiting her best friend. She might even tell us something without realizing how important it is. Myrtle Honeysop's our best lead, and we'll see her tomorrow morning!"

"Speaking of tomorrow," Ollie faltered, "when are we going home? And *how* are we going home?"

"I don't know," Anastasia admitted.

"I think we're in America—in California," Gus said. "We're in a redwood forest, aren't we? I did a project on redwood trees in fourth grade, and I remember reading that the only redwood forests in the world are in California."

"Oh, *Bundt cake*," Ollie swore. "We really *are* halfway across the world."

"You and Anastasia could morph and fly to Switzerland," Gus said uncertainly.

"I'm not ready for that kind of trip! The farthest I've flown is from Gruyère Gutter to the palace, and that only took ten minutes," Anastasia said. "What if I changed back into a girl halfway across the Atlantic Ocean? Besides, Gus, we'd *never* leave you."

"Then maybe Moona will help us," Ollie said. "She could magic up some plane tickets. Or—well, do you suppose she could loan us some flying brooms?"

"Do you think she'll even let us leave?" Gus murmured.

"What do you mean?" Ollie asked.

Gus shifted up onto his elbow so he was facing the other hammocks. "Stinking Crumpet is a *secret witch village. We* found it. Do you think Moona will just let us go back to our Morfolk families? *We're at Perpetual War with the witches,* you know. Moona seems to like us, but that doesn't mean she'll trust us not to share witch secrets with her enemies."

"Oh no!" Ollie moaned.

"Didn't you notice how Moona sent us to bed without even *mentioning* our parents? She didn't say any normal grown-up things about how worried our families must be," Gus said. "I bet it's because she *can't* let us leave."

"Q must be wondering what happened to us," Ollie quavered. "Pippistrella, too."

"I'm sure *everyone* knows we're missing by now," Gus said.

Anastasia imagined the Merrymoon-Wata-Drybread search party scouring the Cavelands for the vanished Morflings, and her eyes brimmed with tears. "I'm sorry," she whispered. "It's my fault we're stuck here."

"*I'm* not sorry," Gus said. "I'm glad to be sitting in a tree house in a redwood forest, breathing fresh air and mist and listening to rain and hearing night birds! I've been waiting my entire life to get out of Nowhere Special, and now I *have!*"

"Well, you'll have to go home *sometime,*" Ollie snuffled. Anastasia suspected he was trying not to cry. Or perhaps he was already crying and was trying to stop.

"Sure," Gus said. "But tonight I'll just enjoy being here."

"I might never go back," Anastasia said softly. "Witches are forbidden in the Cavelands, remember?"

Gus gulped. "Wouldn't the queen make an exception for you?"

An owl hoot drifted through the porthole.

"I don't know. *She* might," Anastasia said doubtfully, "but the rest of Morfolkdom wouldn't." She stared at the tree rings grooving the ceiling. "Besides, I'm not going home until I find Nicodemus and my father. I'm too close to finding the Silver Chest to just give up!"

"Do you think Calixto buried the Chest in this forest?" Ollie asked.

"It's *somewhere* in Stinking Crumpet," Gus said. "It can't be far."

"No," Anastasia agreed, "it can't." She got up and lifted the firefly jar off the nightstand, and then she padded to the window and gazed into the darkness beyond. The forest was very dark indeed, untouched by electric light or moonbeam or starshine. Anastasia unscrewed the lid of the jar, and she set it on the windowsill. The fireflies bumbled over the glass lip and thrummed into flight.

All the darkness in the world cannot extinguish the light of a single candle, Gus murmured, stepping up beside her. "Francis of Assisi said that."

Anastasia turned in surprise, but in the gloom-drenched tree chamber she could not see his face. Yet his hand found hers, and Ollie's cake-sticky fingers slid into her other palm and clasped it tightly.

And the three children watched the fireflies twinkle off into the night, a handful of stars venturing forth to forge their destinies.

* * THE AUTHOR WISHES TO THANK * *

Brianne Johnson,
Fairy Godmother-Agent

&

Shana Corey,
Fairy Godmother-Editrix,
for their starbright storybook magic
for their bibbidi-bobbidi-boo extraordinaire
for guiding the Beastly Dreadfuls ever onward

* * * * *plus a million thank-yous to* * * * *
The Marvel-Working Joy-Practitioners at
Random House Children's Books

HOLLY GRANT is the author of the League of Beastly Dreadfuls series and the picture book *Wee Sister Strange*, illustrated by K. G. Campbell. When she isn't writing, Holly enjoys sipping tea and munching crumpets and visiting bats at the zoo. She lives in Colorado with a clowder of cats and an eight-legged moth connoisseur named Matilda. Holly is also a pancake eater of some renown. Follow her on Twitter at @HollyMMGrant.

JOSIE PORTILLO was born and raised in Los Angeles, where she works as a freelance illustrator. She did not attend the Pettifog Academy for Impressionable Young Minds. She draws inspiration from mid-century design, vintage children's animation, and her surroundings (fortunately, she does not live underground). When she's not illustrating, she can be found spending time with her two dogs (she does not own an electric eel) and playing soccer (though she hears rowing a gondola is also excellent exercise).